The Tour

The Tour

Peter Aspinall

Matador
9 Priory Business Park
Kibworth Beauchamp
Leicestershire LE8 0RX, UK
Tel: (+44) 116 279 2299
Fax: (+44) 116 279 2277
Email: books@troubador.co.uk
Web: www.troubador.co.uk/matador

ISBN 978 1780880 990

British Library Cataloguing in Publication Data.
A catalogue record for this book is available from the British Library.

Typeset in 11pt Garamond Pro by Troubador Publishing Ltd, Leicester, UK
Printed and bound in the UK by TJ International, Padstow, Cornwall

Matador is an imprint of Troubador Publishing Ltd

To Gillian, Ben, Emily and Robert

Thanks to members of Wigan Cricket Club for their inspiration and most of the chuckles.

Cover art: Winston Higham

ONE

Crawford cricket club had never really nestled.

Perhaps some time in the past it may have harboured such a lofty ambition, but the surrounding landscape in the late spring of 1981 was far more chip shop than country Cotswolds. To the side of the ground and uncomfortably close to the mock Tudor pavilion thundered the main railway lines heading north and south. The days of blackened smoke billowing from the steam trains of the Jubilee and Britannia classes and covering the popping crease with a light covering of tangy soot were none-too-distant memories. But time had moved on and modern diesel locomotives now rattled the fading framed photograph of F.R.W.Morthouse's splendid knock of 208 not out (fifteen fours, five sixes) back in the summer of 1952 as the great man himself defiantly gazed out over the snooker table in the back games room.

On the other side of the immaculately tended square lay the former Grammar school, a seat of learning for classical scholars before media studies and domestic science had got the better of

Pliny and Herodotus, but the row of rather imposing Victorian villas whose rear gardens overlooked the outfield was a gentle reminder of a more dignified past.

In the middle of this architectural muddle, groundsman Bernard Gazelle rocked back in his Wellington boots and took in an empire he regarded very much as his own. By his own admission this was one chap content with his working lot. His task was to tend and nurture the cricket pitch, to keep the outfield brisk, flat and green. Drainage and a deep suspicion of marauding strangers with an intent to trespass were part of a self-imposed remit. But while pride in the job extended all the way to the ropes that marked the long boundary down by the warm pile of grass cuttings, the inner sanctum that was the cricket square was his main concern.

A few strips of grass 22 yards long were his world, the protection of which was high priority. The square was protected even during the week when the only visitor may be a passing Airedale and while a few wooden posts linked together by a thickly woven rope was in fact a reasonably effective deterrent, Gazelle often dreamed of beefing up his defences. A moat house, ramparts and a phalanx of archers would surely not go amiss. Wasn't there the opportunity for a boiling oil facility to ward off undesirables, to keep the ordinaries away from his castle? The only concession he had managed to squeeze out of the club committee was a dozen extra 'keep off the grass' signs. Gazelle had painted them all an iridescent canary yellow. Even in the depths of winter they could be seen from the front bar.

The groundsman was jolted out of his day-dreams by the urgent pressing of a car horn as a vehicle chugged into the club via the driveway on the far side of the field. Gazelle – or club chief executive as he fancifully imagined himself to be –

squinted and scowled as a rusting Morris Marina trundled behind a sight screen before emerging into sharper focus. Gazelle's pained expression eased as he recognised the club captain behind the wheel. He still wondered what he was doing there on Monday lunchtime though. But as Dave 'Wobbler' Carter heaved himself out of the driving seat, along with his wife, all became clear. The cricket club was a handy stop-over for a spot of shopping in the nearby town centre.

'Hey up Gazelle,' bellowed the new arrival (even though it was his surname, Gazelle was rarely called anything other).

'Hey up Wobbler,' came the reply without fear of causing offence. (Even though Wobbler was a less-than-flattering nickname and was entirely due to the skipper's fondness for a fish supper, he was never referred to by his parents' original choice on his birth certificate). He didn't mind though because he was only too aware that Gazelle would have happily piled on a couple of stones himself if this would have provided him with the ability to swing a cricket bat or cast down an arm ball in only the way Wobbler could. He walked over and addressed the groundsman. 'How's the pitch coming along? The new season's only a few weeks away and it looks in fine fettle.'

'So it should be,' smirked Gazelle. 'It's probably had more care and attention than your missus this winter.'

Wobbler grinned and nodded his head slightly in tacit agreement. 'It's probably had more use of the heavy roller too,' he retorted, his agreeable smile turning into a self-congratulatory chuckle before he attempted to catch up with his wife who was heading off in the direction of the town centre. 'Self parody, you can't beat it,' he muttered to nobody in particular before turning back to Gazelle and shouting: 'And don't forget the committee meeting on Thursday night.'

TWO

A committee meeting, especially one so early in the season, represented the ideal opportunity for all club members to gratefully gather under one roof again, staff and players alike. It provided the excuse to open the bar early and, for many, marked the end of a winter misery which had involved the watching of far too much tedious rugby union on cold and draughty Saturday afternoons. The anticipation of long, balmy days of the cricket season that lay ahead was now a reality.

Wicket-keeper Alan 'Sammy' Samson was one of the first to arrive. He had spent most of the winter drinking heavily, cultivating his moustache and honing an accent that had its origins on the other side of the world. The moustache, a beast in residence above his top lip, was a life form in itself and one that was charging across his face at an alarming rate. The cultured facial hair was part of an image though, an alter-ego almost. Sammy firmly believed he was an Australian and didn't mind propagating the deception. His place of birth, for anyone gullible enough to believe him, was Adelaide. In fact, he desired to be one Australian in particular, Test cricketer and fellow wicket-keeper Rodney Marsh and there was nothing Sammy liked better than when opposing players remarked on the similarity. His chest, already opened up like a burst settee, would expand to 32psi and the phoney accent would become even more Clive James. In his flannels out there on the square he would take the opportunity to look and play the bellicose Aussie to perfection. Sammy had been sledging opponents long before the word had been re-invented.

Before the first committee meeting of the new season convened, Sammy was to be found in even more familiar territory, perched at the bar and appreciatively eyeing Laura, the new barmaid, before ordering vast quantities of drink. The unfortunate girl – on deboo as Sammy the aspiring Australian would have said of her first night behind the bar – was about to discover exactly how much out of her depth she really was. Sammy lured her over to his web of entrapment with a seductive wave of a crisp five pound note and an irresistible stroke of his enormous moustache. When he leaned over the top of the bar his bushy grin seemed to straddle both bitter and lager pumps.

'A Botham shandy for me and a schooner of whatever you fancy for yourself my dear,' he crooned in his best down-town Sydney drawl.

Not surprisingly, Laura didn't have a clue what made up the constituent parts of a Botham shandy, which suited Sammy down to the ground because the mysterious request merely provided more chances for cheesy one-liners.

'What on earth is a Botham shandy?' she enquired, by now most suspicious of the leering walrus about to topple into the drip tray.

'A double rum and coke with lots of ice, a slice of lemon, a small plastic sword, but no umbrella,' triumphed Sammy before rocking back on his stool in gales of laughter. 'Better keep them coming. It could be a long night.'

The barmaid could not have agreed more.

But just as Sammy's reptilian features threatened an end to the girl's fledgling bar career before it had barely started, a welcome cavalryman appeared on the horizon. Wobbler poked his head into the room and snapped: 'Sammy, the meeting's about to start. Get yourself in here pronto.'

Sammy managed one last leer in Laura's general direction before striding manfully into the games room. He lifted a hand of acknowledgement to a clutch of more senior players gathered around the snooker table before cuffing and scattering a cabal of juniors who had the audacity to be sitting on the front row.

Sammy folded his arms and looked stern and fierce. This was cricket. This was serious.

The top table housed the committee and groaned under its burden of maturity and experience, none weightier in both these departments than club chairman Norman F. Billington for whom cricket had been a lifetime passion. No-one really knew his age, but folk-lore told that he had captained the third team when he was 59 and had continued umpiring and running the club ever since. In his younger days he had carried a dashing bat and had once made a treble century against Old Swan, the original scoresheet providing the evidence of his mastery of the willow behind a glass frontage hanging on the wall three feet to the left of the dart board.

Some of the holes in the frame had been explained away as woodworm, but suspicions ran deep.

Today Norman F. Billington lived in one of the Victorian

houses overlooking the square and the clubhouse. He would keep daily and nightly vigils looking over his garden wall, some of which lasted for hours. Gazelle certainly knew what it was like to have your boss on your case.

Norman F. Billington called for order, cleared his throat and read out the agenda for the night. The list was comprehensive and in need of earnest debate. It ran as follows: Approval to re-appoint first team captain; a change of brewery; the appointment of a full-time groundsman; the appointment of an overseas professional player; a feasibility study into a first-ever tour down south.

Gazelle was standing at the back of the room not taking a lot of interest in proceedings, poking a listless finger into a section of mis-shapen plaster in the wall where a snooker ball had evaded the clutches of short extra cover at a rather raucous end of season party back in '76. Once again there was no mention of reinforcements out there on the square – boiling oil wasn't even up for discussion – hence his indifference and spot of amateur grouting.

But suddenly Gazelle stood rigidly to attention and listened intently. A full-time groundsman and a tour? Why had nobody mentioned such life-changing proposals before?

Gazelle had never been on a cricket tour before. In fact, a few days in Blackpool on a school trip was the nearest he'd ever got to a cosmopolitan lifestyle and even then the illuminations hadn't been switched on. Gazelle was a simple chap whose life prior to joining the cricket club had consisted mainly of a non-event. He had never married, had no children and had shown little inclination towards either of these pursuits. Women were creatures who spent money on hair spray, strangely-fitting undergarments and knitting patterns, activities that served no practical purpose. Once, while waiting for an MOT for his car, he had read in one of those fancy men's magazines that kids were like clichés and should be avoided like the plague. It was the cleverest joke he knew.

After half a life-time working as a bus conductor, Gazelle's career had been cut cruelly short by new-fangled vehicles with automatic doors at the front and drivers who did all the work, including the collection of fares. At the age of 48 a handful of summers ago, he had taken a modest redundancy packet, bought the small terraced house he had rented for years and had looked ahead to filling the years that stretched into the distance with no small amount of trepidation.

The job working on the cricket pitch had been a life-saver. It was only a part-time role, but Gazelle's commitment was full-time. To be actually paid for the hours he spent cutting the outfield and oiling the inner workings of the old mechanical scoreboard was the stuff his dreams were made of.

As a relative late-comer to cricket, Gazelle found it a constant source of irritation and frustration that he actually wasn't very good at the game he now loved, although it wasn't through a lack of trying. Having erected the practice nets as part of his duties, he would spend many long evening hours inside them trying to master the finer points of batting, the juniors only too happy to trundle down their leg breaks and googlies as Gazelle defiantly defended his stumps. He knew that age wasn't on his side, but perseverance and the outbreak of a dodgy pie-related stomach bug among the lower ranks had meant six appearances in the third team the previous summer. The pride that accompanied this achievement was fuelling a desire for more involvement and now at the first meeting of a new season, he was suddenly faced with pressing concerns on two fronts.

Gazelle raised an urgent hand at the back of the room.

'Mr Chairman. Am I getting this full time groundsman's job, and where's the tour going to?' he blurted out, hoping he'd got his priorities right.

It quickly became apparent that he hadn't.

Norman F. Billington shot him an exasperated glance from the top table and barked: 'Gentlemen. Can we please have some order and stick to the order of items up for discussion.'

'That's right,' came some unlikely support from Sammy on the front row as he lifted himself out of his seat and his glass to his lips. 'What's all this about a new brewery then?'

Norman F. Billington threw down his pencil in despair. It bounced off the table and ricocheted neatly into Sammy's Botham shandy.

'Owzat!' Sammy exclaimed before eagerly turning to face the audience in search of critical acclaim, of which there was none forthcoming.

On the back row, leg-spinner Cameron Cunliffe made a rude gesture followed by an undignified heckle. Weighing in at sixteen stones and with lank hair that reached half way down his back, Cameron Cunliffe had attracted the rather unfortunate nickname of Meat Loaf to which Sammy had staked the original claim. Meat Loaf had never quite forgiven him.

Norman F. Billington's increasing frustration caused his voice to rise: 'Gentlemen, order and I mean order. The first item on the agenda is the re-appointment of the club skipper. Does anybody object to Wobbler – I mean Mr Carter – carrying on in this regard next season?'

Wobbler swivelled his considerable frame in his chair and surveyed all around him like a rear gunner in a Lancaster bomber searching for incoming enemy patrols. Assorted nods of the head indicated there wasn't going to be a squadron of bandits at two o'clock.

Norman F. Billington wrested control once again.

'Right, that's sorted then. Let's move on. We shall need funds as ever, so I shall now ask the treasurer to address the meeting.'

Young Matt Fairacre was sitting alongside Norman F. Billington on the top table. A recently qualified accountant and exceptional second slip, he climbed to his feet nervously to report excellent news on the fiscal front. The idea to spend £3,000 on refurbishing the adjacent second bar and so create a venue for wedding receptions and old-time dance evenings for pensioners at the start of the previous summer had been a resounding success. Gazelle's immaculate green outfield had proved to be an attractive backdrop for many couples celebrating their nuptials. The all-day drinks licence and the chance of al fresco boozing while watching Saturday afternoon games in the sunshine had enamoured brides, grooms and guests alike.

Sammy had been particularly pleased because now even complete strangers thought he was Rodney Marsh. One guest – and a best man to boot – had made this very mistake, but even Sammy had to begrudgingly acknowledge that the downing of a fourth pint of premium strength lager before midday could have clouded the best man's judgment, not unlike the groom's choice of life partner in Sammy's considered opinion.

Matt Fairacre revealed that the vast increase in bar takings alone meant there was surplus money to spend on matters cricket and that breweries were falling over themselves to dispense their ales to a grateful and thirsty public.

There was, he assured members, a deal to be done.

They could virtually take their pick of suppliers and with breweries offering discounts and all manner of incentives, the club found itself in a strong negotiating position.

'In terms of our alcohol-related turn-over, we're forty per cent proof,' he chuckled, the accountant rather than the court jester quickly adding that such an encouraging financial outlook had a direct and positive bearing on the next three items on the agenda, the appointment of a full-time groundsman, an overseas professional and a tour later that summer. All three, in his humble opinion, were within their grasp.

Gazelle couldn't bear the agony any longer. Wringing two snooker balls in the palm of one hand like two over-sized worry beads, he again tried to make himself heard from the back of the room.

But on the front row Sammy once again beat him to it. The beer-soaked wicket-keeper had hit upon an inspirational idea, so clambered to his feet and barked at the chair.

'If all these breweries are so keen to sell their ale here why can't they sponsor us? They could chuck in towards the tour too. We could make a banner and drape it alongside our tour bus. Perhaps we could even squeeze a free barrel of booze out of them and take it with us?'

Sammy was so excited by the prospect that tiny specks of spittle appeared on the tips of his moustache. He made his excuses and retired into the lounge bar to pester the new barmaid with a renewed vigour. The meeting was adjourned for refreshments in some disarray.

THREE

Sammy's rant at the chairman's meeting had not been an entire waste of hot air. Even though his ideas sprang from a flimsy base of unashamed free-loading coupled with an overwhelming desire to enjoy himself as much as possible, more sober minds had identified more realistic possibilities.

Matt Fairacre had officially been charged with finding a new brewery, one with a generous disposition and some quality beverages. He had made meritorious progress. In a position of some strength on both the financial and negotiating front, the young accountant had made two and two add up to five and had some tremendous news to impart.

He had met with a senior representative from Furner's Fine Ales and both parties had welcomed each other on board. The brewery was offering the first six weeks sale or return on all beers, a half price spirits night which they would sponsor and a free trial of an experimental new ale they had just produced called John Peel. To sweeten the deal still further, one free barrel would be offered to the club on a trial basis.

It was Matt Fairacre the sensible accountant who could see the financial benefits to be gained rather than the need for an instant party, but in his excitement the master of the purse had rather recklessly confided in the one man for whom the pursuit of hedonism was a full-time career. When Matt Fairacre told Sammy the good news, the deal-broker was immediately clattered between the shoulder blades with a hefty palm to congratulate him on a job well done.

'So, we get a full barrel of this John Peel stuff all to ourselves then,' guffawed Sammy. 'Top stuff young Matthew. Better keep it that way though. If word gets out there are free and gratis pints behind the bar the punters will come piling in from miles around. We'll need to box clever on this one. Any ideas?'

Matt Fairacre, still reeling from Sammy's pat on the back straight out of a rugby league coaching manual blinked rapidly and tried to compose his slightly muzzy thoughts. He had to admire Sammy's clear thinking and frank admission that he was putting himself and his fellow cricketers before all others. He considered mentioning that Sammy's pint pot was hardly overflowing with a generous brew of human kindness, but quickly decided that this was neither the time nor the place to antagonise his older and far more belligerent colleague. Instead he opted to saunter jauntily along the same boulevard of unashamed self-interest.

He said: 'It would be better if we served it up on a quiet night when there aren't too many guests or visiting players and spectators staying on for a drink. A Sunday night would be good. An early finish on the pitch, a quick win followed by an early start. The old dears will be ballroom dancing next door, but they tend to keep themselves to themselves and use their own bar. Come eight o'clock we should just about have the lounge to ourselves. What do you reckon?'

'Top bloody banana Matthew,' roared Sammy. 'You'll do for me, my lad,' and once again thanked his second slip by leaving him with the distinct impression that he was playing in the second row for Dewsbury.

FOUR

The day of the John Peel night dawned fair and sunny, the cricket scheduled for a 2.00pm start despite Sammy's official request to the committee that they ought to start an hour early because his aged aunt in Thatto Heath had been taken poorly.

The official reply – 'err, right Sammy' – somewhat lacked the chairman's customary gravitas.

The visitors, East Lytham, won the toss and elected to bat. The sense of urgency among the home side to remove the visitors was even more tangible than usual. Behind the stumps Sammy was animation personified. He stretched every sinew, checked every limb for full and correct movement before advising the slightly rotund incoming batsman that there wasn't any need for much gardening because he wouldn't be around for long.

Wobbler opened the bowling to a tremendous roar of encouragement from his fielders who could already sense a tremendous thirst coming on.

The first ball left his grasp at a surprising lick, lifted off a sprightly, well-rolled track and struck the batsman firmly in the mid-riff. The shout for an lbw decision went up man and boy, the umpire totally unimpressed.

Sammy seized his chance: 'That ball hit you with more of a splash than a thud,' he smirked. 'Wait until the quick guy gets his chance.'

Pace bowler Pete Skidmore duly proceeded to skittle his way through the demoralised opposition batsmen at an impressive rate. All out for 122 in time for an early tea at 4.20pm, Wobbler and young Matt Fairacre then steered the home side to their target without the loss of a wicket to the delight of Sammy who had spent the innings padded up and pacing impatiently along the nearest boundary rope having promoted himself up the batting order. He wasn't needed, and when the East Lytham players climbed aboard their coach to travel home after a trestle of tea and stickies – Sammy ushering the last man aboard the charabanc with undue haste and urgency – the party could commence.

The barrel of free beer was duly connected up by Wobbler, Sammy the first at the bar to sample the wares. The first pint foamed and fizzed into the glass, Sammy eyeing it up and down suspiciously before dispatching it in one.

'That hit the spot,' he remarked approvingly. 'I'd better have another to make sure.'

Wobbler called Matt Fairacre over to the other side of the bar and had a quiet word in his ear. 'It's six per cent proof this stuff. Strong for a draught beer you know. Do you think we should tell them?'

Matt Fairacre daringly suggested they let them find out in the morning, before wondering if he really was still concussed after paying far too high a price for pleasing Sammy so much.

Wobbler raised a slight eyebrow before joining the non-too-orderly queue behind the John Peel pump.

And so the evening commenced and the longer it went on, the more unruly it became. Sammy took on all-comers on the snooker table, lost £2 to Wobbler, an inveterate gambler and supreme schemer who was mixing his John Peel with lemonade in the hope that he may yet get his Morris Marina re-sprayed courtesy of the drunken bravado of others on the green baize.

By ten o'clock Sammy had taken off his shirt, rolled up his trousers, eaten a bowl of hyacinths and embarked on a slow fox trot with a 92-year-old spinster after straying into the pensioners' ballroom dancing next door. For a man several times over the drink drive limit, Sammy was remarkably sure-footed. Pete Skidmore was sick on the piano, Meat Loaf managed to lose his moped in a particularly fraught game of three card brag in the games room after which a minor scuffle had broken out, while an elderly lady fainted when Sammy decided the waltz was best performed wearing a jock strap only.

They brought her round by gently lifting her head and wafting a small cream sherry under her nose.

All in all the night was deemed a roaring success, Matt Fairacre sensibly calling time ten minutes before midnight, Sammy only placated when it was pointed out to him that the free barrel of John Peel was in fact empty.

Sammy unceremoniously hauled a snoozing Pete Skidmore out of a comfy chair and announced they were walking home. They staggered into the crisp night air together and rather outrageously decided to take a short cut straight across the cricket field, Sammy demonstrating with great relish and vigorous arm movement how he had stumped a flailing tail-ender earlier that day before relieving himself of his last three pints of John Peel all over the popping crease.

As the two miscreants weaved their way across the outfield to the exit adjacent to the Victorian houses alongside the ground, a familiar face suddenly appeared over one of the back walls. Norman F. Billington peered over his reading glasses at the two cricketers as they waltzed towards him. The two drunkards glanced up like school kids in the naughty corner and were halted in their tracks. For once, Sammy and Pete Skidmore were sharing the same thoughts. They were in deep mire. Urinating on the cricket square had to be a capital offence in Uncle Norman's rule book. They slowly approached the chairman's bobbing head with much trepidation and braced themselves for a broadside of wrath and disapproval. But Norman F. Billington merely leaned gently to one side and then the other before lifting his arms above the top of the wall. On each hand was perched a small metal tray of neatly cut sandwiches.

'Ham or cheese boys?' he asked. 'My wife made them.'

Sammy, in a state of utter disbelief, was struggling to come to terms with this most unexpected reaction from a chairman he had long regarded as bit of an interfering old fuss-pot.

'Err, cheese, err, no ham I think sir,' he stuttered. 'Thanks a lot, cheers, err, I mean thanks.'

'Err, I'll have the cheese then,' slurred an equally agog Pete Skidmore.

And so the two desperadoes disappeared into the night chomping on a most unexpected and undeserved late supper. Sammy resolved there and then that this was a fine yarn worthy of saving for his grandchildren.

As long as he could remember it in the morning of course.

FIVE

As well as providing surprise midnight snacks, Norman F. Billington had also been cooking up other plans.

As ever, the first committee meeting of the season had left many issues still to be resolved, but the chairman had long since decided to take matters into his own hands. He had been aware of the club's new-found financial health for some time, a welcome state of affairs which meant he was at last able to put the finishing touches to a lifetime's ambition.

Norman F. Billington had long desired to bring an overseas professional player to the club. Such an appointment at Crawford would mean added status and respectability. Hopefully it would also introduce a fine young cricketer to the side. Scouring the ranks of the better junior leagues in Queensland and combing the network of contacts he had built up on the other side of the world over the years, the chairman believed he had pinned down the man – well, youth really – who would happily become a Pom for a year.

A rising talent called Stuart Latham had consistently been

racking up a string of impressive scores in one of the better divisions and was a useful pace bowler to boot. The fact that the young cricketer had an agent at just 21 years old demonstrated the potential to be explored and after speaking to his rather brash deal-broker on the telephone, Norman F. Billington had secured a six month contract. He was convinced he had landed a fine sportsman, but one or two details still rankled.

Firstly, he had heard from reputable sources that Stuey – as he preferred to be known – was a bit of a knave. He was a long way from undiluted evil, but certainly knew a good time when he came across one. The chairman had found inner solace by reflecting on Sammy Samson's nefarious social life. He reasoned that if he could keep a reasonably tight tether on one loose cannon then a young Aussie a long way from home surely wouldn't present too many problems.

The second niggle was that the player's agent had squeezed the chairman for far more money than he really wanted to spend. The contract was a generous one, leaving little spare cash to pay for extras such an accommodation and expenses which would have to be kept to a minimum, especially if he was going to successfully run this one past his fellow committee members.

But in a moment of rare inspiration whilst hardening off his pansies in his back garden one Wednesday afternoon, Norman F. Billington had looked over the back wall to watch Gazelle lovingly tending the cricket field and had hit upon one brilliant solution to both of his concerns.

Bernard Gazelle, as the humble groundsman was soon to find out, was to be invited to play a major part in the chairman's ambitious plans.

SIX

The letter that lay on Gazelle's rather tired hall carpet caught his eye immediately.

He recognised the chairman's handwriting – Norman F. Billington was for ever leaving him irritating notes on the door of his tool shed – but this was one missive he picked up with a due sense of anticipation. It would be about the groundsman's job and about time too because Gazelle had left the committee meeting fretting about matters still very much up in the air.

But the letter only contained a handful of paragraphs inviting him to a meeting at the club. Gazelle tutted in exasperation. Would he have to wear his one and only suit or would he get away with his other pair of cords?

The meeting with Norman F. Billington was due to commence at 7.00pm prompt. Gazelle arrived early for the rendezvous and felt surprisingly nervous, the formal nature of it all rather unsettling. The chairman breezed in, issued a friendly smile, waved Gazelle into a private side room and chair before sitting down himself and starting to speak.

'Now Bernard, (only Norman F. Billington ever called him Bernard) I have a proposition to put to you and crave a few minutes of your undivided attention.'

Gazelle shifted uncomfortably in his seat.

Norman F. Billington continued: 'You will doubtless be aware that we are considering making the groundsman's job a full-time position and naturally you would be our first choice to fill that post.'

Gazelle felt less ill at ease.

'However, there are conditions attached and while these will be set out on a formal basis at a later date to constitute part of a contract between the committee and yourself, I can't stress enough that we would regard your compliance in this issue as being in the interests of the club and its future success.'

Gazelle didn't have a clue what he was talking about.

Norman F. Billington twigged from Gazelle's blank stare that he needed to sound less like a home secretary and more like a club secretary. He coughed politely. 'Basically, we want you to do us a favour and you'll get paid for doing it. We intend to appoint our first ever overseas professional player this summer. He's a young Australian called Stuart Latham and we've given him a six month contract. We would like you to provide a roof over his head and look after him. In return for the additional responsibility you are taking on board you will be rewarded appropriately and handsomely in my humble opinion. Obviously you will be able to charge a reasonable rent and the committee will pay all of that. In addition, your groundsman's job at the club will be made full-time and your wages increased accordingly. Is that fair? What do you think?'

Gazelle was having trouble thinking at all. He blurted out:

'Do you mean this guy comes and lives with me?' and immediately regretted his bumbling reply.

Norman F. Billington was, as ever, the diplomat. 'That's exactly what I mean,' he cooed. 'Stuart will be a stranger in an unknown land and will need help and guidance from a man boasting a mature experience of life and one who is fully conversant with the ways of our own little cricket club and the colourful members who make up its character. We believe you are that man.'

Norman F. Billington was rather proud of the persuasive flattery he had doled out and awaited a response. The reply he received surprised both men.

Gazelle and spontaneity had rarely been familiar bedfellows over the years, but on this occasion they were snuggled together under a goosedown quilt with a hot water bottle thrown in for good measure.

He said: 'It's a deal. I'm pretty sure I'll do it, but if I do agree, I want to go on tour to play cricket this summer.'

Norman F. Billington was almost as taken aback as Gazelle himself by this abrupt and unexpected demand, but as no immediate objection sprang to mind, sagely nodded his head in agreement.

'Well, I see no problem with that at the moment,' he replied slowly. 'However, I think we should both go home and sleep on it. Better not to be too hasty, but let's shake on it for the time being.'

Both men exchanged handshakes and bade their farewells, Gazelle tripping gleefully into the lounge where Sammy was perched at the bar ripping the heart out of a Botham shandy.

'Where are you lot going on tour this summer?' Gazelle cried across the room.

'Not too sure,' replied Sammy. 'Somerset I think.'

'Marvellous,' said Gazelle leaving the room with a smile on his face and a spring in his step.

He went straight home, plonked himself down in his comfy chair in front of a glowing real coal fire and thought about nothing else. The more he churned over the proposal in his mind, the more he became convinced that he'd made the right decision, albeit a precipitous one.

He was surely on a winner.

In the plus column were three considerable benefits: He would be on full-time pay, he would receive rent and he would get to go on tour.

The downside – and hopefully such a creature wouldn't even exist – was that he would have a lodger in his spare bedroom. He made a mental note to move the wardrobe over the damp patch on the wall by the chimney breast.

Gazelle was rather accustomed to being alone. He had been virtually fending for himself ever since his bone idle father had made him take up a paper delivery round when he was 12 years old. But his landlord role was only for the summer. Surely he could put up with anything and anyone for six months or so, even an Australian.

Informal chats in the club house had led him to believe that mainly first team players would be putting their names down for the tour. This would leave him out of his depth on the sporting front, but a week away down south with the boys was an opportunity that needed to be grabbed with both hands and given a welcome embrace. He would tell Norman in the morning that he was definitely on board.

Gazelle celebrated by throwing another shovelful of coal on the fire.

SEVEN

It was universally agreed that the sensible head perched on top of Matt Fairacre's young shoulders was eminently qualified to organise the tour.

An early blueprint had already been drawn up.

With partial financial backing from the club and a personal contribution from all those electing to take part in the summer sojourn, the Crawford club would take on cricket sides of equal standing in the south west, or that cider country as Sammy had already decided to call it. Matt Fairacre decided to dispense with a formal committee meeting to discuss the finer points, opting instead to invite Sammy Samson, Wobbler Carter, Meat Loaf and Pete Skidmore to sleeves-rolled-up, beer and sandwiches, round-the-table talks in the lounge bar early one evening.

The only item missing was the sandwiches.

Matt Fairacre outlined his grand design to an attentive audience. They would hire two large minibuses for mid-July. One would seat at least 14 in comfort, the argument being that they needed at least this number to fulfil their commitments on the cricket field and in this way, over four days of matches, all the players would get a day off. The other minibus would be more utilitarian, to transport all the kit and to accommodate Sammy and his personal stash of booze for the journey. Matt Fairacre was getting the hang of this comedy lark. Sammy shot him a threatening look, but he remembered the free John Peel night – just – and refrained from hurling a broadside of insults.

Matt Fairacre was of the opinion that a large bed and breakfast hotel needed to be booked, nothing too posh, obviously, but one that met their requirements. He had already located accommodation he considered would fit the needs of a troupe of overgrown kids off on a summer jolly. Its facilities included a large bar with at least one premium strength lager and two bitters, cask, not keg, a pool table, a dart board, a juke box, Chinese and Indian take-aways within walking distance and a willingness from the owner to keep the bar open late on request.

He would, he assured his small audience, also establish if there was a single room for Sammy and his socks.

There was a murmur of agreement among the gathered few that their organiser was on top of his game, especially when it came to ruining Sammy.

However, Matt Fairacre realised that one free barrel of beer would not mean immunity from his victim's wrath for much longer. A large vein in Sammy's neck was beginning to tick alarmingly, so Wobbler decided to intervene.

He addressed the floor: 'I reckon young Matt's done a grand job. Sammy's reputation's in tatters and we've not even set off. But seriously, I think we can make this work. We need to make an impression though. Something that will make us stand out from the common herd, something to bind us all together, a kind of common identity. I've given it some thought and come up with a couple of ideas.'

Now Wobbler was a man wholly motivated by money.

In many ways this was no bad thing because presented with the task of raising funds for the club, he had no peer. He may well have been sluggish with a buck himself, but when it came to other people's hard-earned beer vouchers, he was a captain of enterprise.

It was inevitable that some unfortunate soul would end up poorer than when they started and this indeed looked certain to be the case as he applied his miser's mind to a four day trip south of the border. But Wobbler believed that his ideas were original and inventive and felt sure he could sell them to his colleagues. The common uniting theme he was so keen to promote involved the mass adoption of the same hat. He unexpectedly pulled a rather dapper straw trilby from under the table and placed it on his head.

He said: 'I got a dozen and a half of these on the seafront at Scarborough the other week. Smart aren't they? They cost a quid each by the way,' he exclaimed as Sammy reached across the table and grabbed one for himself.

Pete Skidmore put one on his head too, nods of approval from the floor spurring on Wobbler.

He added: 'The thing is, we're going to be wearing these all the time and we have to make sure that we do just that, so we need some rules to stick to. Apart from when we play cricket of course, the hats must be worn everywhere we go. That means at breakfast in the morning right through to the pub at night and to make sure everybody joins in. I reckon we should have punishments for the rule-breakers. Anyone not wearing his hat at any time can be fined ten pence by any other member of the tour party and chucked into a general kitty.'

Matt Fairacre won the personal bet he had just made with himself. He just knew there would be cash involved.

But Wobbler hadn't finished yet: 'I've come up with another ruse as well. As there's the high likelihood that we'll be enjoying the odd glass or two of something more toxic than diluted Delrosa on this holiday, I reckon we could raise some money here too. I reckon we should ban right-hand drinking. Everybody has to drink left-handed all the time and that includes cups of tea at breakfast, soft drinks and stuff like that. The same ten pence fine applies to those who don't obey. What do you reckon guys?'

Sammy, who could feel his wallet swelling even as Wobbler spoke, was the first to take him to task.

'And what's happening to this mountain of cash from all these fines Rockefeller?' he demanded. 'Is it funding your early retirement?'

Wobbler's rapid response unit was fully loaded.

'We'll pool it and put it all towards the last night farewell bash on tour. I daresay you'll be filling your boots Sammy. I suspect you'll get your money's worth no matter how many times you forget the rules.'

Sammy unexpectedly nodded his head, took a swift pull of his pint and declined to make further comment. He even pushed a pound across the table to pay for his new hat because he actually quite liked it.

Wobbler may have over-looked a flaw in his plan for the time being, but Sammy hadn't.

He was left-handed.

EIGHT

Stuart Latham clambered off the plane in England.

Someone back home in Australia had told him this was going to be the trip of a lifetime and it felt that way already. The 32 hour flight had taken its toll on his back, his stamina and more importantly, his hair. The first three items Stuey needed most in his new country of residence was a bed, a shower and a mirror, not necessarily in that order. The last thing he needed was a scruffy 54-year-old groundsman waving the back of a Weetabix box in the air on which had been scribbled in green crayon: 'Stuart Latham – your carriage awaits you.'

Earlier in the day, Gazelle had thought this was a rather good idea.

Under pressure from Norman F. Billington to meet and greet the club's new professional and his lodger at the point of arrival, the debutant landlord had stifled his initial objections and decided to go along meekly with the request. It had been Sammy who had pointed out late in the day that his fellow Australian would have no means of recognising a groundsman from the cricket club meeting him at the airport unless, of course, Gazelle kept on his workboots and whitewash-splattered overalls, in which case he would be unmissable. To make sure, Sammy had suggested Gazelle take along his lawn rake as well.

Gazelle had snorted in derision, dug out his pair of lucky interview cords and headed resolutely for the airport in his car.

He stood nervously in the arrivals hall, shuffling from foot to foot as passengers pushed and heaved mountains of luggage on trolleys that seemed to have a sense of direction all of their own. One peak looming at the back was particularly towering and the one-man reception committee suspected that he may have spotted his intended target.

Gazelle suffered from a shallow grounding in many aspects of life, but he was aware that any self-respecting cricketer would have all his own equipment in tow, and lots of it. He waited until half the Himalayas was pushed up to the front of arrivals hall and then edged nervously forward, converted Weetabix box held sturdily aloft above his head.

'Is that you Stuart?' he ventured half-heartedly.

A tousle of blonde hair came poking around the blindside of a suitcase covered in Western Australia travel stickers and a picture parade of various marsupials.

'Yeah mate, that's me. Jeez, what's that above your head?'

Gazelle drew down his greeting card as hastily as he had made it and stuck out a hand of welcome. 'I'm Gazelle. You must be Stuart. Welcome to England.'

'Gazelle! What a great name,' the young Australian replied enthusiastically. 'Why do people call you that?'

'Actually my real name is Bernard. Gazelle is my last name, but that's what everybody calls me. I don't mind really.'

'I prefer to be called Stuey if you don't mind really,' came the flat, almost disappointed reply.

Gazelle held his nerve and helped Stuey push the trolley on to the lift up to the multi-storey car park where their carriage indeed awaited.

By now Gazelle was most conscious that his 14-year-old Triumph Herald was far removed from the luxury transport that perhaps Stuey was expecting. But the young man made no comment as they crammed kit bag, suitcase and hold-alls into both boot and back seat before setting off into the night and heading for home. Five minutes out of the airport and Stuey was slumped in the front seat fast asleep.

Gazelle glanced over at the comatose new companion in his life and wondered what the future might bring.

NINE

Norman F. Billington had no intention of going on tour.

He had no objection to the trip, indeed he had wholeheartedly agreed to sanction the club's partial funding of the jaunt at an earlier committee meeting and felt sure that the benefits would outweigh the potential pitfalls, of which there were plenty.

Norman F. Billington was a gentleman of the old school. He would wear a dark-coloured suit and sensible tie even on the warmest of match days while the former solicitor could look back on an upbringing and education lacking even the odd indiscretion. Ordinarily he would have chucked the rule book at Sammy and Pete Skidmore following their outrageous drunken trespass on to his precious cricket square. Personally he wouldn't have dreamed of trays of sandwiches for late night revellers, but there was one part of his life that cast a long and unwanted shadow. It was Mrs Billington who had insisted on the midnight feast for the uninvited, and as his good lady had spent most of the day making friends with a bottle of gin – an annoying habit which was rapidly turning into an alarming addiction – her husband had deemed it prudent to comply and so avoid yet another late night domestic.

Despite the drunken late night antics of a few, Norman F. Billington still held the current crop of players at the club in high regard and afforded them no small amount of respect. The sacrifices they made were considerable and he appreciated the fact. Most summer weekends were completely given over to cricket while many of them socialised in the club house at night, often into the small hours.

But Norman F. Billington was also aware of the knaves within. Sammy was no serial criminal, but he Meat Loaf and Pete Skidmore could career off the tracks after a few drinks as they had only recently vividly demonstrated on John Peel night. And while more sober-minded souls such as Matt Fairacre, Dave Carter and even Bernard Gazelle were reliable props on which many of the younger players could surely lean, in agreeing to a tour, the chairman had still erred on the side of caution.

Liaising closely with the eminently level-headed Matt Fairacre, the chairman had tried to ensure that the tour would be both a memorable adventure and a sporting challenge, yet one that dove-tailed comfortably alongside late night yards of ale and the occasional three pie sprint without making the scandal and uproar columns in the local press. To this end, the hotel they had booked was designer.

It was designed to keep Sammy and the crew out of bother.

It was located in a relatively small, peaceful village, a self-contained entertainment centre with its own darts board and snooker table, simple pleasures which Norman F. Billington felt would be sufficient to keep a group of reasonably behaved men and accompanying adolescents out of mischief. He had also organised three games of one day cricket against reasonable opposition, choosing clubs in relatively docile hamlets far removed from pleasures of the flesh and similar temptations he felt would only lead to hassle.

This was why the next telephone call he received filled him with dread.

The chairman's many sporting contacts formed a complex web in England as well as Australia and news of the tour being organised had travelled quickly among the lower ranks of the cricketing fraternity in the rural south west.

News had even reached a higher place.

Norman F. Billington had served in the RAF during the Second World War. As he helped to protect his country, it had been a source of great irritation and frustration that he had failed to make the rank of pilot because of one deformed toe on his right foot.

The pilots got all the glory, all the girls and the pen-pushers didn't. That was the truth of the matter and, at the time, was all that seemed to matter. Norman F. Billington had cursed his rotten luck as he endured near terminal disappointment. But as the conflict deepened and the death toll among the pilots rose, he grew to realise that one deformed little toe had almost certainly saved his life.

Another frustrated ace of the skies, whose desire to tackle the Luftwaffe was never fulfilled, was his good friend and peer Ronald Richardson. His childhood asthma had accompanied him into long trousers and beyond and had thwarted his dreams of dog-fights over the southern counties.

The two men, united in their good fortune to be alive at the end of the war, had also been drawn together by a common love of cricket, and the long days of feet under the desk in the RAF would be relieved by the prospect of a sunny weekend spent at the crease. They established a strong bond and remained in touch long after their de-mob suit had fed the moths and, on the sporting front at least, their careers had followed remarkably similar paths. Both men had carried on playing their beloved game long after the medical journals had recommended retirement, their interests given the kiss of life by taking up administrative roles with some gusto. Ronald Richardson was the chairman of the rather high-flying Renwick cricket club in Bristol.

It was Ronald – Richie to the likes of old chums such as Norman F. Billington – who was on the telephone:

'Billers old boy (Norman had always disliked his RAF nickname) how the devil are you? I believe you're coming down to God's own county on tour. You'll be coming to play us of course. I believe you've got a handy young Australian who can teach us a thing or two.'

Norman F. Billington had rather optimistically hoped that the rural grapevine of Somerset might not extend its tendrils to the city. The chairman had cogently reasoned that a bustling Bristol wasn't a smart choice for a first tour, but it seemed that his plans were crumbling. They were about to turn to dust.

Ronald Richardson continued to bark down the telephone: 'I've pencilled you in for a game at our place on the Friday, your last day. It will give your boys the chance to let their hair down a bit in the big city, eh, what? It will be great to meet up again and have a good yarn. We're all looking forward to it already.'

Norman F. Billington was stranded between the wickets with nowhere to go. He could not refuse an old friend, especially one who was already so much in the know, and so told the kind of half-truths that could always be forgiven.

He said: 'Lovely to hear from you again Richie. I was keeping the last day vacant so we could play your boys Renwick and make it a surprise get-together. But news clearly travels fast down your way. We'll make all the arrangements and I'll be in touch soon. It's certainly going to be an experience for all concerned. I'll speak to you again soon about the details and timings and such, but I'll see you in the summer Richie. Bye for now'.

Norman F. Billington replaced the receiver with a hefty weight on his mind as the ramifications of the telephone conversation began to sink in. He now felt personally honour-bound to go on tour, if only for the final day in Bristol, the fraught last leg of a mission not without its risks already, he mused to himself.

Sammy, Gazelle, Meat Loaf and the swinging city was a combination he had been rather hoping to avoid and then there was the relatively unknown quantity that was Stuey, the wild card from Down Under on the biggest holiday of his short lifetime.

He telephoned Matt Fairacre to tell him of the developments, explaining that he would now also need to book a hotel in Bristol for the last night of the tour following their game against Renwick.

Matt Fairacre replied that it wouldn't be a problem. Norman F. Billington was inclined to disagree, but kept his thoughts to himself before deciding to sleep on it.

TEN

Stuey awoke and thought he was still asleep and dreaming.

Everything around him was unfamiliar, wood-chip walls, an ancient oak wardrobe pushed unusually close to the fireplace, shabby curtains that didn't quite meet in the middle and he didn't have a clue what time of day it might be. He closed his eyes again only for reality and memory to come rushing in. It was his first day as a stranger in a foreign land in a strange house while a strange bloke had shown one weary traveller into a strange bedroom a bewildering amount of hours earlier. All this strangeness was quite overwhelming and if that wasn't distressing enough, he really did need to wash his hair. Wearing only a pair of Speedos and a bemused look on his face, Stuey abandoned his bivouac, shinned hand and foot down the narrow staircase and stepped straight into the lounge.

A sitting Gazelle, a plateful of pilchards on toast staring up from his lap, turned to greet his new lodger. After directing a travel-weary Stuey straight into bed the night before, Gazelle had booked the morning off work to further accommodate and help acclimatise his jet-lagged Australian guest.

He had started to worry that he would need the afternoon off as well.

'Hello there Stuey,' he said. 'Did you sleep OK?' 'Fine thanks,' Stuey replied with a gaping yawn. That flight left me tuckered out. What time is it?'

'Just before noon. This is my lunch, err, pilchards on toast,' Gazelle added, pointing to twin straggly lines of unappetising tinned fish on two insipid slices of half-browned bread slowly going cold on his knee. 'I have to leave for work soon. I'm the groundsman at the cricket club, but I think you know that already,' he added nervously.

Stuey looked around the room and wondered how far he had stepped back in time and exactly what period of time it might be.

The wood-chip wallpaper would seem to have come as a job lot while a rickety clothes-airer festooned with half-dry Wellington boots and murky gardening overalls stood in front of a fireplace containing a mound of cold grey ashes that had long since ceased to serve a useful purpose. A battered wooden clock with silver Roman numerals ticked wearily on top of a shabby slate surround. A pair of socks had been lodged underneath the clock so that two fraying feet dangled in mid-air above where a fire ought to have been. The dusty hearth at the front, abutting a frayed carpet, was occupied by a half-full, lop-sided coal scuttle which rested awkwardly alongside two chipped tea cups stained by brown rings. Half-chopped kindling was strewn over the remainder of the stone surface. There was only one comfortable chair in the room and that was taken, the row of dead-eyed pilchards staring into mid-space just below Gazelle's bulging stomach now starting to make Stuey feel quite nauseous. But as his survey of the sparsely-clad room neared its end, Stuey became aware of an unusual omission.

There was no television. Domestic bliss seemed even further away.

'Nice place,' fibbed the Australian, 'live here on your own then?'

'Well, I did', replied Gazelle, 'but now there are two of us.'

'What do you do for entertainment at night then?' asked Stuey. 'You've not got a television. Down the pub all the time are you?'

'Hardly ever,' replied Gazelle. 'Don't go much for that nasty beer. I stop in because I like to read, do crosswords or just watch the fire burn.'

'You watch the fire burn!' exclaimed Stuey.

'That's right,' said Gazelle. 'It's my faithful friend and the flames are never quite the same from one night to the next.'

Gazelle realised instantly that his reply, although honest, had made him out to seem slightly odd, even bordering on the eccentric. So he mumbled a few lame excuses, rose to his feet, ditched his stone-cold pilchards in the kitchen bin and explained that he really did need to go to work.

He slammed the front door behind him leaving a bemused Stuey in his new home, cold, confused, all alone and with far too much to fret about.

ELEVEN

Stuey had already arranged a meeting with Norman F. Billington to take place later that same afternoon and it could not come soon enough.

It was meant to be an informal, welcoming chat leading on to all matters cricket, but Stuey had far weightier issues on his mind. He was ready to admit that he hadn't given his decision much time, but he was already convinced that he and Gazelle living under the same roof wasn't going to work.

He took a seat in Norman F. Billington's kitchen, accepted the offer of a lukewarm can of beer, and with dead-eyed pilchards and peculiarly placed wardrobes floating in front of his eyes, started to outline his worrying predicament to a mentor three times his age.

Stuey was still slightly wary of the club chairman, the man who was paying his wages after all, and so was careful not to let off too many maroons. He tactfully explained that he didn't think he and Gazelle were particularly well-suited, which was in fact the finest piece of understatement he'd mustered in his entire 21 years. He felt the age difference was too great, there was a lack of common interests while he wasn't particularly impressed with the accommodation on offer or his landlord's unsettling habits.

'The place is grubby, the guy's not even got a television and he eats dead fish in front of a fire that's gone out,' whined Stuey.

Surprised and intrigued, Norman F. Billington drew in a deep breath and leaned back on his worldly experience. He had, if he was being honest with himself, been expecting something like this. Gazelle's recruitment as a makeshift landlord been a push-over really, now all he had to do was sweeten Stuey, although in private Norman F. Billington had been somewhat taken aback to learn that Gazelle didn't have a television. How could he possibly not watch Test match special?

He dismissed such thoughts as he spoke to the young Australian in a fashion designed to be a soothing blend of a firm hand inside a comforting glove lined with understanding and compassion.

'This is an arrangement that surely has to be given some more time,' he purred as reassuringly as possible. 'You've only spent one night in the house so that's hardly allowed you two to get to know each other. Gazelle is a decent man at heart and you have to remember that all this is new to him as well. We've given you a top class contract to come over here and play for us and in that agreement is written that we provide the accommodation. I think you'll find Gazelle loves his cricket just as much as you do and that once the initial shock of everything being so new and different has worn off you'll get on like, well, like a house on fire.

'What kind of fish does he actually eat then?' he added, curiously.

Stuey looked at him askance: 'Pilchards. Pilchards on toast with dead eyes and they looked quite horrible,' he replied, failing to disguise the surprise that he'd even been asked the question.

'I think sardines may be more palatable for all concerned,' replied Norman F. Billington, not quite believing the surreal diplomatic territory into which he'd strayed. 'And on the television front, well, I think I can sort that out. I'll have a word with the committee because I feel sure that under the circumstances they will pay for one to be installed in Gazelle's house. Your lot – err, I mean the Australian national cricket team – are coming over later this summer and who would want to miss that? I'll tell the members that a television is needed so you can both watch the Test matches at home. That's the ticket. In the meantime, all the players are getting together for a few drinks after nets tonight. I've told them all about you and this is your chance to meet everybody socially. There's far more to Crawford cricket club than Bernard Gazelle you know.'

Stuey fervently hoped that the chairman was right, but despite the relatively reassuring nature of his chat with the chairman, he was still determined to engineer an early escape from the man who dried his socks under a clock. He and Gazelle could be nibbling lightly-poached fresh salmon on French rye bread while watching the cricket on a 24 inch colour Pye and Stuey was convinced it still wouldn't work.

But he was already hatching a devious plan.

He needed to tell Gazelle something about himself, a startling revelation which he felt sure would ensure a rapid showing of the exit door with a hefty groundsman's boot aimed at his dastardly backside whether he wanted to leave or not. He grinned at the prospect, stood, polished off his warm beer with a slight grimace and thanked the chairman for his hospitality.

Stuey left the house looking forward to his first bash in the nets that evening followed by the chance to blow the froth off a couple of chilled lagers with his new Pommie companions, most of whom he hoped weren't also still living in the 1950s.

TWELVE

Sammy was particularly keen to make the acquaintance of his fellow Australian. He felt certain they would have lots in common, not least a huge moustache you could lag a loft with.

Sammy arrived in the nets early, bristling with anticipation and imagination, grabbing a sturdy willow and pretending he was a swashbuckling mid-order batsmith proudly playing for his native Australia at the Sydney Cricket Ground, crashing a huge six, a mighty blow that clinched the fifth and decisive Test over a shabby bunch of hapless New Zealanders. He and Rod would be sharing plenty of tinnies whilst indulging in lots of manly back-slapping and hilarious reminiscing that night.

Meanwhile, back in the real world, Stuey had somewhat reluctantly accepted a lift to the ground in Gazelle's battered Triumph Herald, choosing to clamber out on the main road that ran adjacent to the club and walk across the car park on to the outfield.

Sammy had just picked up the man of the match award

from the Australian Prime Minister in front of an adoring 65,000 crowd at the SCG when he spotted the newcomer arriving. His disappointment was almost tangible. There was no walrus moustache, no sprouting chest hair and not even the slightest hint of ale swell in the stomach region. Instead, a tall, slim youth with a tidy mid-riff and blonde streaks in his hair strolled nonchalantly into their midst and said: 'G'day all. Bonza evening, Stuey's the name.'

At least the accent was thoroughbred antipodean, but as far as Sammy was concerned, this was the only hint of authenticity so far. He was, however, prepared to give the new kid on the block the benefit of the doubt, so he elbowed a protesting Meat Loaf in the ribs and pushed him roughly to one side before bustling to the front of the gathering to be first to shake his new team mate's hand. The Australian accent he had honed all winter had to be perfect: 'G'day mate. Sammy Samson's the name. I'm a long way from home too.'

'Yep, that's right, a whole mile and a half away from home,' piped up a rib-clutching Meat Loaf, before adding: 'And don't be fooled by that fake accent Stuey, Sammy's about as Australian as I am, and I don't even like lager.'

Another throbbing vein in Sammy's neck was the encouragement Wobbler needed and he quickly intervened. Norman F. Billington had already mentioned that he expected the club skipper to take some responsibility for the general behaviour of the players in the presence of their new professional, so here was an ideal opportunity to put his authority to the test.

Wobbler said: 'Boys, boys. Can we keep a focus? Stuey's not travelled half way around the world to listen to you lot bickering and squabbling. We're a team and Stuey has to be

45

made to feel welcome and part of that team so let's try and behave like one. Meat Loaf will introduce you all to Stuey one by one and then we'll get on with the practice session in the nets. A quid says I take three wickets.'

Meat Loaf glowered at Sammy, but dutifully introduced Stuey to his new colleagues accompanied by hand shakes up there in the high teens, Sammy's glad-handing so sincere that it made the Australian wince.

A hundred yards away Norman F. Billington was surveying proceedings from behind his garden wall, his eyes screwed tightly together above his half-lens reading glasses. But as the players dispersed into the nets, he pushed open his gate and strolled across the field to join a handful of fellow committee members and partake of a closer and clearer inspection of their expensive overseas investment. After the accommodation wrangle and tour complications, the chairman needed some reassurances that at least one part of his plan was on course.

Stuey did not disappoint.

Aware that he was under watchful scrutiny, the young Aussie made an effort to show what a splendid all-round cricketer he was. His third ball up-rooted Meat Loaf's leg stump much to Sammy's delight, Sammy himself faring only four balls better as Stuey's deceptive pace impressed one and all. At the crease he demonstrated his ability with the bat, crashing Pete Skidmore for a straight six back over his head, even Wobbler's fiendish off-spin failing to trouble the dashing new arrival.

Down near the long grass, a recently-arrived Gazelle somewhat begrudgingly conceded a reluctant admiration, while nearer to the action, Norman F. Billington was quite delighted. The considerable amount of money he had invested in their first ever professional seemed to have secured the club a prized asset and suddenly even the trip to Bristol seemed even slightly attractive rather than downright daunting.

The chairman was, however, delivered a swift reality check when Sammy suggested they all repair to the lounge bar half an hour early to welcome their new member in the time-honoured fashion, Stuey agreeing at once which rather alarmingly seemed to mean decision made.

Behind the bar, Laura smiled for the first time for days as Stuey flashed her a winning grin, ran his fingers through his blonde rinse, introduced himself, leaned over the bitter pump and started talking hairdressers.

Sammy, trailing close in his wake, grimaced and was forced to give his new chum his second chance of the night, a decision made that much easier when Stuey announced that the first round was on him. The Australian nodded with vigorous approval when Sammy enthusiastically detailed the make-up of a Botham shandy and promptly ordered one for himself, an occasion for the immediate forgiveness of early trespasses in Sammy's book.

The night was a huge success, pints quaffed, yarns swapped and Laura volunteering for an extra hour manning the pumps which was certainly attributable to the presence of one coiffured antipodean and did not go unnoticed.

And even though Stuey felt as though he had inherited an over-protective father when Norman F. Billington rolled up shortly before midnight and insisted on giving the new recruit a lift home, he did not put up a lot of resistance. He was fairly mellow to say the least after spending most of the night in Sammy's company and if he was being honest, he wouldn't have a clue how to find his way back to Gazelle's house on his own.

On the way home, as Norman F. Billington droned on about the start of the county championship season and the need to visit Bristol on the last night of the tour later that summer, Stuey resolved that he would deliver the news that would result in his immediate expulsion from Gazelle's home, assuming his landlord was still up and awake of course, which he very much doubted.

But as Norman F. Billington pulled up outside the terraced house there was a flickering light behind the curtains. Stuey wished his chairman goodnight, walked across the pavement and pushed open an unlocked front door.

Gazelle was indeed still up, sitting in his comfy chair in front of a glowing coal fire.

He turned and spoke as Stuey entered the room: 'Hello there. I thought I'd wait up for you, not least because I've not given you a front door key yet which was stupid of me. I've made you a couple of rounds of chicken sandwiches. They're in the kitchen. Bring them through if you wish.'

Stuey mumbled a half gratitude and went to fetch his supper. As he came back into the lounge and settled in front of the fire on the small wooden stool thoughtfully provided, he could feel the resolve to deliver his devastating news ebbing away. He was still determined to go through with it, but was slowly convincing himself that this was not the right moment.

Firstly there was the completely selfish and practical point of view.

If Gazelle took the news really badly – and there was every chance that he would – then he might just boot him out there and then which would mean no bed for the night. But what was really worming into Stuey's mind as he chewed appreciatively on his second chicken sandwich was the fact that the house seemed so much more homely and hospitable with a real coal fire glowing in the grate. He took that thought with him as he thanked his host and retired for the night and while he was soon asleep, it had taken a firm mental resolution of: 'Jeez, I've gotta get out of this place,' before he slipped safely into the arms of Morpheus.

THIRTEEN

The next day was a Saturday and heralded the start of the new cricket season which for Crawford meant a home tie against Sutton Heath.

Gazelle was spending the morning at home before driving to the club to put the finishing touches to the wicket at lunchtime which meant he was sitting at the small table in the kitchen drinking a cup of tea when Stuey came tumbling downstairs at 10.00am. Despite his dishevelled appearance and hair all over the parish, Stuey's mind was a tidy stratagem of layered tactics. He believed he had worked out exactly what he needed to say in order to get kicked out of the house. As he accepted a steaming cup of tea from his landlord and pulled up a chair, Stuey delivered his opening salvo.

Mustering as much apparent indifference as possible, he said: 'By the way Gazelle, is there anywhere I can get my hands on any grass around here? I haven't had a decent smoke since I flew in from Australia.'

A puzzled Gazelle looked up from his tea cup not at all sure how to react or even if he'd heard him correctly.

'Grass?' he replied, but his voice was pitched too high for the required innocent tone and he sensed that his cheeks were reddening. 'Are you talking about the grass on the field at the club?'

Stuey didn't know if Gazelle was bluffing or just plain stupid and didn't really care.

'No man, grass, the stuff you put in joints. You know, marijuana, cannabis, weed, I don't know what you guys call it over here. I just need to know where I can get some and when I do, will it be OK to smoke it in the house?'

Having launched both his best shots deep into enemy territory, Stuey braced himself for some explosive return fire.

In his head, he was already packing his suitcase.

In Gazelle's head, it was a complete mess. Complex, contradicting messages bounced around his brain, none of them making the short cerebral leap to any kind of cogent reply.

Gazelle didn't know what to say. He knew what he wanted to say – even ought to say – that he didn't want any drug-smoking hippy under his roof and that he'd better be out of the place pronto, feet not touching the ground as he did so. But despite the fact that Stuey's outrageous candour had knocked him back completely, in the few seconds it had taken these audacious requests to sink in, Gazelle had worked out that he was skewered on the horns of a deep dilemma.

He knew only too well the benefits of having a lodger. Let's face it, he'd thought about little else ever since Stuey had breezed into his life and living room. Gazelle realised that under normal circumstances he would not have hesitated and chucked him out. He wasn't having some pot-head weirdo taking mind-altering, illegal substances in his home. No way.

But these weren't normal circumstances. Stuey brought his problems, but he brought his positives for Gazelle too, including a full-time job, a considerably increased monthly income and a coveted place on the tour.

Both men were sitting on opposite ends of a kitchen table staring at each other without saying a word.

But the silence belied the mental turmoil seething just below the surface, Stuey's mind now a ferment as well. He had fully expected a furious Gazelle to blow his stack at once which would mean one scheming Australian caught up in the torrent of red hot lava streaming down the upper slopes. He would go with the flow he had smiled to himself. But while he could see that Gazelle had clearly been deeply troubled by his audacious requests, the volcano merely smouldered.

It was Stuey who broke the silence.

He said: 'So, have you got a problem with what I've just asked Gazelle? If you have, just say so and I'll go find myself somewhere else to live.'

Gazelle still didn't know what to say. He needed time to think. There was far too much at stake to come up with an instant decision, especially over an issue as contentious as illegal drugs. He decided that he must have breathing space and said: 'Err, I need more time to consider what you've asked me. I just can't think at the moment. I've got to go down to the club now. I'll speak to you later today.'

And with that Gazelle swept out of the room, leaving a bewildered Stuey as lost for words as his landlord had been two minutes earlier.

But he still had a roof over his head which was a surprise in itself.

FOURTEEN

Sutton Heath batted long and hard into the afternoon. This suited Gazelle as he paced up and down the boundary rope because it provided the time he needed to ponder his predicament. He watched Stuey pound in to bowl. His sprightly pace and accurate length troubled all the batsmen and of the three wickets that had fallen as an early tea was taken, the Australian had two of them by his name. Why such a talented young athlete should desire the need for artificial mental stimulation niggled at Gazelle, but he was sensible enough to realise this was not the issue demanding his attention at the moment.

Sutton batted too long for a winner to emerge, an honourable draw declared as the light started to fade in the relatively early Spring evening. Gazelle packed away the stumps and assorted kit before roping off the square and heading off towards the lounge bar.

He really did need a word with Stuey.

He found the Australian in big demand, not least from

Laura whose alluring new dress had already attracted Stuey's attention much to the annoyance of Sammy who was relegated to the role of mere by-stander, a Botham shandy in each hand as he waited patiently to talk over the game with the new professional whose company he was finding increasingly pleasurable.

Gazelle knew that he had to wait his turn as well and after losing two straight pints to Wobbler on the snooker table, seized his chance when he spotted Stuey making his way to the toilets.

Gazelle headed him off, diverting his target on to the empty ballroom dance floor next door. He dragged him over to a corner, looked furtively over both shoulders before getting straight to the point and testily firing off a broadside of questions at a bewildered Stuey.

'Right then, about what you asked me at breakfast this morning. I think I'm ready to talk about it, but first I want some answers. How much of this stuff do you smoke? Do you take any other drugs and if you get caught, am I going to get into trouble as well? And when you do smoke it, what does it do to you? Do you turn into a gibbering wreck and see reptiles climbing up the walls and things like that?'

Stuey struggled to respond.

This was not the outcome he had expected or had particularly wished for. Nor had he anticipated being bombarded with so many questions. So he shrugged his shoulders and decided to tell Gazelle the truth, or as near to it as he dare stray. He said: 'Look, I only smoke two or three times a week and then only late at night and I've never even tried any other drugs, not been tempted to really. I've not seen any crocs crawling along the mantelpiece so far, but if I do, I'll let you know. Look mate, if this habit of mine troubles you so much then I'll move out like I said before. I reckon that's only fair dinkum.'

Gazelle looked at him long and hard before adding: 'I can't claim that I'm happy with what you do in your spare time, but you can still stay if you want to. All this is new and strange to me. It must be a generation difference and I'll get used to the idea. I suppose I'll have to. But it has to remain a close secret between you and me and in answer to your earlier question, no, I haven't got a clue where you might lay your hands on some of your, err, stuff.'

Stuey had to privately admit to himself that he felt a modicum of relief to be told he could stay despite his earlier determination to quit the place. He had, if he was being honest, spent far more time of late thinking about the lovely Laura rather than the need to move house. On the restricted occasions he had talked to her – when he had managed to escape the attentions of the over-possessive Sammy – he had found her to be an attractive, engaging girl with hidden depths. The barmaid's job turned out to be a temporary affair, just for the Easter holidays. Laura was a second year student studying psychology at Bristol University which went some way to explaining why she had so little time for Sammy's obvious overtures. Hadn't Norman F. Billington mentioned something about Bristol? He resolved to find out.

And to score some weed of course.

FIFTEEN

The romance between Stuey and Laura blossomed quickly.

She had volunteered to show him the local beauty spots in her car one afternoon, and after that 20 minutes was finished, the two of them had spent the rest of the day talking and kissing in the back seat. The fact that Stuey had kept his hands to himself was a clear indication of his depth of feeling for his new companion. He had never imagined that a Pommie Sheila could be so irresistible and yet somehow untouchable.

Time and fate however were adversaries. Laura had only a week of her Easter vacation left before she quit working behind the bar to return to her studies in Bristol. Stuey talked about Norman F. Billington mentioning Bristol, Laura's geography lesson for the day teaching her new Australian boyfriend that the city lay at the hub of the West country, near to where the summer tour was taking place. It was quite likely that Bristol was on the agenda.

But the present was far more important and Laura and Stuey spent their last few days together hand in hand, feelings of mutual affection growing ever stronger.

As a result, Stuey spent very little time at Gazelle's house. He would return after midnight every night, long after Gazelle had gone to bed and rise the day after at some time in the mid-morning, long after Gazelle had gone to work.

Drug-related fretting seemed like a distant memory for Gazelle, but after Stuey had waved an emotional farewell to a university-bound Laura on the railway station a week later, real life was soon to come knocking on the groundsman's front door.

Stuey's full-time love life had also left little opportunity for late night Botham shandies, much to Sammy's dismay. Stuey had even been late for nets one night, Sammy officially appalled and blowing several fuses as the session started without their star professional. But when Stuey did eventually turn up, Sammy was surprisingly subdued. The players all knew where the Australian had been – their lurid minds waywardly imagining what he might have been up to – and while Sammy was particularly upset, there was little sign of outward displeasure, at least when Stuey was in the vicinity.

Sammy's emotions were riding a rollercoaster all of their own. He felt jealous, but jealous of Laura for being with Stuey which was surely the wrong way around. Sammy's logic told him that he was missing Stuey, which had to be a bit of a worry to say the least.

He chucked the cricket ball viciously from one glove to the other before hurling it and a few choice insults at Meat Loaf who had the temerity to sit down after three lacklustre overs of medium pace bowling, the sweat pouring off his brow in torrents as indeed it did most of the time.

Sammy's one consolation throughout these troubled times was the fact that he knew Laura would be returning to university soon, after which he would surely be welcoming Stuey back into his drinking club for the 'after-fun' as he liked to call it.

But Laura's departure had no such effect on Stuey.

After evening nets on the first night without his girlfriend, Stuey made his excuses before heading straight back to Gazelle's house on foot. En route, he called at a newsagent's shop for some single rolling papers and half an ounce of tobacco. He also nipped into the late-night grocery store next door. He hadn't laid his hands on any grass in his adopted home yet, but he'd stashed a small amount in the torn lining of his cricket bag back before leaving Australia.

This hadn't been smoked yet, but it would be tonight.

Stuey pushed his way through Gazelle's front door at 9.00pm to find his landlord still up and the coal fire burning brightly. There were two new additions to the room, another armchair by the fire and a large television in the corner.

Gazelle shifted in his seat and smiled at Stuey: 'I got the other chair from a charity shop and the committee's paid for the TV. There's not much worth watching though, not until the Test cricket starts later this summer. I was beginning to think they were both a waste of time and money because I've seen so little of you recently. I believe you've been courting strongly.'

'Something like that,' replied Stuey evasively, not too sure what courting actually meant and keen to quickly change the subject. 'I reckon you're right about the television though. Most of the stuff's rubbish so I'm not bothered. You can leave it switched off for me. I'm going to roll up a joint now anyway, if you don't mind of course.'

Gazelle's mouth turned dry, but he remained calm, nodded his head slowly and accepted that the moment he had thought about so much and dreaded for so long had finally arrived. He hurriedly picked up the evening paper and buried his head deep inside it even though he'd already read it from cover to cover.

Stuey legged it upstairs for his grass, nipping into the kitchen on the way back down, picking up a small stool which he placed between his legs when he returned to the lounge. He pulled three single papers out of their packet, glued them together before tearing down one side to create a long-sided rectangle into which he gently coaxed some thin strands of tobacco to form an orderly line down the middle. Reaching for the grass out of his pocket, he gently sprinkled some of it on top of the tobacco before rolling the whole lot into a thin tubular cone, sticking a piece of tightly rolled up cardboard into one end. He raised his head and looked over at Gazelle who was peering around the side of the amateur sports section watching his every move in absorbed fascination.

'That's it, finished,' proclaimed Stuey. 'I don't suppose you've got an ash tray by any chance?'

'I don't suppose I have,' replied Gazelle.

'Didn't think you would have, that's why I borrowed one from the cricket club last week,' said Stuey, bounding back up the stairs and returning with what looked like a multi-coloured frisbee emblazoned with beer adverts.

Stuey settled back in his comfy chair and lit the joint, pulling the pungent-smelling smoke deep into his lungs before exhaling at his leisure. He repeated this several times, stopping to re-ignite after a few minutes before carefully extinguishing the joint with just less than half of it remaining.

'I'll save that for later,' he said, before relaxing deep into his chair and pushing his bare toes nearer the warming fire.

Three feet away Gazelle was a man filled with fascination,

tormented by a million questions he desperately needed to ask. What was going through Stuey's mind? What would he do next? Would he start talking strangely? Would he behave in a bizarre fashion? Could he already see strange scaly creatures crawling out of the plaster? Would armed police screech to a halt outside at any moment and break down the front door? Would civilisation come crashing to an end?

After about ten minutes of non-event silence, Stuey suddenly clambered to his feet and walked over towards the kitchen.

'Where are you going?' Gazelle blurted out far too anxiously.

'I'm going to get a can of lager out of the fridge. Do you want one?' replied Stuey.

'Err, yes, I think I might, err, thanks,' stuttered Gazelle, amazed by the normality of it all. Here he was, in own lounge with a foreign bloke whose brain was on the brink of total breakdown after bombarding it with an illegal substance, yet everything was as it should be, or at least as close to as it should be in Gazelle's own whirring mind.

Stuey returned with two cans and two glasses, poured them both, took a long drink of his own, handed the other to Gazelle before engaging his landlord in conversation. 'This cricket tour we're going on in summer, do you know much about it? Who's in the squad and is it right that we're going to Bristol?'

This was a long way from the incomprehensible babble that Gazelle was expecting, Stuey even coming up with a new and intriguing snippet of information about the tour. Knowing Norman F. Billington as he did, he had rather imagined more rural venues than Bristol, but life was full of surprises these days.

'I, I, I don't really know if we're going to Bristol, Stuey, it's the first I've heard of it,' came his stammering reply. 'I think most of the guys have signed up for it though, Sammy, Meat Loaf, Wobbler, the usual suspects. And I'm going too.'

Gazelle failed to add that his place on the tour was dependent on Stuey remaining as his lodger, reflecting that this was one piece of information that may have to stay a secret for some time.

The two men drank two more cans each and talked cricket for the next hour or so, Stuey proving to be far more entertaining company than Gazelle had ever imagined, some of his more outlandish yarns about his sporting days in Australia raising a chuckle or two and even a modicum of envy in Gazelle. He then grabbed the chance to ask his lodger more about his marijuana habit and found Stuey more than willing to talk about it.

Stuey said: 'It's quite common back home. Guys can grow grass in their own gardens because the weather's so good and that way you don't have to get mixed up with dodgy dealers and all the criminality that involves. And you don't get ripped off. Personally I don't see what all the fuss is about or why the stuff's illegal. Guys get up to far worse stuff when they're falling over rotten drunk on lager and grass doesn't leave you with a stinking hangover either. If you need to chill out or even talk a lot, then I reckon you can't beat it.'

As if to prove his point, Stuey proceeded to smoke the rest of the joint during the latter stages of their conversation

And as an evening of enjoyable, light-hearted banter drew to a close, Stuey once again headed for the kitchen.

'No more drink for me,' piped up Gazelle as his lodger padded across the room. 'I'm going to bed soon.'

'I'm not getting a drink', replied Stuey. 'I won't be long.'

And a few minutes later he duly returned with a large

dinner plate in his hand. On the plate was piled a roughly-hewn cheese sandwich, a tub of coleslaw, a pack of digestive biscuits and a rather large bar of fruit and nut chocolate, most of which he had purchased at the grocer's shop earlier.

He plunged his fork into the coleslaw and shovelled it into his mouth.

'Do you always have such a large late supper then?' enquired Gazelle.

'No, not usually,' replied Stuey, tucking in enthusiastically.

'But I just can't resist this stuff when I'm stoned. Have you never heard of the munchies?'

Gazelle weighed up his reply carefully: 'So, you're only scoffing all that lot because of that grass stuff you smoked earlier. Is that right?'

'That just about sums it up,' replied Stuey. 'You've not got any cheese and onion crisps have you?'

'You'll never get to sleep after scoffing that lot,' remarked Gazelle.

'Oh, but I most certainly will,' Stuey replied. 'I'll sleep like a log. Probably wake up on the fire in the morning.'

Stuey laughed aloud at his own joke, Gazelle smiling ruefully as he rose from his chair to go to bed.

'I'll wish you goodnight then. If you're stopping up, you might want to chuck some more coal on the fire.'

'I might just do that, I could even watch the television for a while', replied Stuey and as Gazelle made his way up the creaking stairs, he grabbed the scuttle and topped up the glowing embers.

The flames were soon licking up the back of the chimney, but as Stuey settled back into his chair again, all thoughts of switching on the television deserted him.

Instead he found himself staring deep into the leaping flames, his bloodshot eyes transfixed as the burning coals danced and flared.

Then an uncomfortable truth hit home. The very same fire that he had found so appalling shortly after arriving in England now seemed rather appealing.

Stuey and Gazelle had both grown up a bit that night.

SIXTEEN

The alarm clock started to jangle at 6.30am on the first Monday of June. Sammy rolled over in his bed, clattered it to a halt with a hefty palm, sat up in bed and indulged in a free moan.

'I really don't see why it has to be me who picks up these bloody minibuses. And to make matters worse, Meat Loaf's coming too. Have you seen how much that bloke sweats these days?'

One pillow along the bed, Angela stirred reluctantly into half-consciousness.

'Did you have to wake me up?' she groused. 'What time is it?'

'Time for me to go,' Sammy replied. 'I'll see you in five days' time. Say goodbye to the boys for me when they wake up will you?'

He kissed Angela lightly on the cheek, dressed, went downstairs and just had time to make a mug of tea before Meat Loaf banged on the front door, beads of perspiration popping out like translucent pearls on his forehead as he barged his way through into the lounge.

Sammy grunted what Meat Loaf assumed to be a friendly word of greeting before they both went outside and chucked a suitcase into the boot and a large kit bag on to the back seat of Meat Loaf's dad's car before the pair set off for the van hire depot ten miles away.

'How's the missus?' asked Meat Loaf as he crunched the car into gear and trundled into the improving light.

Sammy had been married since he was 18 and had known Angela ever since they were school playground sweethearts. They had been man and wife for 12 years, their twin boys aged 11 – one called Rod of course – already fine young cricketers mainly due to their father's studious tutelage.

There were times when Sammy regretted marrying so young and this, he would reassure himself, was another reason why he felt jealous of Stuey. When he was 21, Sammy had been mowing down pedestrians with a pushchair made for two, in stark contrast to Stuey, who, at the same age was a major player in a quite different ball game. This 21-year-old was on the trip of a lifetime 15,000 miles away from home, single and creaming off the pick of the local girls from under everybody's noses, Sammy's included.

But for all his outrageous flirting, Sammy's chat-up lines consisted mainly of bluff, bluster and showing off. Despite his readiness to try and impress members of the opposite sex, a scorecard of infidelity over the last decade or so would read plenty of overs bowled, but no wickets taken.

In some ways he was rather pleased that Stuey and Laura had hit it off because it probably would have irked him more had the Australian turned out to be some serial womaniser working his way through the female population of the northern provinces.

And hit if off Stuey and Laura certainly had.

Laura's return to resume her studies in Bristol after Easter had restricted their time together, but she had spent a large chunk of her meagre grant travelling home most weekends to be by her new squeeze's side which inevitably meant watching hours of cricket until they could get to do some actual squeezing.

Sammy was reminded very much of his early days with Angela when she also spent every Saturday and Sunday admiring the dashing young cricketer in her life before happily volunteering to take to the field with mid-afternoon jugs of chilled orange cordial on the warmer days. Sammy sadly reflected that his wife had only been down to the club once this season and that had been to pick up the boys after a junior game.

Meanwhile, Stuey's popularity had not been limited to one starry-eyed ex-barmaid and university undergraduate. The Australian was a big hit at the club in more ways than one. His friendly, out-going nature and fondness for a drink meant he had dove-tailed neatly into the social scene at the club while his cricketing skills had gone from strength to strength.

Not entirely, but mostly due to his prowess, the side was second in the league having lost only one game. Promotion was already being discussed, a prospect that filled Norman F. Billington with delight and fully vindicated his decision to throw funds in the direction of a full-time professional.

In the light of his presence on the forthcoming tour, Gazelle had attempted to spend more social time at the club during the evenings at the weekend and had found it to his liking.

He marvelled and was bewildered by Stuey's exploits in equal measure.

His lodger had continued to smoke grass at his home two

or three nights a week and after playing cricket at the weekends too, having 'scored himself a dealer' as Stuey had none-too-succinctly put it. When Stuey would disappear for about ten minutes after matches between the end of dressing room banter and the slow trickle into the bar, Gazelle alone knew where he had been…around the back of the building enveloped in clouds of marijuana smoke.

Yet he would slip back into the fold and mingle so well with all-comers, from Norman F. Billington's stone-cold analysis of the day's bowling figures to Sammy's compulsory cheerfulness combined with his infectious determination to have a good time. On the weekends Laura had left her study books in her hall of residence she would take her place by Stuey's side as part of the general mix. Gazelle was intrigued to learn if she was in on the secret too. If not, then he was the only one.

Stuey's seemingly effortless ability to blend seamlessly at all levels contradicted everything Gazelle had ever heard or read about drug-takers, evil wastrels who needed to be treated as rejects on the fringes of society. Far from being a social outcast, Stuey had cast himself as the life and soul of the party.

It had made Gazelle wonder whether this was despite his drug habit or because of it.

SEVENTEEN

The minibuses, Sammy and Meat Loaf at the wheels, rolled up outside Crawford cricket club at 8.30am.

A huge mound of kit was waiting to be loaded alongside a full posse of cricketing aficionados. A hint of drizzle hung in the air, but also the threat of impending enjoyment. A photographer from the local evening newspaper waited patiently to take their picture.

Wobbler opened one of his kit bags and pulled out a tower of straw trilbies.

'There's one of these for everybody and they're a quid each by the way,' he added hastily. 'They have to be worn all the time, otherwise you get fined. There are some rules about drinking as well, but we'll explain more about that on the way there.'

Norman F. Billington picked up one of the trilbies and placed it on his head. The chairman thought it only appropriate as he prepared to deliver a short valedictory speech. He coughed, stepped forward, called for a bit of order and addressed the gathering.

'Now boys, I just want to wish you all a great time on tour and to tell you that I'll be joining you in Bristol for the last game. I hope you'll all be treating this trip as a holiday as well as the opportunity to practise your sporting skills against some unknown opposition. I feel sure it's going to be an unforgettable experience for all concerned and I do want you to enjoy it while always remembering that you are representing Crawford cricket club and that its reputation is in your hands. But as cricketers of the highest order, I know it will be in safe hands.'

Norman F. Billington paused to allow his little joke time to be appreciated, but the only sound forthcoming was the whoosh of an opening lager can from Sammy in the cheap seats at the back. Wobbler was on his case immediately.

'Sammy, you can't drink that now!' he exclaimed. 'Apart from the fact it's quarter to nine in the morning, you're the one driving the kit van down to Somerset.'

'Why me?' whined Sammy. 'I drove it here.'

Wobbler's response reeked of forward planning. 'When you and Meat Loaf signed for the vans at the hire depot, you also became the only ones insured to drive them. Meat Loaf's taking us and you're taking the kit, so no boozing.'

Wobbler turned, caught Norman F. Billington's eye and winked.

The chairman nodded approvingly. The skipper had opened the batting with a steady, sensible knock. Long may he stay at the crease.

Three places along in the same cheap seats, Stuey cracked open a lager can with a whoosh of his own and raised a toast to Sammy to the amusement of all. Sammy cursed under his breath. He thrust his drink into the hands of a startled Pete

Skidmore and started chucking the kit bags into the back of the van with unnecessary vigour. Gazelle started to help him then said: 'I'll come with you in the van Sammy if you like. There are two seats in the front. I'll keep you company.'

And so, trilbies in place and like so many players in a two-bob jazz band, the cricketers headed off, the sun also putting on its hat as they headed off into the great unknown that was life south of the border.

EIGHTEEN

Sammy wouldn't have picked dusty Gazelle as his first choice travelling companion, but at least he had someone to talk to.

As they joined the motorway traffic heading south, Sammy began to realise that perhaps driving the kit van wasn't such a bad option after all. At least he'd distanced himself from Meat Loaf's incessant sweating.

Gazelle started to relax too. He pushed his body down the rather uncomfortable seat, took off his hat and threw it into the space between the top of the bulkhead at the bottom of the windscreen.

Sammy turned to him and smiled. 'Removal of hat only twenty minutes into journey. That's a ten pence fine. Come on, cough up. It's all in a good cause anyway.'

'What's the good cause?' asked Gazelle.

'Getting pissed together on the last night.'

'Quite a worthwhile cause then, but Jeez, this is still going to be real hard for me,' Gazelle replied as he retrieved his trilby, dug into his pocket and handed over his money.

Sammy smiled again and said: 'You do realise that you sounded exactly like Stuey then don't you?'

'Did I?' said Gazelle.

'Yep, you're turning into an Australian just like me and no bad thing either,' sniggered Sammy, before adding: 'Been spending a lot of time with him at your place recently?'

Gazelle replied: 'I hardly saw him at all while that girl Laura was up here for Easter, but since then he's been stopping in a lot at night during the week. I think he misses her.'

'I think you might be right there,' replied Sammy, before adding: 'Do you and Stuey get on alright then? He's not got any weird habits has he?'

Gazelle eyed Sammy suspiciously and wondered if this was some kind of test for him or character analysis of Stuey.

Deep down he would have liked to share his lodger's marijuana secret with someone else for a number of reasons. Primarily this was because he wasn't too sure how much of a big deal it really was. He was aware there were worse drugs out there, but how would other people react if they knew? He could have gone running to Norman F. Billington as soon as he found out and told him exactly what Stuey was up to.

But that would make him a real tell-tale sneak. For all he knew half the players at the club might smoke grass which would make him the most unpopular guy in the place. Perhaps Sammy used the stuff – he certainly worked his way through enough cigarettes – but he just didn't dare ask him because he simply didn't know what his reaction would be. He might laugh, pull a joint out of his pocket and spark it up there and then. Or he could be so offended that he would fly into an uncontrollable rage and chuck his nosy passenger out of the van on to the hard shoulder without a second thought. Gazelle imagined both outcomes rather unlikely if the truth be known, but even so, not for the first time in recent weeks, he didn't know what to say.

Gazelle decided to joke his way out of his dilemma: 'You know what you Australians are like, you're all completely weird. Seriously though, Stuey's alright really. He's a rare cricketing talent isn't he?'

'He's certainly that,' replied Sammy. 'And a lovely lad too.'

Gazelle was a tad surprised to hear the abrasive Sammy reveal such a tender side, Sammy himself also slightly taken aback by the startling frankness of his own admission. He quickly drew a line under his moment of weakness by flashing his headlights and waving an angry fist as a jeering Meat Loaf and the rest of the crew passed them in the second lane.

'Matt Fairacre said that we're all stopping at the next service station for a late breakfast,' he barked across at Gazelle. 'Last van there picks up the bill and watch out for illegal right-hand drinking because we can make a bloody fortune,' he added, before pushing the accelerator to the floor and bouncing up and down in his seat.

NINETEEN

The Swan at Little Nettleford had seen better days.

The rambling old coach house was losing the rendering plasterwork which had spoiled its good looks in the first place while a laurel bush was growing out of its crumbling main chimney stack. Nettles and dandelions were winning the battle for space with the neglected tea roses along its unkempt borders.

The two minibuses pulled up into the car park late in the afternoon. Matt Fairacre, paperwork tucked neatly into a folder, announced that he would go and book them in, leaving the rest to unpack and explore.

Sammy left the kit in the van, walked through the entrance and immediately spotted a large empty bar behind the main reception.

His inspection was thorough.

He discovered it boasted a premium strength lager, two ciders, a choice of three bitters and a mild, while a chalk board next to a rack of spirit bottles advertised home-made cheese and onion pasties. At the far end of the room was a pool table, a dart board and a juke box on which there was to be found not one Cliff Richard track.

Things were looking up already.

Sammy was joined by Stuey and Pete Skidmore and the three of them climbed the staircase to the first floor off which ran three long landings. The place was huge and they could only guess that it had at least 20 bedrooms, Sammy inspecting them by kicking open the doors with his boot and sticking his head inside.

They were big and airy, shabby but clean.

Most of the rooms contained twin single beds a sink, a couple of painted wardrobes and needed decorating. One of them was completely empty except for a full-size table tennis table in the middle. Three bats and two crushed ping-pong balls lay on the top. There was no net.

At the end of each corridor was a bathroom with a communal toilet, a bath and a sink. There didn't seem to be anyone else staying in the place.

In short, it was perfect.

'We can't cause a lot of damage in this place which is probably exactly why we're here,' remarked Sammy dryly and totally accurately. 'Come on, let's go downstairs and grab a pint. I really need to get this taste of no beer out of my mouth.'

A tall, slim youth followed them from the main reception and took his place behind the bar.

He smiled, introduced himself as Rob and said he was the son of the owner.

'I assume you're the guys on the cricket tour. You're very welcome,' he said. 'How come you're all wearing the same hats?

'It's so we can recognise each other when we get plastered,' sniggered Pete Skidmore.

Sammy ordered two pints of bitter, a pint of lager, change for the pool table, change for the juke box and two sets of darts.

'We'll soon liven the place up a bit,' he said.

'It could do with livening up,' replied Rob. 'It's the first time we've had a cricket team stay here. This is the busiest we've been for weeks.'

Meat Loaf, Matt Fairacre, Wobbler and Gazelle then sauntered into the bar, adding their nods of approval as they took on board the facilities on offer.

'Apart from the odd game of cricket, I don't think we'll ever need to leave this room,' remarked Wobbler, before turning his attention to the drinkers at the bar and adding: 'That's a ten pence fine Stuey. You're drinking your pint with your right hand.'

'Jeez, this is going to be real hard for me,' groaned Stuey.

Sammy cast Gazelle a knowing glance as Gazelle's eyes reached for the heavens.

TWENTY

It was unanimously agreed that the first night at least would be spent at the Swan, not least because the place already felt like home.

Wobbler, Matt Fairacre, Gazelle and some of the juniors walked into the nearby village to find somewhere to eat and have a bit of an explore, vowing to return soon, while Meat Loaf, Sammy and Stuey decided food was for wimps and carried on boozing.

When the scouting party did return in the early evening, Stuey and Meat Loaf were much the worse for drink, locked in what appeared to be mortal combat on the pool table while Sammy, alarmingly red in the face, was perched precariously on a teetering bar stool telling a bemused Rob about his early up-bringing in Adelaide. Wobbler claimed 30 pence in fines off all three hatless drunks before placing his own money on the side of the pool table and offering to take on both Stuey and Meat Loaf for 50 pence a game. He had noticed that all three were drinking premium strength lager and not making a lot of sense, so had decided this would be an ideal time to use his own sobriety to full advantage. The plan was to have his Marina resprayed free of charge by the end of the summer.

At the bar, Sammy was still coming over all Australian to Rob who was by now seriously beginning to doubt the authenticity of the yarn being spun to him by an incoherent stranger. Sammy was joined by Stuey who, having lost horribly to Meat Loaf on the pool table, suddenly realised that he was far more drunk than he had thought and indeed ought to be so early in the evening. Stuey listened to Sammy's phoney Australian accent and the pack of lies heading in Rob's direction, but opted to leave him to it.

He decided he ought to be feeling hungry – it was eight hours since they had dined at the greasy spoon café masquerading as a motorway restaurant – but the intake of far too much gassy lager since had left him with a queasy, bloated feeling and no appetite. Stuey knew the cure though, one of the two pre-rolled joints in the top pocket of his jacket and with scant regard for the consequences, made his way unsteadily to the gents' toilet, bouncing off a couple of walls as he did so.

The washroom was huge, a relic of late Victorian architectural excess, and Gazelle was already in there, quite sober and staring intently ahead as he splashed a slab of porcelain towering at least two feet above him. Stuey staggered in, mumbled a slurred greeting before informing Gazelle that he was about to use one of the sit-down cubicles to smoke some weed.

'Is that wise?' warned Gazelle. 'Anybody could walk in.'

'I've not got a clue how to get out to the back garden of this place or if it's even got a back garden, so I'm smoking in here,' slurred Stuey defiantly and drunkenly. 'You can stand guard.'

'Stand guard!' gasped Gazelle. 'And what exactly am I supposed to say? Oh, sorry, you can't come in here because this is Stuey's drug den?'

'Say what you like, I really don't care,' replied Stuey, and with a dismissive wave of the hand stumbled into the cubicle at the end, locked the door and sat down on the toilet. Seconds later, plumes of aromatic smoke started to float up through the open top.

Gazelle sighed, but before he could take up sentry duty or any other kind of vigilante posting, the main door was flung open with some force and an ale-soaked Sammy stumbled into the room.

'Hey up Gazelle, you don't want to be hanging about in here for too long. Folk will start talking.'

Sammy unzipped his fly and started to relieve himself in the middle urinal. He was just about to boast about the high tide mark he had achieved when he suddenly turned to Gazelle and hissed: 'What's that smell?'

Gazelle was growing quite weary of being lost for words.

'Err, err, I really don't know. What smell?'

But Sammy had the answer already. He finished urinating, grabbed Gazelle's arm, propelled him to the far side of the wash room and jabbered excitedly in his ear: 'Somebody's smoking wacky baccy down there in that end toilet. I would recognise that smell anywhere. I wonder who it is. It's not one of the boys is it? Shall we hang about and find out?'

Gazelle thought about feigning surprise. At that moment, he wished he'd stopped in the hotel bar drinking strong lager all afternoon, that way he too just wouldn't care. Gazelle's next move was going to a tricky one, but he was rescued when a disembodied Australian accent floated up from the toilet into the upper atmosphere along with the last of the smoke. Stuey had turned his convenience into a confession box, the occupant requiring the services of a high priest presumably.

'It's only me, Stuey,' he announced, emerging from the toilet and grinning inanely before flicking the dead end of the joint into the gutter of the urinal Sammy had just vacated.

A startled Sammy looked at Stuey and then at the cardboard roach as it swirled its way down towards the drain.

Gazelle held his breath as he awaited Sammy's response.

Now Sammy had been a strictly beer and fags man for more than a third of his 30 years and he didn't have a lot of time for illegal substances. He had tried smoking cannabis on a couple of occasions when offered it at parties in the past and had not been particularly impressed. As far as he was concerned it turned normal conversation into gibbering nonsense and he knew that if he'd caught some waster such as Meat Loaf smoking the stuff then the unfortunate bloke would have been on the wrong end of a good telling-off to say the least.

But this was different.

This was Stuey, fellow Australian, fine chap, soul buddy and as far as Sammy was concerned, the best thing to have happened to Crawford cricket club for many a long, hot summer. He therefore piled all his prejudices into a storage box of forgetfulness, placed it in a dark corner under the stairs and summoned up a response only his best chum deserved: 'Bloody 'ell, Stuey mate, you might have saved some for me. I haven't had a decent smoke in ages.'

Relief coursed through Gazelle's mind and body.

He was mainly happy because Sammy hadn't asked Stuey to pick his window and then chucked him through it, but he also felt quite a weight lift off his shoulders because at last somebody else knew about Stuey's secret and apparently didn't care.

Stuey felt quite a weight lift off his shoulders too, but this was only because he was so light-headed, the effect of the marijuana on top of all the afternoon's alcohol more pronounced than usual. 'Do you want some smoke now Sammy?' sniggered Stuey. 'I've got another joint in my jacket pocket.'

'Yeh, why not,' chuckled Sammy. 'We're on holiday after all. Come, let us repair in haste to your drawing room where we can partake in private,' and burst into gales of laughter as he propelled Stuey back into the toilet.

Gazelle urgently needed a swift exit and took it, leaving Sammy and Stuey chest to chest behind a locked toilet door chuckling like two naughty school kids skipping maths.

Gazelle felt every one of his 54 years as he made his way back to the bar, but he also felt relieved, reminding himself once again that now he wasn't the only one sharing the Australian's drug secret.

Now it was he and Sammy…or so he thought.

During their entry to and exit from the washroom, all three miscreants had failed to notice that the door to the first toilet cubicle was closed and locked and hiding a fly on the wall who had heard every word. Matt Fairacre had been in there all along, not to spy, but for the one legitimate reason that anyone would choose to use a toilet.

The young accountant was now riddled with guilt about his eavesdropping. But he hadn't felt the need to speak early in the episode and simply hadn't dared to speak as scurrilous scandal had unfolded so quickly just feet away.

He hadn't seen a thing, but hadn't needed to. The twin

senses of sound and smell had painted a picture of surprising and revealing clarity.

After Stuey and Sammy had stumbled and giggled their way out of the toilet and then out of the washroom, Matt Fairacre poked his head out of his cubicle, checked the place was at last empty and quietly returned to the bar.

He was frankly staggered by the events that had just taken place, but what exactly he was going to do about them was about as clear as the air he had just left behind in the toilets.

TWENTY-ONE

Wobbler strode into breakfast the morning after ready to take on the world.

But he was the only one.

The rest of the party were in various states of distress as hangovers hit home. Even Gazelle was feeling rough. After his surreal experience in the toilet, he had taken to drink to forget. It hadn't worked.

Meat Loaf and Pete Skidmore listlessly pushed some greasy bacon and egg around a plate while Stuey and Sammy ignored theirs completely. A couple of cheese and onion pasties in the middle of the evening had blotted up some of the alcohol intake, but late night cards and darts accompanied by more copious amounts of lager had taken a heavy toll.

Wobbler, having dined out earlier in the evening and then stuck with wholly predictable shandies all night in order to clean up on the pool table, was bursting with health and more than happy to make as many of his colleagues as possible feel even worse than they already did. He poured himself a glass of orange juice before presenting his case in a most prim and proper manner: 'I can count six heads without hats while Stuey and Meat Loaf have been drinking tea right-handed ever since I sat down which means fines totalling at least eighty pence. This is a very good effort boys. At this rate we'll be able to afford two last nights.'

Rob the barman, who was also doubling up as head waiter, shuffled into the dining room carrying two racks of toast and wearing a straw trilby left behind after the previous night's shindig. He too was suffering, but mainly from a lack of sleep. It had been 2.30am before he had finally managed to close the bar and he had been on kitchen duty four hours later.

He half-heartedly asked if everything was alright. A most chipper Wobbler answered on behalf of everybody else.

'Most things are fine my dear boy. Indeed, I have only one complaint. Why is it every time I turn on the cold tap in the bathroom I tune into Radio West?'

A chuckle of approval circled the table and raised spirits a tad.

Stuey smiled, lifted his aching head off his folded arms and decided to take a stab at this peculiarly dry English sense of humour: 'If we're all paying up for not wearing hats and drinking with the wrong hand and all that stuff, then I think we ought to fine Meat Loaf for sweating at breakfast,' he said, a jocular remark which brought a round of critical acclaim, especially from Sammy who was beginning to derive a strange pleasure from sharing Stuey's drug secret, feeling jealous even that Gazelle was also in the know.

But deep down Stuey was a fretful young man and it was more than a passing hangover that was troubling him. At the time, sharing a joint with Sammy had seemed harmless enough.

Drunk and silly, it had provided several chortles and had even seemed like a rather good idea at the time.

But in the cold light of day, there was more than a twinge of regret. Stuey was well aware that not everyone shared his liberal values. Even back home in Australia, cannabis was frowned upon by many of the older generation while in England the more free and easy days of flower power and drug-fuelled psychedelia in the sixties had been overtaken by more authoritarian and, in Stuey's opinion, misguided times.

This was just one reason why he had intended to keep his secret in as tight a circle as possible, but now that circle was expanding. In his drunken and stoned stupor, Stuey had failed to impress upon Sammy the need to keep his discovery under his hat. He should have reminded him that on tour at least it would also save him ten pence a time.

Stuey was roused from his mental meanderings by the sound of the annoyingly healthy Wobbler who had climbed to his feet and was banging a spoon and an empty tea pot together to both attract the attention and irritate everybody around the breakfast table. The good news was that they had the morning free to undertake whatever mischief they may care to come up with before they all met at noon outside the hotel to board the minibuses for their first fixture of the tour.

Stuey's head sank back into his arms. He had never felt less like mischief or playing cricket in his life.

TWENTY-TWO

The cricket ground at Bleighdon-Under-the-Water really did nestle.

Perched prettily in the lee of a small grassy hill on the outskirts of a 200 hundred-year-old village, a brook meandered along one side of the manicured square flanked by weeping willows which appeared to have stooped to take a drink from its shallows. A small stone bridge almost engulfed by a climbing rose merely enhanced its tumbling beauty and demanded its presence on the prettiest of postcards.

Stuey was cheered as soon as he set eyes on the idyllic scene. Australia had its finer points, but nothing quite so quaint.

The two minibuses disgorged their contents in front of a club house which was also pleasing to the eye, its wonky stone-tile roof and aged oak frame forming a verandah at the front, offering a pleasant, carefree welcome.

Sammy's appreciation of bucolic bliss lasted less than a minute.

'Do you know why this place is called Bleighdon-Under-the-Water?' he scoffed.

'Thrill us, Sammy,' replied Meat Loaf sardonically.

'Because that's what it becomes when that stream floods. I wonder if the bar's open yet?'

Sammy had been given the day off. He had brought along a large transistor radio to listen to the first day of the England versus Australia Ashes Test at Headingley and as the sun was already beating down from a cloudless sky, his plan to crash out in the long grass beyond the boundary rope accompanied by several glasses of something long and chilled from behind the bar seemed be one that was made in heaven.

He told Stuey of his grand design who was immediately consumed by envy.

'Jeez, why didn't I book the day off?' he whined.

'Go and tell Wobbler you're ill,' replied Sammy. 'He'll be fine with that.'

'I am ill. I feel bloody awful, this is one stinking hangover,' griped Stuey.

'I've got a cure for that,' said Sammy. 'A large port and brandy. I might even have one myself.'

And before Stuey had time to object, Sammy had sprint-walked to the bar, been served, and returned with a glass of rich, amber fluid in each hand. Even Stuey didn't think that strong spirits before a cricket game was a good idea, but he shrugged his shoulders, quaffed his potent spirit mix in one and smiled for the first time since before breakfast. Half an hour later and Stuey had volunteered to open the bowling, feeling surprisingly invigorated and yet in need of physical punishment to purge himself of the toxins within.

Bleighdon CC may have enjoyed a rarely delightful setting for a cricket field, but its members' sporting prowess was far less impressive. They certainly had little to offer in way of resistance when confronted by a lithe young Australian paceman hungry for action, with or without hangover. Stuey flattened two sets of stumps in his first four deliveries, batsman number five late to the crease as he struggled to pad up in time. Stuey glanced over to beyond the mid-wicket boundary where Sammy had risen from the horizontal to lift a glass to his team mate's early success, while eagerly beckoning him over with his spare hand. Stuey smiled to himself and resolved to join him in the long grass before the sun went down.

Meat Loaf and Pete Skidmore helped Stuey skittle out the West Country side with a meagre 58 on the scoreboard, a total surpassed in less than an hour as even Wobbler, the original Captain Sensible, chucked his bat about. So with victory achieved before tea was due to be taken, Stuey jogged over to Sammy and flung himself on to the grass where he gratefully accepted the longest Botham shandy he had yet to set eyes on.

Sammy was suddenly overwhelmed by affection for his young visitor. It was deep and genuine yet at the same time embarrassing enough to mean that he felt compelled to thrust such thoughts from his mind. He did so by relating news of the Ashes Test he had been listening to on the radio, but he was still troubled by his feelings for Stuey, emotions he had never encountered before or had realised he was even capable of.

He felt relieved to be able to talk about cricket. 'Your boys have started well in the third Test. John Dyson's on his way to a hundred. But it's a great all round Aussie team. Well, it would be with Rod Marsh in the side wouldn't it?'

Stuey felt tremendously relaxed and lay flat out among the meadow flowers. It was the best he had felt all day. He replied: 'And Allan Border. Now that guy is what you call a fair dinkum Australian.'

Sammy and Stuey stayed behind the boundary rope drinking and chatting for another hour. Only as the sun started to dip behind the hill did Sammy think about the rest of the players socialising in the bar and only then did it occur to him what they might think of two grown men lying in the grass together as the shades of night approached. Sammy hauled himself to his feet, picked up a tray of empty glasses and said: 'Come on Stuey, let's go and have a beer or two with the boys.'

Later that evening, Wobbler and Meat Loaf volunteered to drive back to the Swan, Sammy quickly establishing that Wobbler had simply lied about the insurance restrictions on the hired minibuses, a ruse the club skipper still considered to be hilarious.

The full squad marched into the main bar and were surprised to see several customers in there already, the pool table and dart board occupied, the juke box blaring. Several heads turned in surprise, but this was the effect that a dozen blokes wearing the same straw trilbies tended to have. The cricketers had discovered that their 'uniform' was a nuclear-powered ice-breaker and were also about to find out that their presence in the village was not without its novelty value, Rob explaining with some delight that most of the people were in the bar merely to satisfy their curiosity.

'It's often deserted in here on a Tuesday night,' he said as he pulled two pints in tandem. You guys are quite an attraction. The first round is on the house. You're not planning on going anywhere else this evening are you?'

This was highly unlikely; Wobbler the eternal entrepreneur had espied the opportunity to fleece the locals as well as his own mates and ten minutes later, a pool and darts competition was under way while Matt Fairacre had used some of the fine money to purchase a net, a bat and three balls to re-commission the table tennis table upstairs.

Stuey volunteered to play table tennis after he had telephoned Laura. She was back home with her parents for the summer and it was beginning to dawn on him that he missed both her and her steadying influence. After the heady events of the previous night, a relatively low profile was needed.

A spot of ping-pong seemed perfect.

TWENTY-THREE

Matt Fairacre was a young man skewered on the horns of a huge dilemma.

Before the tour had left, he had assured Norman F. Billington that he would monitor events and inform him of any brewing or actual bother that needed to be relayed back to base camp. While Wobbler was effectively in charge, Matt Fairacre was responsible for communication, in other words, the settling of Norman F. Billington's fraying nerves. He knew that the visit to Bristol was bothering the chairman, a drug scandal before they had even crossed the city boundary was simply unimaginable.

But precisely what action he was supposed to take after his inadvertent spot of espionage in the gents' toilet was a question that both vexed and baffled him. He felt an obligation to report what he had stumbled across, but he harboured so many niggling doubts and unanswered questions. Matt Fairacre was fully aware that in the eyes of the law at least both Stuey and Sammy had done wrong, although where exactly this left

Gazelle was a real puzzler. The groundsman – as far as he could tell from behind his own locked lavatory door – was, like himself, an innocent by-stander, albeit one who had taken this remarkable turn of events very comfortably in his stride.

Gazelle had barely passed comment as drugs were smoked in a public place. He certainly hadn't kicked up a fuss, another issue further muddying the waters and in need of an answer. But the most demanding question that Matt Fairacre faced was this one: What actual damage had been done and would it not be better if he just pretended the whole episode had never taken place?

He had once read that people who smoked marijuana protested their innocence because there was no victim, and therefore no crime.

And he had to admit that there was no victim in this instance.

The only person suffering, he reflected ruefully, was himself and he could hardly walk into a police station or a hospital casualty department complaining that he was suffering from a bad dose of mental turmoil. He was pretty sure they didn't issue legal guidelines or a prescription medicine for indecision.

And could he face the embarrassment of telling anyone of the shameful circumstances in which he had come across this insider information? How he had sat in guilty silence on a lavatory seat and taken it all on board without daring to breathe a word.

What kind of toilet snake did that make him?

After much anguished deliberation, Matt Fairacre reached the conclusion that he couldn't decide what to do and therefore decided to do nothing.

For the time being at least.

TWENTY-FOUR

Day two of the tour brought another clear blue sky and a visit to Chimmiford CC.

The ground wasn't as pretty as Bleighdon had been the day before, but still snuggled cosily next to a steep gorge in the depths of the Mendips. Gazelle wasn't too concerned with imposing backdrops though. He had been picked to play and as this touring party was to all intents and purposes a first team squad, his selection represented a considerable promotion from last season's sporadic appearances in the ranks of the thirds. His nerves jangled that bit more when he learned that Sammy was to be skipper for the day.

Wobbler Carter had awarded himself the day off and had decided to hire a car along with Matt Fairacre to go sight-seeing and shopping in Cheddar. Sammy was officially appalled and indulged in a free moan about his skipper's shameful disregard for the quality of life.

'Fancy going sight-seeing when you're on holiday, the bar's open all afternoon and the Ashes Test is on the radio,' he bleated to anyone willing to listen as the minibus pulled into Chimmiford. 'The bloke's got no sense of adventure. I'll bet he doesn't even come back with any home-made cider.'

Sammy had long since decided that intimidation should be a crucial weapon in his arsenal as he led his invasion force deep into enemy territory and to this end produced a rare and surprise example of forward planning as the two sides mingled in the players' lounge before stumps were set.

Sammy was wearing a t-shirt especially commissioned for the occasion of his captaincy. Emblazoned across the front in bold capitals proclaimed the legend: 'Get 'em in, get 'em out....gloat.'

Sammy strutted around the lounge like a walking bill-board, chest fully inflated to 42psi to the bemusement of the Chimmiford players who didn't know quite what to make of their colourful friend from up north. The whisper around the room labelled Sammy as a pumped-up version of Asterix the Gaul, not that anyone had the temerity to make the comparison to his face.

But Sammy's choice of intimidatory clothing merely served to inspire the Chimmiford bowlers and with Meat Loaf, Pete Skidmore and two juniors back in the pavilion with less than 30 runs on the board, Gazelle and Stuey came together at the crease to form a most unlikely mid-innings partnership. Gazelle was a quivering bag of nerves, even more so when Stuey beckoned him down the track for a mid-wicket tactical talk.

'Just try and defend your end and stay there,' said Stuey. 'These quick guys are tiring, we'll be OK. We can still be here at tea. You never know, with a bit of luck we might be having tinned pilchards.'

And with a sly grin, Stuey retreated to the bowler's end, leaving his unamused landlord facing a quick guy showing little sign of aforementioned fatigue.

His first delivery had pace, but strayed down the leg side, Gazelle managing a thin edge past the flailing dive of the wicket keeper, the ball's barely halted momentum carrying it all the way to the boundary rope.

'A four for the leg-glance specialist!' bellowed Sammy who was jumping up and down in front of the dressing room, his loud and spirited applause lifting Gazelle's confidence and moral.

A combination of good fortune and gritty determination produced a personal best of 37 not out for Gazelle, which was 29 more than Stuey who had been comprehensively bowled by a 'tiring' paceman several overs earlier.

And as Gazelle walked off the square back to the small, but perfectly formed pavilion for tea, one of the great events of his life occurred, and let's face it, there hadn't been many. The entire Crawford team rose to their collective feet and gave their groundsman a standing ovation, while it took only a small prompt from Asterix the Gaul to persuade the opposition players to join in.

Gazelle felt humble and magnificent at the same time. No-one had ever stood and clapped him before and for this to happen as he walked off a sporting arena in front of his cricketing peers was surely a moment that would live with him for as long as he did. As Sammy, Stuey, Meat Loaf and the rest cheered and clattered him between the shoulder blades, a lump formed in his throat and a small tear moistened the corner of one eye. But the overwhelming emotions were of exhilaration and utter joy. Suddenly, all the negotiations with Norman F.

Billington, the hassle with Stuey, the bizarre drug scene back at the hotel, all seemed to fade into insignificance, even seem worth it.

Just an hour with a cricket bat in his hand on an obscure field in deepest Somerset and Gazelle was in seventh heaven.

TWENTY-FIVE

Matt Fairacre, in stark contrast, hadn't even made first heaven.

He had returned to the Swan in the evening after a less than enjoyable day out with Wobbler only to be told by barman Rob that some posh bloke called Norman F. Billington had been on the telephone twice and could he ring him back, urgently. Matt Fairacre's dithering in the wake of those eye-opening events in the washroom had at last caught up with him. Now he had to ring the chairman with a moral dilemma bearing down on him like a great weight descending from a dizzy height. If Stuey and Sammy did get into trouble because of drugs on tour and it became clear that he had been aware of what had been going on all along, then Matt Fairacre was in deep mire. But then again, what Norman F. Billington didn't know couldn't harm him he reasoned, so he picked up the tatty payphone in the main reception, dialled the number and drew a deep breath. He was determined to keep this brief.

Norman F. Billington was already annoyed with the normally reliable Matt Fairacre. Three days of the tour had elapsed and his personal attaché still hadn't been in touch. Something must be amiss. So when the telephone did ring and it was Matt Fairacre on the line, his opening question came as no surprise.

'Matthew!' he exclaimed. 'Why haven't you been in touch before. What's wrong?'

'Err, nothing's wrong', came the reply. 'Everything's fine.'

'Why didn't you ring on Monday night to say you'd arrived safely?' demanded Norman F. Billington.

'Yes, right, sorry about that. We had quite a bit to drink in the hotel that night and it slipped my mind. We've been playing cricket ever since.'

'Quite a bit to drink!' exclaimed Norman F. Billington. 'I hope there was no bother. That Sammy Samson wasn't up to mischief was he?'

'Err, no, we all just got a bit drunk that's all. There's really nothing to worry about.'

Norman F. Billington suspected that Matt Fairacre wasn't his customary calm, collected self, but decided not to pursue the issue.

He added: 'How's the cricket been going? Have we won a couple?'

Matt Fairacre had to make a real effort to disguise the relief in his voice as the subject was changed.

'Well, we beat Bleighdon quite easily yesterday, but lost to Chimmiford today apparently. Wobbler and I didn't play, but Sammy informs me that Gazelle got a few runs and was the man of the match. The boys are all in the bar now getting pis…err, playing pool. My money's running out Norman so I have to go. So long, see you Friday.'

TWENTY-SIX

The last day of cricket in Somerset meant a 20 mile trip to Mewley and it was the longest drive of Gazelle's life.

He was sitting in the back of the jarring, rattling minibus, eyes closed, shoulders slumped and regretting every minute of the previous night's festivities.

At the time it had been great fun.

Sammy had insisted that Gazelle's fine knock – he had been caught at first slip two runs short of a half-century – was worthy of an almighty drinking session in the Swan and as the man of moment, Gazelle had little to offer in way of resistance. Not that he really wanted to object. He intended to revel in his fifteen minutes of fame. If only it had lasted fifteen minutes.

Sammy had insisted that early evening cocktails were the order of the day, inspired, by none other than Wobbler Carter. The captain had confounded Sammy's earlier accusations of being the most boring man on earth by returning from his day out with two large flagons of local cider for general consumption, payment for which, he hastened to add, would be taken out of the fines money. Sammy pulled the cork out of the first flagon, raised it to his lips on the crook of his elbow and swigged a deep draught.

The howls of protest could be heard in the next village.

'Spot on that stuff,' enthused Sammy. 'I must remember to get some for myself before we go home. I still reckon we can pep it up a bit though.'

The cocktail mixed by Sammy would have impressed Molotov himself. Borrowing Rob's stainless steel slop bucket and giving it a cursory wipe down with a handy bar towel, Sammy poured the remainder of the cider into the vessel before skipping behind the bar and hoisting it under the top row of optics. He then proceeded to run the bucket along the row, releasing a measure of spirits from each bottle as he did so, several shots of whisky, vodka and gin gushing into the general melange below as Rob desperately hit the buttons on the till trying to work out some kind of bill. Sammy lifted the bucket to his nose, took in the sweet, sticky bouquet and declared his wicked witch's brew available for general consumption, Rob quickly handing round half pint pots, including one for himself.

Guest hero Gazelle was invited to drain his first glass in one to mark the commencement of the evening's merriment which he duly accomplished, only grimacing twice in front of an approving audience. And when the first bucket of firewater was replaced by another, the rest of the night was dispatched into the hands of half-forgotten history.

Ten hours later in the minibus and the only item in Gazelle's hands was one throbbing head containing a brain operating at about fifteen per cent of usual capacity somewhere beneath a skew-whiff straw trilby. Gazelle had been pencilled in to play cricket again that day, but as soon as he stepped tentatively off the minibus in Mewley he groaned audibly before asking Wobbler if he could be moved down the batting order, preferably to about fifteenth man. The pious club captain – whose wholesome, reverential ways on this tour were even beginning to get on Gazelle's long-burning wick – decided it was time for Thought for the Day.

He hectored: 'Gazelle, you really should know better than to drink any potion that Sammy's concocted. Personally I stayed away from that terrible cocktail he came up with. Fancy drinking out of a bucket. What a disgrace. You should have stayed with me. I had three pints of bottom-weight bitter, two bags of salted peanuts and feel as right as rain. I raised £1.90 in fines and won £2.50 on the pool table. Now that's what I call a great night out.'

Gazelle couldn't decide what he wanted to do most, deck Wobbler with one single punch to the chin or curl up in a corner and die. Death seemed the more attractive, albeit less sensible option, but as he suffered in silence on a wooden bench near the entrance to the club house along came a smidgeon of heartening news.

Wobbler had redeemed himself somewhat by winning the toss and electing to bat which hopefully meant a couple of hours at least before Gazelle's cricketing services would be called upon. Gazelle decided that lethargy was not going to defeat this hangover and so embarked on a walk. A few laps of yet another pretty cricket field on yet another sunny day would surely hasten the return of some good juices. By the time he had commenced his second lap, Gazelle had company. Matt Fairacre was also a late order batsman and had asked Gazelle if he could join him for a couple of circuits.

Gazelle didn't know Matt Fairacre too well. There were almost three decades between them and most official business concerning the up-keep of the ground back at the club was dealt with by Norman F. Billington. He certainly didn't know of the intrigue that was gnawing away at the back of Matt Fairacre's mind.

Events in the washroom were still very much in Matt Fairacre's thoughts, particularly Gazelle's seeming indifference to drug-taking, compliance with its use even. Matt Fairacre reasoned that as Gazelle and Stuey shared the same home then perhaps he knew more about the Australian than most imagined. This nagging curiosity just wouldn't go away and as Stuey was out there in the middle of the pitch facing Mewley's finest strike attack, this might just be the opportunity he'd been waiting for.

Matt Fairacre watched Stuey lift a half-volley over mid-off, nodded in his direction then ventured to Gazelle: 'Great young cricketer that lad. What's he like as a lodger or as a person for that matter? Any strange or unusual habits?'

Even from under the cloying fug of his horrible hangover, Gazelle could detect a familiar bell ringing. First it had been Sammy and now Matt Fairacre who was pursuing some kind of character analysis of the bloke in his spare room. Was this just coincidence or was there more to it?

The motivation behind such interest was beyond Gazelle. He really felt too ill to even think about it, but he reasoned there was no way Matt Fairacre could suspect Stuey of nefarious drug-taking. He still needed a way out of this conversation though and beat a hasty path to the exit door.

He said: 'Stuey's fine. Let's face it, he's the only reason I'm here on this tour having such a great time. Now if you don't mind Matt, I'm going to that long grass over there for a while. I think I'm going to be sick.'

TWENTY-SEVEN

All members of the tour party were sorry to say farewell to Rob, mine host, part-time waiter and full-time friend.

The feeling was mutual.

Despite four late nights on the bounce, a pack of lies from Sammy and Wobbler's demon hustling on the pool table, the cricketing tourists had breezed into the Swan like a welcome, warming scirocco and had doubled the bar takings in the process.

Now the most welcome guests of the year were gathered in the bar shortly before 11.00am ready to make the short drive back up the motorway to Bristol for their final fixture of the tour followed by their last night together. Straw trilbies in place as required and embarking on their farewell pints left-handed to a man, the cricketers reflected on the fine time they had enjoyed so far and toasted the imminent big city adventure that would inevitably make their tour immensely unforgettable.

There was one notable absentee. Sammy had commandeered the kit bag minibus shortly after breakfast to 'do a bit of shopping' and had promised to be back in time for the farewell froth-blowing. Sammy and shopping normally made for most unhappy stablemates, so it was a matter of some intrigue among his peers as to what exactly he had gone to purchase.

True to his word, Sammy's mini-bus careered into the car park of the Swan at the top of the hour, tyres objecting, brakes squealing in protest. He climbed out, slammed the door and sauntered jauntily into the lounge where his lager laid in wait on the bar. He took an appreciative slug before turning round to face a host of inquisitive faces preparing to hang on his every word.

'What?' asked Sammy.

'We're all fascinated,' explained Wobbler. 'We've never known you go shopping before so we want to know what you've bought.

'It's got nothing to do with you lot, it's just for me.' Sammy snapped.

'I reckon it must be a load of drugs if it's such a secret,' smirked Meat Loaf. 'That's it, we're all going to be wanted drug-runners chasing the dragon on the road to nowhere.'

The heads of Stuey, Gazelle and Sammy lifted as one while an adjacent Matt Fairacre thought he was going to have a heart attack. Meat Loaf's off-the-cuff jape had raised more blood pressure than he could ever imagine, but at least it elicited a truthful, albeit reluctant reply from Sammy.

'Alright then, if you really want to know, I've bought two flagons of farmhouse cider. It's in the back of the kit minibus. That's where it's staying and you lot can keep your grubby paws off it. It's supposed to be dynamite stuff and it's all mine.'

'Where did you get it from?' asked Wobbler.

'Well, I struggled for a while to find some to be honest,' replied Sammy, scratching his head and drinking his lager at the same time. 'I didn't want any of that village shop eye-wash that Wobbler bought, I wanted the real home-made stuff. So I drove out into the countryside and because it's called farmhouse cider, I decided to call on a few farms. It made sense to me anyway. I drew a blank at the first two, but this old bloke at the last one I tried had a fresh brew in his back shed. He said that he didn't usually sell it, but didn't mind if I bought some off him. Very reasonable it was too.'

'I read somewhere that they put dead rats in home-made cider in this part of the country,' chipped in Pete Skidmore. 'Brings out the flavour or something.'

'You really don't want to believe all those stupid old wives' tales,' snapped Sammy in reply. 'Anyway, you lot aren't going to find out because I paid for it and it's all for me. I'll get some more drinks in right now though. Who wants what?'

But before Sammy could spur Rob into action behind the bar, Matt Fairacre intervened: 'Err, lads, sorry to break up the party before it's even started, but we really do have to go. We're under strict orders to meet Uncle Norman at this Renwick cricket ground at half past one and before that we have to find this new hotel in Bristol and check in. Norman will be furious if we're late or anything goes wrong because as some of you may already know, the chairman of this Renwick club is one of his old RAF chums. So basically, no more ale and let's hit the road. But before we do, Stuey wants a quick word with you all.'

Stuey shuffled his feet and edged forward awkwardly, surprisingly nervous and suddenly feeling slightly ill-at-ease with the news he had to impart. 'It's nothing really boys,' he mumbled uncertainly. 'I just want to tell you that I won't be able to come out with you lot on the thrash in the city tonight. Laura's catching the train down this afternoon and I'm going to be spending the evening with her. She's got some kind of summer seminar at the university for the rest of the weekend, so we thought we'd take the opportunity to, well, err, just meet up.'

Stuey's little speech tailed off in front of a wall of embarrassed silence. Most of the players were disappointed to lose Stuey on their last night of the tour together, but no heart was heavier than Sammy's. He felt really upset, cheated in a strange way, and to the surprise of many present, was prepared to say so in public, choosing language he hoped Stuey might understand.

'Jeez, Stuey mate, this is our last chance for a few schooners together on holiday. I've got this night club lined up and everything. Can't the Sheila wait?' he beseeched.

'Sorry mate, it's been arranged for some time,' Stuey answered. 'It's only one night and I'm sure you'll all have a great time without me. There will also be more fines money to go round which means more free drinks for you and none for me.'

Sammy wasn't even cheered by this prospect, but the debate was brought to an abrupt close by an impatient Matt Fairacre who realised the conversation was going nowhere and that there were far more pressing matters to attend to.

'Right lads, come on, we really do have to leave.'

TWENTY-EIGHT

The hotel in Bristol was forbidding and grey.

The terraced, three storey, pebble-dashed building was streaked with dirt from the traffic fumes off the busy main road next to which it stood. One of downspouts was severed halfway. Below, slimy green moss was making a decent living on the wall. Their new home for the night was only 46 miles from the Swan. It could have been a million miles. If the hotel had a redeeming feature, it could claim to be a short walk from the city centre.

It was to be its only one.

Inside the entrance hall there was no improvement. Dark and uninviting, dusty and dying ferns sprouted out of two cracked terracotta pots next to a dank reception desk on which sat a half-full ash tray, an ink blotter and a bell that didn't work. Sammy led the troupe through a swinging door, looked the place up and down with some disdain and was decidedly blunt for the second time that day.

'This place is a bit of a dump isn't it?'

Just as he finished speaking a heavily-jowled, unshaven man wearing only a grubby vest and low-slung trousers appeared behind the reception, scowled, tutted, stubbed out a cigarette and pushed open a heavily-thumbed signing-in book. 'You must be the bloody cricketers. One night only I see. I'll have payment in advance in that case. Who's in charge?'

'Matt....Prince Charming wants a word,' was Sammy's sullen reply. Matt Fairacre elbowed his way to the front and glared at Sammy who was just about as miserable as he'd ever known him.

'We'll pay in advance if you wish, but we weren't informed this would be necessary. Will a cheque be OK?'

'No it bloody well won't,' the surly owner replied. 'It will take too long to clear, so I want cash.'

'Everybody dig deep into their pockets for the master of the workhouse', groused Sammy. 'After a bowl of thin gruel, he'll be selecting a couple of the juniors to sweep the chimneys.'

'Sammy, will you please let me deal with this,' pleaded an agitated Matt Fairacre, before turning back to the increasingly hostile hotel owner who was now glaring menacingly at Sammy. 'I've got the cash if you prefer. Can the rest of the party go to their rooms now?'

The hotel owner lit another cigarette and from behind his desk pointed a grubby pen in a sweeping arc at the new arrivals. 'There are two big rooms on the second floor. Numbers eight and nine to accommodate you all. But there are strict rules. No smoking or alcohol in the rooms, breakfast at eight sharp and the front door is locked at eleven thirty at night on the dot. It will not be opened for anyone who is late and there are no spare keys. Have I made myself quite clear?'

'Yes, yes, right, that's fine' replied Matt Fairacre hurriedly.

'Now can we get on and just chuck our stuff in the rooms. We have to be at the cricket ground in less than an hour and there'll be hell to pay if we're late.'

Sammy stomped off first up the stairs muttering darkly under his breath. He unceremoniously booted open the door to room number eight and surveyed the scene. It wasn't so much a hotel room more a school dormitory for the Bash Street Kids. Several bunk beds were scattered at random across a half-carpeted floor, a plywood wardrobe was managing with just one door, the curtain-less draughty sash windows desperately in need of a clean.

It made the Swan look like the Savoy.

Stuey walked into the room behind Sammy. He had maintained a diplomatic silence for some time since his cry-off speech back in the Swan, but decided it was time to speak: 'Sorry about letting you down tonight Sammy, especially as you've ended up in this dive,' he said.

Sammy grunted and replied ungraciously: 'I suppose you've got yourself some fancy love pad for the night with heated carpet slippers, electric curtains, self-emptying ashtrays, the whole nine yards.'

'Actually we're staying in Laura's hall of residence,' said Stuey. 'I don't suppose it's going to be unbridled luxury, but it's got to be better than this place.'

Sammy replied: 'I'm not bothered about this dump or even old misery guts downstairs. It's tonight that worries me. It's going to be so boring without you coming along Stuey. I know that Gazelle, Meat Loaf, Pete Skidmore and a few of the lads will turn out for a few beers, but where's the fun in that? Wobbler will probably stop in reading Bleak House or something, counting his money like Fagin in a pair of those fingerless gloves. But what's really bugging me is that a mate of mine recommended this little night club called Stella's. I was going to haul us all down there as a bit of a surprise. I don't feel like going now.'

Stuey's guilt coursed through him. He wanted to make it up in some way to his disgruntled chum, but he could hardly tell Laura that he had decided to go clubbing with the lads at this late hour. Suddenly he had an idea. It wasn't the best in the world, but it was all he could come up with on the spur of the moment and in the circumstances, would have to suffice.

'Err, Sammy, I've got a couple of joints here in my jacket. You can have them if you like. I don't, well like, smoke in front of Laura, silly of me really, but that's the way it is so I won't be needing them. I realise they're not going to turn the night into a head-banging experience or anything like that, but err, I just thought they might help.'

Stuey placed the two joints in the palm of his hand and offered them to Sammy.

Sammy looked at them and then lifted his head and looked at Stuey. Despite feeling almost totally brassed off, his affection for this young man again prevailed. Sammy could not find it within himself to feel angry with Stuey or even to let a cross word come between them. Even though the Australian was the direct source of his unhappiness and distinct unease, Sammy realised that he was blaming everybody except the person at the heart of the matter.

He also realised that he found it difficult – no impossible – to tell Stuey of his true feelings, of how he had lied about enjoying drugs in the past either to impress him or just to stay in his good favour. It was becoming more and more apparent that never in his life had he felt this way about another man.

Sure, he had his friends, his cricketing colleagues and his many boozing partners while even losers such as Meat Loaf were afforded small amounts of respect.

But with Stuey it was different and had been different all along. He had looked forward to meeting him, had enjoyed being with him and now was in a fearfully bad mood just because he was losing him to a woman for one night. It was all becoming too much.

Sammy looked at the drugs in the outstretched hand and briefly toyed with the idea of some frank admissions. The reality, when the words tumbled out, was another tissue of half-truths. Taking the reefers and placing them discreetly in the top pocket of his jacket he said: 'Cheers Stuey, nice one. It still won't be the same without you this evening, but I appreciate the gesture. I'll drink your share of the ale and then tell you all about Stella's. Apparently the place is crawling with....'

At this point the door burst open and Meat Loaf, sweating profusely after climbing up two flights of stairs fully laden, noisily heaved his way in and chucked two large hold-alls on to the floor, one of which was Sammy's. Meat Loaf started to moan.

'I'll tell you what Sammy, why don't you leave all the hard work to us while you and lover-boy here have a cosy chat. Matt Fairacre's tearing his hair out downstairs and he's not got all that much to tear out. He says that if we're late, we're dead.'

Sammy growled: 'Meat Loaf, why don't you go and boil your head,' and roughly pushed his way past him into the corridor outside.

Stuey shrugged his shoulders and followed him.

TWENTY-NINE

As the two minibuses pulled into Renwick CC, it came as no surprise to see Norman F. Billington pacing up and down outside the clubhouse checking his wrist-watch every few seconds.

Against all the odds, the touring party had arrived on time – just – the chairman so relieved to see them that all his anxieties disappeared in an instant. He hugged a somewhat taken aback Wobbler as he heaved himself out of the driver's seat, Wobbler immediately handing down an on-the-spot fine for the non-wearing of hat.

'But you never even gave me a hat to wear in the first place', protested Norman F. Billington half-heartedly.

'Possession is nine tenths of the law,' said Wobbler, a statement which was as baffling as it was irrelevant, but still served to silence the smiling chairman who gladly dipped into his pocket to pay his dues.

As the rest of the players stepped down from the minibus, a large silver-grey Jaguar crunched its way noisily across the gravel forecourt and pulled up alongside them. Out of it climbed a dapper, well-groomed gentleman, tall and debonair with a moustache that was the same colour as his car and almost the same size. Within seconds Norman F. Billington was hugging then vigorously pumping the hand of the suave Jaguar driver, a man approximately his own age. He turned and spoke to his cricketers. 'Boys, this is Ronald Richardson, the chairman of Renwick club, a dear friend, fellow sportsman and a former colleague in arms. Believe me we go back a long way.'

Ronald Richardson stepped forward resolutely and spoke with great clarity as he proceeded to shake hands en masse. 'It's an absolute delight to meet every one of you. I believe there's a celebrity Australian in your midst,' he said as he worked his way through the throng, but when he happened upon Sammy, he stopped and said: 'Ahh, you must be our antipodean friend. That moustache reminds me so much of Rodney Marsh.'

The dark thunder cloud hanging over Sammy drifted to one side for a moment to allow a sparkle of sunbeams to come shining through. He initially considered maintaining his customary pretence for as long as possible, but quickly thought better of it. Even Sammy realised this was an important day for Norman F. Billington. 'Err, it's not me actually, but thanks for the compliment. Our cousin from Down Under is over there at the end. He's the good-looking guy with the blonde streaks.'

Ronald Richardson did not deflect from his hand-shaking line-up, Meat Loaf, Gazelle and Matt Fairacre all afforded the VIP treatment before the Renwick chairman worked his way along to Stuey. He looked the young Australian up and down with ill-concealed admiration before speaking: 'I've been looking forward to meeting you so much young man. You've earned yourself quite a reputation back home Down Under and

I believe you're making one for yourself over here as well. But I think you'll find you're up against some pretty stiff competition today. My boys are no push-overs, all of which must make for a spiffing game of cricket. May the better team win.'

Formalities over, Wobbler led his players towards the dressing room and as they made their way across the car park, Norman F Billlington took Stuey gently by the elbow and held him back from the rest of the group.

'May I have a quiet word in your ear Stuart,' he said.

'Whatever Norm,' grunted Stuey obligingly.

'You may already be aware of this, but Ronald and I are close friends and served together in the war. But when it comes to all matters cricket, we're also great rivals. Here in Bristol, Renwick are in a higher league than us, so they're expecting to win, possibly quite comfortably. It would mean an awful lot to me and everyone else at the club if we could beat them, at the very least leave the ground with our heads held on high. I certainly don't expect you to achieve this all on your own. David Carter, Peter Skidmore and Matthew Fairacre to name but a few all take their cricket very seriously, but as our finest player and our very own club professional, I feel sure you will appreciate there is possibly an even greater onus of responsibility resting on your shoulders today. What do you think?'

Stuey turned to Norman F. Billington and said: 'Who's David Carter?'

Norman looked at Stuey in a perplexed state.

'Pardon?'

'David Carter. Who is he? I don't know who he is.' Stuey repeated firmly.

It dawned on Norman F. Billington that Stuey was being

quite serious. He really didn't know who David Carter was.

Norman F. Billington said: 'It's Wobbler. I can't believe you didn't know that.'

'Oh him,' replied Stuey, a hint of disappointment in his voice, before adding: 'Nobody ever calls him anything else but Wobbler. I wasn't to know.'

A slow smile came to Norman F. Billington's lips. He recalled that Dave Carter's wife had telephoned the cricket club one night last year and even she had asked if Wobbler was there.

He couldn't believe that at the time either.

This didn't alter the fact that Stuey had still managed to steer himself away from the most important issue of the day, but Norman F. Billington felt sure he had done so inadvertently and without malicious intent.

'So', resumed Norman F. Billington, 'are we going to win today?'

Stuey dove-tailed his Australian and English colloquialisms skilfully.

'No worries Norm. We'll batter these men.'

THIRTY

Battering these men proved easier said than done, even in an Australian accent.

Batting first in a 40-over encounter, Crawford struggled to make much progress and lost wickets steadily, a total of 74 runs with four batsmen already back in the pavilion and half the overs bowled was starting to look like a lost cause indeed. A badly out-of-sorts Sammy made just two before being stumped trying to smash the opening paceman into the next county, a flop which did little to improve his rapidly deteriorating mood. Stuey came to the wicket with Matt Fairacre and set about rescuing the side – and possibly more importantly Norman F. Billington – from embarrassment that was straying uncomfortably close to humiliation.

Just as Gazelle in the previous game, Matt Fairacre was inspired by Stuey's mere presence out there in the middle of the park and dug deep, even if his concentration was impaired by the constant niggle that his batting partner may well have been smoking weed that very morning.

While Matt Fairacre grafted and consolidated at one end, Stuey unleashed his entire range of attacking flair at the other. The Australian felt inspired, the source of which he couldn't quite pin down. The imminent arrival of Laura and the weight of expectation placed upon him by Norman F. Billington were both prime candidates, but deep below the surface Stuey had felt surprisingly moved by the reaction of his peers when he had told them of his alternative plans for their last night. The uncaring Australian inside him told him not to come over all emotional just because of a load of whinging Poms, but he had been touched by guilt and had to admit to himself that he was paying off a debt of honour with the bat in his hands.

Stuey pushed the score along at a cracking rate and at the end of 40 overs had steered the side to 220 for nine with a swashbuckling personal tally of 106 not out, the standing ovation for his century led by Norman F. Billington who, for the first time in his life, had almost stepped on to a chair.

There was the scent of victory in the visiting camp as tea was taken, news of a thrilling finale to the Ashes Test at Headingley filtering through after Ian Botham's splendid knock of 149 had rescued England from complete ignomy the day before. Even as Botham and Bob Willis in particular were driving a coach and horses through the Australian batting, Wobbler and his team were attempting much of the same deep in the Severn estuary.

Early success for the bowlers was limited.

The Renwick batsmen were diligent and determined. They knew they weren't chasing a huge total so were digging in defiantly, drip-feeding themselves toward their target rather than thrash and hope.

After 20 overs they were 102 for two and set fair for victory when soft drinks were served on the field

Wobbler gathered his players together for a pep talk as thirsts were slaked.

'By way of a tactical switch, myself, Stuey and Pete are coming off and Meat Loaf and Matt Fairacre are taking over the bowling. I think these batsmen might be tempted to cut loose to try get it over quickly and so take a few risks.'

After some early set-backs – Meat Loaf's first two balls dispatched to the boundary – Wobbler's plan began to reap rewards.

One batsman then another were caught deep in the outfield and when Matt Fairacre secured himself an lbw decision by dint of being awfully polite to the umpire, Renwick were beginning to feel the pressure. They still had five wickets standing though and with Meat Loaf threatening to disappear completely due to vast amounts of sweating, Wobbler and Pete Skidmore returned to the attack.

Pete Skidmore asked his skipper: 'Wouldn't Stuey be a better option? He's fitter than me.'

'He'll need all his energy tonight, Laura's in town. Come on, we can do it,' insisted Wobbler.

But they struggled. Just one more wicket fell and with four men still standing and just 40 runs required in eight overs, Renwick had again established themselves as firm favourites.

Wobbler called over Stuey and invited him to bowl his remaining four overs. The captain couldn't work out whether Stuey was in need of any more motivation, but thought he would chuck some at him anyway.

He said: 'The lad who brought out the drinks reckons that Australia are going to lose that Test at Headingley which frankly is unbelievable.'

'That can't be right,' replied Stuey. 'The entire team only needed 130 to win. What's going on there then?'

Wobbler replied: 'Apparently Bob Willis has been inspired by Ian Botham's amazing batting yesterday and now he's skittling through the opposition with the ball.

'Perhaps you'd better show us all what a real Australian's made of.'

Stuey nodded gravely and glanced up at the pavilion where Norman F. Billington was looking to the heavens. Next to him stood Laura, newly-arrived off the train. She waved cheerfully and blew him a kiss. Stuey caught the ball with one hand and ran his fingers through his hair with the other.

If some kind of fate was reaching out to him, he needed to be looking his best.

His first ball was quick and short, lifting sharply off the bone-dry track and whistling past the batsman's head as he took evasive action. The batsman glared menacingly at Stuey who in turn glared back.

The next four balls were as short and hostile as the first, the batsman flailing but failing to make contact, the umpire having a quiet word with Stuey about making his bowling more playable. The last ball of the over was eminently playable, the frustrated batsman heaving it high over mid-on where Meat Loaf took a great catch five feet short of the boundary rope.

There was much cheering and many moist embraces.

Stuey's wicket maiden had animated the contest, but also served to make Matt Fairacre increasingly nervous. He was the only recognised bowler with overs remaining and he also recognised that he wasn't in Stuey's league.

He needed to be accurate and tight, but the facing batsman

knew he was up against the weaker of the two bowlers and took six runs off six balls.

The next two overs were also fruitful for Renwick, the requirement reduced to just 20 before Stuey struck again, the wicket-keeper caught at mid-off for a single, leaving the home side needing 19 to win with three overs and two wickets remaining.

Matt Fairacre was growing increasingly tense, not least because he now looked certain to be bowling the last over. He silently cursed Wobbler for his lack of foresight.

The nerves unsettled Matt Fairacre. His next six balls cost 14 runs including a six and a four and with Renwick only needing to score five off two overs, Crawford's fate seemed settled.

Stuey prepared to bowl his last over. He decided not to turn and face Norman or Laura in the pavilion, but still felt their eyes piercing into him. He felt every eye on the ground piercing into him, so he drew a deep breath and steadied himself.

His first ball boasted venom, but lacked direction, the batsman flicking it down the leg side for four, a shot Gazelle would have been proud of, Stuey reflected ruefully. His next ball was bowling perfection wrapped in a leather casing, just short of a length, full pace, nipping back off the seam and taking out middle and off stumps. Sammy picked up the debris, smiled and shouted encouragement down the wicket, his first of the afternoon.

The last man of the innings did a bit of gardening, took his guard and looked stern. Stuey's next three balls were bowled with too much enthusiasm and zeal to command the necessary accuracy, the tail-ender allowing each one to pass innocuously through to Sammy, smiling as he did so.

One more ball to survive and his established partner would have an over of Matt Fairacre's soft oranges to score just a single run to claim victory. Stuey stamped the ground in frustration and looked to the heavens in despair. He allowed himself a glance over towards the pavilion where Norman F. Billington now appeared to be praying to the heavens above whilst holding Laura's hand.

Norman was a calm person, always thinking, Stuey reflected. His last ball needed to be full of thought, not anger, not overloaded with passion, delivered with a due sense of deliberation and purpose. He had about thirty seconds to come up with a plan and it needed to be good. He told the umpire he was shortening his run and going round the wicket. The batsman was duly informed and Stuey marked a new start in the grass less than five yards from the delivery crease. More than anything he was determined to unsettle the batsman and then make him play the ball.

Stuey cantered rather than ran to the wicket before releasing a slow, measured delivery. He then chased after it. The batsman, both eyes fixed intently on the ball which he had already decided he would have to play, moved forward out of his crease and put a defensive shield up to it. The ball bounced a tad more than he had anticipated and struck the shoulder of the bat. It wasn't much of a deviation, but it was enough. Stuey's outstretched hand on the end of his diving body scooped it up before it hit the grass. The catch was made and a stunning victory belonged to Crawford.

Stuey threw the ball high into the air and fled towards the pavilion as though his life depended on it.

Meat Loaf was chasing him for a big hug.

THIRTY-ONE

The scene in the Renwick CC lounge was one of unrestrained joy and celebration.

If there had been a VIP chair at the top table, Stuey would have been sprawled all over it, bedecked in ermine, while nubile young ladies decanted ice cool champagne into cut-glass flutes. As it was, he had to be content with a creaking bar stool, a pint of cooking lager and a delighted Norman F. Billington shaking his hand for a full two minutes while expressing his complete indebtedness and undying gratitude.

The chairman's decision to bring over an overseas professional was now totally vindicated. The young man had turned out to be everything he had hoped for, and today, a little bit more. Gracious in defeat, Ronald Richardson was happy to sign up to the ever-growing ranks of the Stuart Latham appreciation society, noisily announcing that there was always a place for the dashing young blade at Renwick, should the cookie ever crumble that way.

Stuey's last-gasp inspiration was sharing a tandem with

news of England's even more sensational Test victory at Headingley, Bob Willis charging in to take eight wickets as the Australians fell 18 runs short of their meagre target. It was being reported that bookmakers had been offering surreal odds of 500-1 against England winning the game followed by rumours that a couple of the Australian players – Rod Marsh one of them – had been tempted to bet against their own team before the last day's play.

Sammy, whose bad mood had only marginally improved after his side's victory, was appalled to learn that his hero could even contemplate such treachery and slumped back into his dark depression.

He resolved to take it out on the drink that night.

THIRTY-TWO

The fines money for the last night on the thrash in Bristol had been boosted by a most generous £25 donation from the back pocket of an eternally grateful Norman F. Billington.

The visiting players said their thanks and farewells in Renwick and after leaving the minibuses in a side street near the hotel, the more senior players opted to take their share of the kitty and walk into the city where they settled in a quiet corner of the Saracens Head to partake of the opening toasts of the night. Firstly, glasses were raised to absent friend Stuey who had left the Renwick club arm in arm with Laura and secondly, well, it was Stuey again whose exceptional feats on the cricket field had doubled the booze kitty.

Sammy was also doubling up, throwing back the lager at an alarming rate and quite prepared to complain to anyone who wasn't up to pace. Wobbler, both hands on the purse strings, took him to task. 'Sammy, we're supposed to be having fair and equal shares of this kitty, so take your time will you? We've got all night you know. Why are you drinking so quickly?'

'I'm drinking to forget,' replied Sammy snappily

'Forget what exactly?' asked Wobbler. 'What's eating at you man?'

Sammy didn't know what to say. He couldn't even bear to admit the truth to himself so the chances of frank and open revelations in front of his cricketing peers were slim indeed. Deep down, he knew the real reason for his simmering bad mood. He missed Stuey. He didn't feel jealous of his cricketing prowess, he didn't really begrudge him his night out with Laura. He just missed him and wanted him to be there. The fact that he felt this way was as upsetting as Stuey's absence itself.

He said: 'I'll be fine when I've had a few more lagers. Come on, let's move on and see if we can find this night club my mate recommended.'

The cricketers embarked on a pub crawl of the city centre, Gazelle's sneaky half of mild in the Firkin and Bucket duly noted and made the subject of a mass reprimand, but the early evening hours passed pleasantly enough without rescue flares soaring into the night air. Sammy's desire for them all to attend Stella's was overpowering though and it was mainly to keep the disgruntled one happy that they all agreed to go along with his plan.

The night club was located near the bottom of a seedy alley, some distance away from the city centre and would most certainly have been overlooked had it not been for Sammy's dogged insistence. Wobbler was convinced that a group of half-drunk blokes wearing daft hats wouldn't be allowed in anyway, but the woman who opened then peeked through the fortified front door raised no objections, merely asking for a modest entrance fee.

Stella's was surprisingly quiet and spacious and while it was far more attractive inside than out, was still no palace. As they walked in, there was a small bar on the immediate left and an empty dance floor in the centre, off which ran a raised walkway leading to a series of side rooms. Closer inspection revealed that the club seemed to be more of a games hall than a night club, two pool tables in one room, several one-armed bandits in another and a full-size snooker table in a separate large lounge where drinks were also being served.

Wobbler was tremendously impressed. Even their own cricket club back home couldn't lay claim to a full-size snooker table, the general concensus being that this one was the genuine article with a real slate base and ornate wooden legs.

Matt Fairacre, Pete Skidmore and Meat Loaf took little persuading to join him in a doubles tournament – a kitty to be organised for the winners of course – Sammy and Gazelle less enthusiastic. Sammy, already armed with a monster Botham shandy, announced that he was off to play the one-armed bandits, sullenly adding that he had never realised it was going to be this quiet and would prefer to be alone.

The rest nodded in agreement tinged with relief. Sammy in such a bad mood was best operating solo.

Gazelle had no appetite for snooker either. He wasn't even any good at pool and if the truth be known had taken on board his fill of alcohol for the night.

He espied his chance to buy himself a quiet orange squash without being labelled a lightweight. He resolved be a real devil and drink it right-handed.

Gazelle said: 'You boys carry on with your snooker in here. I'm going to sit at the other bar near to where we came in. I'll see if they've got a newspaper I can read or something.'

'Are you sure Gazelle?' said Wobbler. 'Don't you even want to watch me win a boat load of money off these losers?'

Gazelle offered a weak grin and replied: 'No, honestly, I'll be alright. I'll see you guys later.'

Gazelle walked back across the dance floor and pulled up a stool at the bar which was deserted apart from a woman near the end sipping a long, pink drink through a straw. She was in her late thirties, smartly dressed with short-cropped blonde hair and seemed to be on her own. She looked across, smiled and then spoke as Gazelle sat down.

'I like your hat,' she said. 'Do you always wear it inside?'

'Err, yes, I'm afraid it's compulsory at the moment,' replied Gazelle.

'Compulsory?' giggled the woman. 'I've never heard of a compulsory hat before.'

'Err, we have to wear them because we're all on a cricket tour together,' offered Gazelle uncertainly. 'My mates over there are in the snooker room. They're all wearing them as well.'

At this point the barman appeared and asked Gazelle what he would like to drink.

'Err, just an orange juice please,' before he hesitated, glanced awkwardly down the bar and added: 'And perhaps the lady would like a drink as well.'

'That's very sociable of you', the woman replied. 'I'll just have a half of lager and I'll come and join you if you don't mind.'

The woman lifted and carried her stool along the bar, settled down next to Gazelle, lit a cigarette and said: 'Tell me all about this cricket tour then and what's your name by the way?'

'It's Gaz...err, Bernard,' replied Gazelle. 'What's yours?'

'Estelle,' she replied and offered her hand. 'You're not from around these parts are you?'

'No, we're from up north. Like I said, we're all on a cricket tour down here. We've spent three days in Somerset and today we played here in Bristol. Renwick I think the club was called and we won. This is our last night.'

'That's a shame,' said Estelle.

Suddenly Gazelle found himself telling his new female friend lots about himself and even more about the tour. For more than an hour, he described in some detail the recruitment of Stuey from Australia, how he had become his lodger back home and how he had made nearly half a century in a place called Chimmiford. He even told her all about Norman F. Billington and his own job as a groundsman. Apart from his mother, Gazelle had never spoken to a woman for so long before in his entire life. He tried to keep the conversation flowing because he had half expected his new companion to make her excuses and leave or even worse, fall asleep. It had happened in the past.

But Estelle had listened attentively to every word, accepted another two halves of lager and had even made small talk herself, asking Gazelle where he was staying.

'We've got a hotel on the other side of the city. It's not too far though. We've walked it here,' he replied.

Estelle extinguished her third cigarette, swivelled her shapely legs off her stool, stood up and said: 'I've won't be a moment. I've just got a bit of business to attend to. Keep my place warm for me.'

And with a flick of her hair she walked off towards the ladies' toilet.

Gazelle was feeling rather pleased with himself. Without trying too hard, without much effort at all really, he had managed to meet a rather pleasant lady, one who was actually interested in what he had to say. She had smiled in the right places, even laughed on occasions and had seemed content in his company.

And it was all down to his hat…and a dash of his own very special charisma of course.

He made a mental note to congratulate Wobbler on his fine choice of head attire. Not wearing it might have cost him at least one limb in fines over the last few days, but tonight it was worth every penny and although he still wasn't sure exactly where the night was taking him, he was sure that it had to be better than boozing and playing snooker.

Gazelle caught sight of Estelle talking to another woman outside the toilets. She pointed over to Gazelle and they huddled together deep in conversation before Estelle strolled back to the bar, re-straddled the stool and lit another cigarette.

'The other girl is called Yvonne,' she said huskily to Gazelle, inhaling the tobacco smoke deeply. 'She's my sister. We've had a chat and because I've told her you seem like a really decent kind of guy, we've decided to cut you a special deal. You can have us both for forty quid. Back at your hotel of course. How does that sound?'

You…can…have…us…both…for…forty…quid.

The words bounced around Gazelle's brain, knocking him senseless.

His mouth moved, but nothing came out.

Why was he always lost for words these days? Why were people always making statements which were no less than vicious right hooks landing on his vulnerable glass chin?

As the full implication of Estelle's offer finally made its way through to some connecting neurotransmitters, the overwhelming emotions flooding into Gazelle's mind were utter dejection and demoralising disappointment. He firmly believed he had won this lady's attention and possibly even admiration by dint of his own charm and personality, with a little help from a rather dapper hat of course.

Now it was becoming clear that she had listened to his cricketing yarns for business reasons only, to engage and seduce the client, to clinch a deal, and now the lady of the night was laying down terms and conditions.

Estelle surveyed the jibbering wreck in front of her for a few moments before a wave of realisation crashed up on to her shore as well. She held a hand up to her cheek and said: 'Oh Bernard, my poor love. Didn't you know? We're all on the game in this place. I just assumed….'

Gazelle looked at her. Even though he felt crestfallen and crushed, his mind was now racing.

He started to think that forty pounds was a crazy amount of money, even if there were two of them, wondering how much Estelle alone would charge and even then if he could afford it.

But could he possibly even imagine taking her back to the hotel from hell with that youth hostel dormitory full of half-drunk yobs and sweaty cricket flannels?

And Sammy.

Gazelle decided that he really needed to put such ridiculous thoughts from his mind, but before he could make his excuses and leave, he was rudely interrupted by Meat Loaf who was making his way to the toilets with Pete Skidmore.

'Hey up, Gazelle's pulled,' announced Meat Loaf as he sashayed nonchalantly across the dance floor and walked up to the couple. 'Who's your new friend Gazelle? She's a bit nice for you isn't she?'

Gazelle ignored Meat Loaf's ignorant remarks and said: 'Her name's Estelle, but she's leaving now and so am I.'

And with that, Gazelle picked up his hat off the bar and headed hurriedly for the door. Meat Loaf stared at Estelle who stared back coldly. He coughed, mumbled incoherently and followed in Gazelle's footsteps.

'Wait for me,' Meat Loaf cried. 'I'm coming too, in fact, we all are. We've got some cans of beer back at the hotel, so we're going back there to play cards.'

'Everybody except Sammy,' added Wobbler, as he pulled on his jacket and joined them. 'He insists that he's stopping on the bandits and finding his own way home later. I'm not arguing with him when he's in such a foul mood. There must be something seriously wrong with that lad because he's even stopped pretending to be Australian.'

THIRTY-THREE

The walk back to the hotel seemed further than before.

It certainly seemed much longer for Gazelle because he was the focal point of attention, Meat Loaf leading the grilling over the identity of the mystery woman in the nightclub.

'I thought you were in there Gazelle,' he sniggered as they strolled along. 'How did you manage to pick up that darling and how come you ditched her so quickly?'

Gazelle wished his brush with Estelle could avoid a public airing, but his top secret file was already full, so decided it was better to come clean.

'I didn't realise it at the time, but Estelle was a lady of the night, a prostitute and she was, err, how do you say it, propositioning me.'

'You're joking!' cried a wide-eyed Meat Loaf. 'And you turned her down? Hey lads, listen to this, can you believe this one? Gazelle nearly got off with a hooker.'

'Two hookers actually,' chimed in Gazelle. 'She said she had her sister with her and that they would both come back to the hotel with me for forty quid.'

'Forty quid!' exclaimed Wobbler, the mere mention of money halting him abruptly in his tracks. 'That's a bit steep isn't it? Forty quid! That's a lot steep. Was she really her sister? That's what they all say you know.'

'Wobbler, you'd think it was steep if they were charging four quid and chucking in a fish supper for afters,' scoffed Meat Loaf.

'And what do you mean, that's what they all say?'

Wobbler changed tack quickly.

'Weren't you tempted then Gazelle?' he asked.

'Well, I was and I wasn't really. But you're right, forty quid is a ridiculous amount of money and then of course there was all you lot dossing down in the same YMCA dormitory. It would have been a complete farce.'

'We all could have watched,' leered Meat Loaf, 'and then joined in.'

'I think you've all just entered the realms of fantasy,' said Wobbler.

'Come on, let's step it up a bit. It's starting to rain.'

THIRTY-FOUR

The advance party arrived back at the hotel which was in total darkness.

Matt Fairacre walked up to the front door and tried in vain to push it open. It was locked and there was no bell.

'What time is it?' he asked.

'Just after midnight,' replied Wobbler.

'That's torn it,' said Matt Fairacre. 'That miserable owner warned us that he was locking up at 11.30 and we've forgotten all about it. What on earth are we going to do now? He's going to go berserk if we knock him up and I'm not even convinced that he'd let us in even if we did manage to wake him. I'm also not convinced that we can wake him. There's a porch and then two more double doors even before the reception. We've got no chance. Anybody got any ideas?'

Wobbler looked the building up and down 'There's no chance of getting in at the front. Let's try the back. There may be a tradesman's entrance, even a fire escape or something.'

The players walked to the end of the terrace, turned right

then right again along a rough track which led to the rear of the premises. They climbed over a crumbling brick wall into what appeared to be a builder's yard. Workmen had clearly been renovating the back of the hotel and their tools of the trade were still on site. A mixer with a tarpaulin hastily thrown over it was encircled by torn bags of sand and cement and a half-used pile of bricks. The back of the hotel was also in total darkness and all the ground floor windows had metal grilles on the outside.

But a long wooden ladder was leaning against the back wall. Meat Loaf walked to it, kicked it and looked up.

'It goes right up to that third floor window,' he said. 'It's bound to be a bedroom. Shall I climb up and see if I can get in?'

'That's just the ale talking,' sneered Wobbler. 'That's one hell of a ladder and one hell a height'.

'I'll be fine, I used to be a window cleaner you know,' replied Meat Loaf. 'You lot just grab hold of the bottom of the ladder and hold it steady.'

Wobbler had serious reservations. 'Meat Loaf, if you fall off and kill yourself, or even worse, fall off and crush us all to death, I will not be held personally responsible. If Norman finds out about this, we're in deep mire.'

'We're in deep mire already,' answered Meat Loaf. 'We've got no ale and nowhere to sleep. It doesn't get any worse than that.'

And with that he set off up the ladder. The wooden rungs creaked and moaned under the strain. He reached half-way, looked down and shouted.

'You're right, it is high. I'm definitely having an extra can for this.'

Pete Skidmore started to shake the ladder from side to side

causing Meat Loaf to squeal and protest.

'Pack it in you lunatics. If I fall, we're all dead.'

Wobbler said: 'He's right, we'd better not mess about. Can you imagine being hit by a bouncing bomb of plutonium-grade perspiration? The stain would have a half life of a hundred years. Leave him be Pete and let's hope he makes it.'

Meat Loaf started to grunt and heave as he pulled his considerable frame up the final few rungs. He managed to raise his head above the window sill where he stopped and drew in several deep breaths. He wanted to wipe away the sweat cascading from his brow, but that would involve the removal of one tightly clenched fist from the side of the ladder. He looked down and shuddered. It might have been worth mentioning earlier that his erstwhile window cleaning round had consisted mainly of old age pensioners' bungalows.

But it was too late now, there was no going back.

He closed his eyes and with a supreme mental effort, prised one hand off the ladder and tapped gently on the lower glass pane which was now just above the top of his head. Nothing happened. So he tapped again with a bit more vigour and a light came on.

Down below, the support troops at the base camp heard an ill-fitting sash window being reluctantly pushed open followed by a garbled conversation which they couldn't make out. They then heard the window being closed, the ladder starting to creak again as Meat Loaf tentatively made his way back down. He reached the bottom rung and with great relief stepped off on to terra firma and into the gaze of four expectant faces.

'What's the script Sherpa Tensing?' asked Pete Skidmore.

A trembling Meat Loaf gasped for air before speaking.

'Some foreign bloke opened the window. I think he's

Dutch. He was a bit taken aback to say the least, possibly even scared out of his wits, but that's not surprising when a complete stranger knocks on your window in the early hours of the morning, especially when you're on the third floor. I told him we were locked out and he had a bit of a moan, but he's agreed to go downstairs and open the front door. Quick, let's go before he changes his mind. I really need a drink.'

The five desperadoes clambered back over the yard wall and hot-footed it around to the front of the hotel. As they got to the door, a light came on in the reception area and a small, middle-aged man in red striped pyjamas pushed his way through the double doors and started to fumble with the lock on the front door. He managed to turn the handle and as he pulled the door fully open was confronted by a grinning Meat Loaf who said: 'Bonny pee-jays, mate. Fancy a game of cards?'

The Dutchman muttered darkly under his breath and swore in his native tongue before walking back into the reception area, proclaiming all Englishmen barking mad and disappearing back up the stairs.

The rest of the cricketers, who were still outside, trooped in sheepishly and with much relief made their way back up to their room. Once safely ensconced, Meat Loaf unzipped a hold-all and threw several cans of lager into some grateful hands before grinning and pulling out a bottle of vodka and a pack of cards. He and Matt Fairacre pushed two bunk beds together to form an impromptu table and battle commenced, Meat Loaf determined not to lose the replacement moped he'd been forced to buy the last time he'd entered the dangerous world of three card brag.

But the atmosphere around the card table was convivial and restrained, a sensible gambling limit ensuring that no internal combustion engines changed hands despite Wobbler's protestations. After half an hour, the playing field was mainly level, not unlike Meat Loaf who had worked his way through half the bottle of vodka and was in the mood for some serious knavery. He glanced up from his fourth useless hand of cards in succession and looked around the room in search of more engaging entertainment.

'Which is Sammy's bed?' he asked of no-one in particular.

'He's claimed the top bunk on his own over there in the corner,' replied Gazelle. 'That's his bag on the pillow.'

'Right, let's sort him out with a little surprise,' said Meat Loaf, rising unsteadily to his feet. Meat Loaf weaved and waltzed over to Sammy's bunk and stood on the lower of the two beds. He lifted the top mattress, peered underneath it and whooped with delight. The base of the bed was constructed of flimsy wooden slats which he could pull out without a great deal of effort. Giggling and smirking, Meat Loaf yanked two, then three slats out of the bed, walked across the room and hid them at the back of the wardrobe, the side that boasted a door of course. He returned and concealed another armful, leaving just three slats on the bed. He placed one at each end and one in the middle before carefully re-arranging the mattress and its covering of a pillow, a grubby sheet and two shabby blankets.

'He's in for a shock when he rolls on to that,' he announced with much sniggering glee. 'It might even cheer him up'.

'I have my serious doubts about that,' warned Wobbler, confidently arranging a more than welcome queen flush in his left hand.

'Especially when he breaks his neck.'

'It's just a bit of fun,' countered Meat Loaf. 'Sammy will be fine with it.'

'I just hope you're right,' said Wobbler. 'Anyway, come and take cover next to me Meat Loaf, it's your turn to play. Perhaps you ought to have a bet on your hand. It may well be your last.'

The card session lasted another 20 minutes before there was a thunderous crashing noise at the door. The noise was made by a size eleven boot opening it. Sammy stormed into the room wild-haired, wild-eyed and in no mood for messing.

'I've had a completely crap night, probably the worst of my life,' he bellowed. 'I lost a bloody fortune on those bandits, I'm sure they were fixed and then you lot buggered off and left me.'

'We hardly left you Sammy. It was your decision not to come with us,' protested Wobbler.

'Yeh, whatever, it's still been a complete stinker,' snorted Sammy. 'And whatever happened to all those prostitutes that were supposed to be in the place? Not a sniff. Sod it. I'm off to bed.'

Sammy stamped angrily across to his bunk, quite oblivious to the fact that every eye in the room was on him and every breath was being held. Sammy heaved himself up to the side of the bunk bed and rolled his considerable frame on to it. The middle slat snapped and cracked like a piece of flimsy matchwood, a Sammy and mattress double-decker sandwich cascading straight through the void and crashing down on to the bed below with a tremendous thud, this bed also collapsing under its unequal tussle with the almighty force crashing down from above.

Sammy's initial shock quickly turned to anger. He snarled, hauled himself to his feet, gritted his teeth and turned purple with fury.

'Whoever did that is dead,' he raged. 'It was you wasn't it Wobbler? Own up now or else.'

'No way, it was Meat Loaf,' whimpered Wobbler without a moment's hesitation, better a snake in the grass than a bunch of fives in the dial his unshakable logic.

Sammy launched himself angrily at a scrambling Meat Loaf who had a split second to prepare a protective barrier. He did so by grabbing one of the pillows off the impromptu card table and holding it up above his face with both hands as Sammy leapt across the beds and started to rain blows down on him. Meat Loaf's shield was mainly effective in as much as it deflected most of the blows while allowing him to reason with the raging bull trying to re-arrange his features. As he covered up he squealed: 'Sammy it was just a joke, a bit of fun, the boys having a giggle on tour, remember?'

Still the punches rained down.

'Ouch, Sammy, ouch, stop it. I was completely drunk and you're not badly hurt are you? Give me a break will you?'

Still the punches came, but as they lessened, mainly due to the fact that Gazelle and Matt Fairacre were pluckily trying to pull Sammy off his hapless victim, a strange question suddenly entered Meat Loaf's head. He was in no position to work out the reason why this puzzler should occur to him as he was in the process of being beaten up, but he daringly poked his head around his makeshift shield and blurted out: 'Sammy, how did you get in?'

Sammy stopped trying to kill Meat Loaf, sat up and glowered at Gazelle and Matt Fairacre both of whom tentatively relaxed their grip on an arm each.

'What!?' he cried threateningly, leaning forward again so his face was only inches away from Meat Loaf's nose.

'What!?'

'How did you get in?' gasped a retreating Meat Loaf. 'Into

the hotel? When we all got back at midnight it was locked up.' Sammy stared aggressively at Meat Loaf with a mixture of disbelief and disdain on his face. 'How did I get in? How did I get in?!' he steamed. 'I'll tell you how I got in. I had to climb up some bloody great big ladder at the back of this dump. I banged on the window and some dozy foreign bloke let me in.'

'You mean he went downstairs and opened the front door for you?' interrupted Wobbler incredulously.

'No, the bugger didn't want to know. So I just pulled myself through his window and climbed over his bed anyway. He didn't seem at all happy and kept ranting on about mad Englishmen. I wasn't really listening because I just didn't care. Then I made my way down here straight into Jungle Jim's bloody booby trap.'

There was a momentary stunned silence before Wobbler started giggling which quickly turned into gales of laughter.

Matt Fairacre joined in, then Gazelle and Pete Skidmore, Meat Loaf slipping surreptitiously off the bed out of Sammy's reach before he too broke into raucous guffaws. A feeling of collective relief made the laughter even more infectious, all five of them chuckling away at Sammy's expense.

Sammy cursed, hurled the cards at Meat Loaf and stormed off to another spare bunk bed on the other side of the room.

'I don't see what's funny about that at all', he groused before punching the pillow into shape, pulling a sheet over his head and closing his eyes.

THIRTY-FIVE

None of the tourists made it down for breakfast for a variety of reasons.

Most were too sleepy, a few afraid of the landlord, the rest wary of Sammy and possibly an axe-wielding Dutchman seeking dastardly revenge. There had been a vague agreement not to languish in bed all morning because they were expected back home in the early afternoon, but it was still past ten o'clock when Wobbler wandered into the reception carrying his overnight bag. He recognised the Dutchman checking out at the desk, waving his arms about as he griped to the hotel owner about the outrageous disturbances in the night. Wobbler turned and tip-toed back up the stairs. The rest were still in their rooms, allowing Wobbler to organise an unnoticed mass exodus and so avoid an unseemly fracas with the management. This they achieved by standing quietly on a first floor landing and waiting until the Dutchman was pointing out the builder's ladder to the highly sceptical hotel owner through a rear ground floor window. Even Sammy had agreed that an ugly confrontation was best avoided, but when the party arrived at the two minibuses parked nearby, his mood was as dark as ever.

After they had chucked the bags into the luggage vehicle and prepared to head home, Gazelle manoeuvred himself into diplomatic territory and said: 'I'll drive the kit bus home if you want. Sammy, do you want to come with me?'

Sammy, who could just about tolerate Gazelle, replied: 'Right, but I'm going in the back on my own with the luggage. It will be for the best, believe me'.

And with that, Sammy climbed in through the double doors and slammed them shut. Gazelle looked at Wobbler who shrugged his shoulders and said: 'Perhaps it is for the best then. Come on, let's go and let's try and stick together.'

It had been many years since Gazelle had driven a minibus and while he navigated his way along the busy roads of Bristol, he lost contact with Wobbler and the rest.

Sammy was quiet in the back. There was a floor to roof metal partition separating the driver from the large luggage area in the rear and even though there were two small windows, Gazelle didn't have a clue what Sammy was doing.

Perhaps he was asleep on top of a mound of batting pads. He hoped so. Gazelle drove on alone, pulled the minibus on to the motorway and headed north in relative silence. But after about half an hour he could detect movement in the back. Sammy was certainly awake now if he hadn't been all along and as the journey continued, started to shift around more and more. The crashing and banging gave the impression that he was re-arranging the luggage. Gazelle tried to turn and look through one of the windows, but his view was obscured and he still had to drive the van.

After several minutes of thrashing about in the back, there

was a knock on one of the partition windows and Gazelle turned his head momentarily to see Sammy's face looming large. He was beckoning Gazelle to stop, shouting his instructions as well, although these were barely audible through the glass and above the road noise.

Gazelle wasn't prepared to pull the van on to the hard shoulder, but he had spotted a sign for a service station a few miles back. They surely couldn't be far away and tried to convey this simple information to an increasingly agitated Sammy via the unsatisfactory media of one-handed signals and miming out of the side of his mouth. He wasn't sure if the message had got through, but at least Sammy's nose was no longer pressed against the glass like the last felon in Alcatraz.

Less than ten minutes later, Gazelle drove the minibus off the motorway and towards the service station, stopping short of the main facilities on the side of the feeder road. He walked to the back of the minibus and yanked open the double doors, Sammy tumbling out, dishevelled, scowling and dragging a heavy-looking suitcase behind him.

Sammy's tolerance levels were still at an all-time low.

He grumbled: 'That's it. I'm really sick of being in that van. I'm off.'

'Off!' exclaimed a startled Gazelle. 'Off where to exactly?'

'Can't say I rightly know at the moment, but this place will do for starters,' replied Sammy.

'You can't just wander off into a motorway service station,' protested a stunned Gazelle.

'You watch me do just that,' countered a belligerent Sammy and stamped off up the road, dragging the suitcase behind him.

'Sammy, come back!' shouted Gazelle. 'What am I going to tell the boys? What am I going to tell Uncle Norman?'

'Tell them exactly what you like', grunted Sammy without turning back. 'I just want to be on my own.'

Gazelle sadly shook his head from side to side as Sammy disappeared around the corner.

He knew that further protestations were futile.

Gazelle held little sway over Sammy, perhaps less than anybody else at the club. He wouldn't even listen to Wobbler anymore, so there was no way he was going to listen to him. He climbed back behind the wheel, started the engine, drove slowly up the road and in the mirror saw Sammy in his shirt sleeves settling down on a grass verge in the sunshine and unzipping his suitcase.

Gazelle turned off and headed back towards the motorway, dreading all the explaining he would have to do on his solo return home.

THIRTY-SIX

The homecoming was lacking a cascade of ticker-tape. There were no adoring fans waving banners on the roof of the club. The red carpet had been taken away for a clean.

There was a one-man reception committee though. After a most agreeable night at the home of Ronald Richardson and only sporadically slipping into gloat mode, Norman F. Billington had made it back home earlier in his own car and was waiting at the club house. He was still feeling pleased with himself, positively smug in fact. The tour had been a great, problem-free success, Renwick had been beaten and man of the summer Stuart Latham had covered himself with a rich gloss coat of crowning glory. There was only one small cloud in an otherwise azure sky; Stuey hadn't travelled home with the tourists, opting instead to spend the rest of the weekend with his sweetheart in Bristol.

Wobbler turned the passenger mini-bus into the driveway leading to the club and spotted the chairman awaiting their arrival in the distance. He turned his head and spoke: 'Best behaviour boys, Uncle Norman's on the prowl. Let's not mention the hotel ladder fiasco and perhaps even the night-club visit might be best over-looked. You know how jittery he can get if there's even a whiff of scandal in the air.'

The mention of the word scandal raised Matt Fairacre's pulse slightly, but the unnerving mental turbulence he had encountered after his experience in the washroom earlier in the week had mostly been replaced by an inner calm. Encounters with illicit drugs had not been repeated, indeed the issue seemed to have gone away, a non-development which could be filed away as good news indeed in the young accountant's ledger of life.

Norman F. Billington greeted the returning tourists like long lost friends even though he had seen them all just the day before. Wobbler was again hugged as he stepped out of the van, the club skipper congratulated on his leadership qualities which had surely contributed much to the welcome lack of unsavoury incidents south of the border.

Norman F. Billington scanned the ranks for Sammy and raised a querulous eyebrow.

'Where's our esteemed wicket-keeper?' he asked, intentionally keeping the banter light-hearted.

'Oh, he's travelled up in the kit van with Gazelle,' replied Wobbler. They should be along soon.'

'Everything alright there as well?' added Norman F. Billington, clearly identifying Sammy as prime suspect in the mischief-making department.

'Was the night out in Bristol an enjoyable one? No-one arrested I hope,' he added with a hollow laugh.

'Bristol was fine, no bother,' replied Wobbler, choosing not to mention Sammy's recent foul mood in the hope that his imminent arrival on home soil would substantially improve his demeanour. 'The hotel was a bit of a dive, but that was Matt Fairacre's fault because he booked it, but we didn't spend a lot of time there to be honest.'

Wives, girlfriends, mates and the odd taxi or two rolled up to take the tourists on the final leg of their journey home, although most of the group waited for their luggage and kit to arrive in the other van.

About ten minutes later Gazelle drove in, the sight of such a large gathering waiting to meet him on the other side of the cricket square – particularly the presence of Norman F. Billington – not a welcome one. Gazelle had even considered stopping at the next service station to ring ahead and warn of surreal developments, but had decided that such action smacked of unnecessary panic.

The minibus crunched over the gravel and pulled alongside the other van at the top of the car park adjacent to the club house. Wobbler beat Gazelle to the back doors to let out Sammy. There was clearly concern on his mind as he turned the handle, concern that turned to dismay as he was confronted by an untidy mound of bags, suitcases and holdalls, but no sign of human life. Wobbler started to lift up the luggage and peer anxiously beneath the layers before Gazelle took him by the arm and led him gently away from the back of the vehicle.

'It's no good looking in there,' he sighed. 'Sammy's gone.'

'Gone?' Gone where exactly?' snapped Wobbler.

'Dunno really,' replied Gazelle. 'He could be anywhere by now.'

It was Wobbler's turn to grab Gazelle's arm before leading him away to the limited privacy that the space between the two vans afforded. 'Quick, tell me what happened before Norman comes over,' he whispered.

Gazelle explained the bizarre circumstances and whereabouts of Sammy's defection in as much detail as he could muster.

'And didn't you try to stop him?' demanded Wobbler.

'Of course I did,' replied Gazelle testily. 'But he was still in a foul mood and wouldn't listen. Let's have it right, he's not listened to anybody for these last couple of days, you included, so I'd got no chance. I just don't know what's wrong with him.'

Wobbler looked at Gazelle and felt a certain sympathy. 'Yep, you're right there and I don't know what's wrong with him either. Oh hell, what are we going to do now?'

'Whatever we do, it's probably best if Norman doesn't find out what's happened, not yet anyway,' replied Gazelle.

But it was too late. Even as Gazelle and Wobbler were winding up their conversation, Norman F. Billington popped his head around the side of the kit van and said: 'Where's Sammy?'

'Err, there's been a change of plan, he's, err, making his own way home', stuttered Wobbler.

'But I thought you said he was in the van with Bernard,' retorted Norman F. Billington indignantly.

'Well he was, but he unexpectedly got out near Birmingham and decided to....'

'Decided to what?' demanded Norman F. Billington.

Wobbler turned to Gazelle for inspiration and help, but a blank shake of the head clearly indicated there was to be none forthcoming. He turned back to Norman F. Billington and said dejectedly: 'We've got something to tell you Norman. Perhaps all three of us had better go inside.'

THIRTY-SEVEN

Norman F. Billington listened attentively to the strange, almost surreal, saga behind Sammy's disappearance, concern turning to worry, worry turning to agitation. The solicitor in him wanted the whole story, one which hopefully would lead to some logical reasons for Sammy's inexplicable behaviour.

Reluctantly, and at times contrary to what he believed was his better judgment, Wobbler recounted the events of the last couple of days, including the visit to the nightclub, the episode with the Dutchman at the hotel and Sammy's fracas with Meat Loaf. Much to Gazelle's relief, his own chance encounter with a lady of the night wasn't mentioned, Gazelle making a mental note to thank Wobbler for his discretion once this was all over.

But Gazelle still had questions to face and was again quizzed by Norman F. Billington over the actual circumstances of Sammy's decision to go walkabout near a roundabout. He repeated the story he had related to Wobbler, but in more detail, adding, for what it was worth, that Sammy had been in a terrible mood for a couple of days, although for what reason he could not be sure.

Norman F. Billington closed his eyes and kneaded his forehead with all fingers. 'So, was Sammy drunk when he left you at the motorway services? I suppose he was unruly and misbehaving himself as well.'

'No, not at all, just the opposite really,' replied Gazelle. 'He'd been drunk the night before and might have had a hangover, but he was sober when I left him and he wasn't causing any trouble. He was just sitting on some grass near the road.'

At this point the door was pushed open and Meat Loaf's head appeared through the gap. 'Err, sorry to interrupt and trouble you guys, but the kit minibus is empty and everybody except me has gone home. There's just one thing, it's not quite empty. Sammy's kit bag's still there and there are a few loose clothes on the floor which nobody's claiming. I think they're Sammy's as well. The socks sure smell like his.'

Norman F. Billington thanked Meat Loaf and told him to make his way home as well, adding that they would sort out the return of the hired vehicles. The three of them then went outside to investigate further. True to Meat Loaf's word, there were clothes scattered on the floor of the van and they did indeed belong to Sammy, Wobbler identifying a Brisbane Broncos' rugby league shirt he'd had sent over from Australia and the beige jacket he'd been wearing during their night out in Bristol.

'The plot thickens,' mused Norman F. Billington, scratching the back of his neck. 'Surely Sammy didn't get changed just to go into a motorway service area? Why on earth would he want to do that?'

Neither Wobbler nor Gazelle could provide any practical solutions, but this was the least of Norman F. Billington's worries. His most pressing concern was what to do next. Sammy had been missing – if indeed missing was the right word – for less than two hours. As far as could be established, he wasn't in danger, wasn't drunk, wasn't injured, wasn't at risk of harming himself or anyone else and was, after all, a responsible adult. Norman F. Billington reflected that he could have cogently argued the case that Sammy was probably the least responsible 30-year-old adult he knew, but quickly dismissed the notion.

His first thought – and the one still nagging at him now – had been to call the police, but he was unsure how they would react when he informed them of his shaky grounds for concern. He would have to tell them that as far as he could work out, Sammy had abandoned the minibus because he was sulking, hardly good reason to call out a search party, but possibly reason for total indifference and even ridicule he surmised. For all he knew Sammy had flagged down a lift and was on his way home even as they fretted and fussed. He may even be home already. Home already…now there was a thought. He didn't want to alarm Sammy's wife, but then again, he didn't need to. He was merely making a polite enquiry to establish if Sammy had yet returned safe and well. If so, then they could all relax.

Norman F. Billington picked up the telephone behind the bar.

THIRTY-EIGHT

Angela Samson pushed a third bundle of dirty clothes into the washing machine, sighed heavily and aimed an irate kick at a stray sock.

Her husband was due back later that day and a sharp tongue armed with several howitzers of home truths awaited him.

Angela was quite accustomed to being alone in the house and taking on the manifold responsibilities and duties that two pre-teenage sons brought with them. Sammy's cricketing commitments and the social life inevitably attached to his beloved sport often meant long hours on her own in the evening and at the weekend, so solitude was no stranger. A five day leave of absence was a first, though, and while Angela wasn't expecting a love letter a day from her husband of 12 years, she felt she deserved at least some form of contact.

But Sammy hadn't even telephoned.

Some wives, she reflected, might feel concerned for their partner's safety in the event of such a lengthy absence, but

Angela was a full load and a final spin away from being anxious. When Sammy Samson was on his travels, no news really was good news, but on this occasion his downright lack of consideration had raised many hackles.

So when the telephone rang in the late afternoon, it fleetingly crossed her mind that this could be her horrible husband. As she went to pick up the receiver from its cradle, she wagered he would be ringing from the club for a lift home. She was ready to launch a fearsome verbal broadside.

The crisp tones of Norman F. Billington came as a surprise.

'Oh, hello Angela,' warbled the club chairman. 'Is Sammy there?'

'No, he's not,' came the blunt, monotone reply. 'I thought you would be better placed to answer that question rather than me Norman.

'You've been with him on that stupid tour. Hasn't he come back with the rest of the team?'

'Well, yes and no,' dithered Norman F. Billington, somewhat taken aback by Angela's abrasive tone.

'He travelled back in the kit bus, well at least part of the way at least. We were just wondering if he's made it home yet?'

'No, he's not', repeated Angela haughtily, 'and I can't say I'm all that bothered either. Can you believe that he's never been in touch all week? He's left me here alone with these two boys off school for the summer holidays, both of them bored silly and nagging me to find them something to do all the time. The thoughtless swine has spent all week boozing and talking mucky with his mates while I'm stuck here at home. It's just not fair and now he probably doesn't want to come home and face his responsibilities as usual. He knows that he's had it when he walks in through that door. Well, I've got some news for him.

Even if he does arrive back this evening, I'm not going to be here. I'm dropping the boys off at my sister's house for their tea and to sleep and then I'm going out on the thrash with my mates. Let's see how he likes it. And if you do happen to see old Walrus-face before I do Norman, you can tell him to stick that in his pipe and smoke it.'

And with that off her chest, Angela slammed down the 'phone, leaving a slightly stunned Norman F. Billington staring blankly into mid-space.

'Relations would appear to be strained,' he said as both Wobbler and Gazelle waited expectantly for the outcome of a most one-sided conversation. 'Sammy's definitely not back home and it's highly likely that he won't be welcome when he does get there either. His wife's furious because he hasn't been in touch all week and frankly she doesn't seem bothered when he turns up, if at all for that matter. The question is, where does that leave us and what do we do now?'

Wobbler, who probably knew Sammy better than anyone, felt confident the issue would resolve itself to the satisfaction of all concerned. He tried to be reassuring when he said: 'I reckon we should just leave things as they are. There's not a lot more we can do now. Sammy will turn up tonight, fend off the odd flying frying pan or two from Angela and then they'll kiss and make up. Everything will be sweet. You mark my words.'

Norman F. Billington nodded his head in agreement, but still harboured a nagging doubt as he added: 'You're probably right David. Gazelle, you drive the kit mini-bus back to the depot, take Sammy's clothes out of the back and then get yourself home. Let's all sleep on it and see what tomorrow brings. I suspect we're all looking forward to our own beds.'

THIRTY-NINE

No-one was looking forward to his own bed more than Matt Fairacre.

If the unassuming accountant were ever asked to describe what kind of animal he was, then he would have to be one that could always be found in the kitchen at parties.

He would be a mouse cowering behind the cooker.

The events of the last few days had been a rollercoaster ride of epic proportions for this timid young man. He had courageously drank far too much alcohol for his own good, had inadvertently stumbled across illicit drug-taking, had visited a nightclub of ill-repute and had witnessed a fellow reveller take his own life into his own hands at the top of an enormous ladder whilst breaking into his own hotel. They were four frantic days that would fill a lifetime of adventuring – or at least a Matt Fairacre lifetime anyway – and as he climbed into bed was forced to admit to himself that he was glad the gallivanting was all over. Now back home in his own snug little flat, he pulled the comforting sheets around his shoulders and relaxed.

He had fretted long and hard since his fly-on-the-wall drugs bust, but there had been no ramifications for which he was eternally grateful. They had even escaped the terrible hotel he'd booked in Bristol without a scene.

And as he drifted contentedly off to sleep he made himself two promises: He would enjoy a long and carefree slumber in bed in the morning and would then give up drinking for at least a month.

He was asleep within minutes.

Unfortunately it seemed like minutes later when he was rudely awoken by the telephone ringing in the lounge. Matt Fairacre cast a pained look at his bedside clock and grimaced. The time was 6.30am and he silently cursed whoever was ringing as he made his way stiffly through the connecting door.

He picked up the receiver and was greeted by a strong Midlands accent on the other end of the line.

'Is that a Mr. Matthew Fairacre? Yes? Good. This is sergeant Jon Swindells from Birmingham Central police station. I'm sorry to trouble you at such an unearthly hour in the morning sir, but I'm afraid we urgently need your help.'

Matt Fairacre's heart sank. His knees felt weak and his mouth turned instantly dry. This would be about drugs. He was going to prison for ever and his fledgling career in the financial world was over before it had hardly started.

'How can I help you sergeant?' he croaked.

'I believe you're the key-holder for the premises of Crawford cricket club,' said the policeman.

'How on earth do you know that?' gasped Matt Fairacre.

'We know this because our colleagues in the local constabulary up your way told us so and then let us have your telephone number from their records.'

Matt Fairacre was indeed the cricket club key-holder. As treasurer and a responsible member held in much trust, he was the person the police were instructed to contact in the event of a fire, a flood or a break-in at the premises. He clutched at what appeared to be a straw dangling before him.

'So there's been a problem at the club then?'

'Err, not quite,' said the sergeant. 'But we think there's a problem with one of your players.'

Sergeant Swindells explained patiently and in some detail how one of his motorway patrols had pulled into a service area south of Birmingham at lunchtime yesterday only to be flagged down by the anxious manager of a coffee shop on site. The manager had told the officers that a man was seriously ill inside, slumped over a table in fact, and that staff had been unable to revive him.

Sergeant Swindells continued: 'The officers tried to bring this chap round, but they failed too. So they searched him to try and find if he had any special medical needs and to establish who he was. The only form of identification they could find was a crumpled cricket club scorecard stuffed into his back pocket. It had the name Crawford cricket club printed on the top. It was all we had to go on. I know it's a bit of a long shot, but is he one of yours?'

Despite the ungodly hour and despite his racing mind, Matt Fairacre realised that the sergeant's story was too much of a coincidence to be a mistake. He collected his thoughts and said slowly: 'A whole gang of us from the cricket club did travel up from Bristol yesterday, but the mini-bus we were in never stopped. There was another minibus as well, but I didn't know anyone was missing from it. Do you have any idea what this chap looks like?'

Sergeant Swindells rustled some papers before clearing his throat and reading out loud: 'Male Caucasian, about 30 years old, unkempt dark hair, medium to heavy build, scruffily dressed, but well-nourished. Particular identifying marks, one huge black moustache.'

'It's Sammy!' Matt Fairacre almost shouted down the telephone.

'You're absolutely sure you know who this person sir and if so, could you be a bit more specific than Sammy?' asked Sergeant Swindells.

'Oh yes, right, sorry,' replied Matt Fairacre. 'It's him alright and his full name is Alan Samson. Sammy's his nickname'.

'And next of kin?' asked the sergeant.

'Next of kin!' choked a startled Matt Fairacre. 'Why on earth would you want to know that?'

'I'm afraid this gentleman is very seriously ill sir. After the police officers failed to bring him round, they called an ambulance crew and they couldn't revive him either. He was taken to hospital and as far as I'm aware is still unconscious and under continuous medical surveillance. So, next of kin please?' Matt Fairacre swallowed hard and said: 'Sammy, sorry, I mean Alan, is married to Angela. We've surely got to tell her what's happened.'

Sergeant Swindells added: 'We'll do that if you wish or you can. It's up to you but before anyone does anything, we need confirmation that it's definitely him.'

'I can sort out both those matters sergeant', replied Matt Fairacre, trying to sound as authoritative as possible. 'Leave it to me. Give me your number and I'll ring you back within the hour.'

Matt Fairacre scribbled down the number, replaced the

receiver and picked it straight back up again. It was still only 6.35am, but Matt Fairacre had to tell Norman F. Billington what was happening right away.

He dialled the number and closed his eyes even though he was fully awake.

FORTY

Norman F. Billington was also surprised to be awoken by a telephone ringing so early in the morning. Experience had taught him that such calls were rarely good news and this one turned out to be no exception.

He listened with rapt attention as Matt Fairacre carefully re-iterated everything the police sergeant had told him.

Norman F. Billington also closed his eyes, trying to block out the dismay brought on by the reality of the crisis unfolding before him while trying to think ahead at the same time. After he had exhausted all the available detail, a bemused Matt Fairacre opened fire with a fusillade of questions.

'So Norman, do you believe that this chap the police found really is Sammy? It has to be him surely. What's happened exactly? I didn't even know Sammy hadn't made it back from tour. Did you know?'

'I did actually', admitted Norman F. Billington, sensing a crimson flush of embarrassment colouring the normal pallor of his cheeks. 'Sammy didn't make it home with Gazelle. It seems that he stormed off from the minibus at a service station somewhere near Birmingham which matches exactly what the police have told us.'

'So you knew he was missing when we all got back yesterday then?' Matt Fairacre interjected.

'Yes I did,' replied Norman F. Billington reluctantly, slightly aggrieved by the accusatory tone of the question.

'Gazelle explained to us what had happened, but neither of us knew that he was ill. Sammy certainly didn't appear to be in any kind of trouble when he walked off. Gazelle just assumed that he was in another bad mood and wanted to be alone. Apparently he'd been like that for a couple of days and while it was a strange thing to do, Gazelle explained that it didn't really come as that much of a surprise if he was being honest.'

'So you think it definitely is Sammy the police were called to help?' continued Matt Fairacre.

'I don't think there can be any doubt about it,' sighed Norman F. Billington. 'The question that needs to be asked is why is he so ill? What could he have taken to make him this way? Unconscious in hospital? Continual medical surveillance? What could possibly have brought that on?'

A cold hand suddenly closed around Matt Fairacre's heart. A very cold hand indeed. One word had suddenly flashed up in his mind and now it was stuck there, a dark and menacing presence forcing liquid anxiety through every pore of his body.

Cannabis.

FORTY-ONE

Angela Samson thought her brain was about to explode.

It was being pounded from all sides by a cacophony of alien noise; bang, thud, ring, ring, bang, thud.

She turned over where she lay and felt herself falling. It was a drop of less than two feet from the top of the sofa to the foam-backed carpet below, but she felt as though she had toppled off a cliff on to jagged, wave-lashed rocks.

Angela groaned, gingerly opened her eyes and looked up. A bright light shining down from overhead made her wince and she closed them again.

A second attempt proved slightly less traumatic and a few pieces fell into place. She was in the lounge of her own home and clearly had been all night or since the early hours of the morning more likely after passing out on the sofa. There was a discarded take-away pizza box containing a half-gnawed garlic bread on the carpet next to her. She had no recollection of buying it or eating it.

Angela had been drunk the night before, horribly drunk.

She had embarked with much resolve on a revenge mission, binge-drinking to take it out on that rat of a husband who had chosen to ignore her all week, to prove to him and herself that she too knew how to party. At the time it had seemed like a great idea, now she wasn't so sure. The logic that had made so much sense just hours ago and which had told her that Sammy would be the victim in all this now rang so hollow. So did her head. The only person suffering was herself.

Angela sat up, leaned against the back of the sofa and clutched her aching brow. The bangs and thuds in her head were the unmistakable calling cards of a hangover from hell, but the ringing noise?

She screwed up her eyes and listened. It was the telephone in the hall. Why didn't it stop? Why didn't the caller just go away?

Angela grimaced, hauled herself to her feet and stumbled her way through the lounge door. The telephone was buried under a discarded coat and an umbrella that wasn't hers.

More gaps that may never be filled.

She picked up the receiver and heard Norman F. Billington's distinctive voice for the second time in as many days. But she didn't listen. Instead, she spoke with as much haste as she could muster leaving the chairman with no chance to explain the exact nature of his call.

'Hi Norman. I assume it's Sammy you want. He'll be in bed. Hang on, I'll go and get him.'

Angela dropped the telephone and gingerly climbed the stairs. Her husband was still in deep mire, but she knew that shouting and an argument were the last things her pounding head needed right now. The flogging of Sammy Samson would have to wait.

She pushed open the bedroom door and stopped abruptly in her tracks. The clean white sheets laid by her own fair hand yesterday morning were unruffled.

The bed had not been slept in.

With a furrowed brow, Angela made her way down back the stairs wondering how she was going to explain this one away. Her semi-functioning, dehydrated brain was offering little apart from the truth. 'I'm back Norman,' she said, trying to sound at least half awake. 'I'm afraid Sammy's not here. I slept on the sofa last night so I wasn't sure if he was in or not. Sorry about that.'

'It is precisely Sammy's absence that I'm ringing you about', said Norman F. Billington, concealing his exasperation and trying to sound patient, efficient and sympathetic all at the same time.

'I assume you haven't heard from him.'

'As I explained before, not a word from the bugger since he left to go on tour,' replied Angela. 'Is there something wrong? Where is he?'

Norman F. Billington drew a deep breath.

He sensed it was going to be a long day.

FORTY-TWO

Sergeant Jon Swindells poured himself a lukewarm cup of tea and turned a downcast eye towards the mountain of paperwork on his desk awaiting his attention.

The usual collection of drunk and disorderly reports and late night car smashes would take up his full morning and make it very dull indeed, but there was one report that was a bit out of the ordinary and had caught his eye in the first place, the case of the mystery man found slumped over a table in the motorway service station.

Sergeant Swindells sifted through the ream of papers until he found the right one and started to read through it in more detail. The officers who had attended the scene reported that the 'victim' – the word had subsequently been crossed out and replaced by 'patient' – did not appear to have suffered any physical harm despite the fact he was unconscious. There was no evidence of bruising to the face or lumps on the head as was so often the case when attacks took place, there was no blood and no broken bones as far as they could establish, while none of his clothing was torn.

An overdose of alcohol was the usual suspect in such instances, but this too had been deemed improbable. The two experienced policemen had reported that the man did smell of drink, but they had dealt with hundreds of drop-dead drunks before and only rarely had they been unable to revive them.

Even one of their better old tricks – a handful of ice-cubes down the back of the neck straight out of the ledger of Oliver Reed's outrageous hangover cures – had failed to deliver the required result.

And on the rare occasions they had failed in the past, ambulance crews had always managed to muster some sign of life. Yet in this case the man had remained obstinately unresponsive, even in the hands of the time-served medics.

Sergeant Swindells pushed the bottom half of his now stone-cold brew across his desk, chewed his pencil and admitted to himself that this case was a real puzzler. Before he had time to deliberate further the telephone rang. It was the hospital that had admitted the mystery man and the news wasn't encouraging. The patient was still unconscious and was being transferred to another hospital in Cheshire where more in-depth tests could be carried out. The bottom line was that the local A and E unit didn't have a clue what was wrong with this patient and were sending him for a specialised investigation.

Sergeant Swindells thanked the doctor for his help, scribbled a few notes, re-located Matt Fairacre's number and re-dialled.

Matt Fairacre picked up the telephone and recognised the Birmingham accent immediately. His stomach wrenched and churned. Deep down he realised that he was over-reacting every time he encountered any semblance of authority, but he couldn't help it. He still felt riddled with guilt despite so many self-assurances that he had done nothing wrong.

Sergeant Swindells wanted to know if the club could yet confirm that the mystery man was indeed one of their own. Matt Fairacre explained the back-up story given by the chairman, adding the certainty of his identity was as complete as it could be without someone actually seeing the person in question.

'I'm glad you mentioned that,' said Sergeant Swindells, 'because someone will have to go along and confirm who he is, not just for our records, but the family need to be sure as well and then perhaps the doctors can research the medical history and dig out a few clues.'

'I fully understand,' replied Matt Swindells. 'We'll drive down there this afternoon. Where is he exactly?'

'Oh, there's been a change on that front actually', replied the sergeant.

'It's a good job you mentioned it, because I nearly forgot.'

There was another rustling of papers.

'Aha, here it is. He was transferred this morning to the Cheveland Royal hospital near Macclesfield. Apparently he's in the tropical disease unit.'

Matt Fairacre's stomach heaved again. 'The tropical disease unit!' he exclaimed. 'What on earth is he doing in there?'

'Can't say I rightly know,' replied the sergeant. 'My best guess is that the medical guys don't know what's wrong with him so perhaps they think it's something foreign that he's eaten or drank.'

Or smoked thought Matt Fairacre, dread, fear and self-loathing joining the flow of poisoned perspiration forming rivulets all over his body.

'Thank you sergeant,' he said, his voice barely audible. 'We'll be in touch.'

FORTY-THREE

Norman F. Billington decided that the delegation visiting Sammy ought to meet at the cricket club first and then travel to the hospital together.

Due to the gravity of the situation, the first team game scheduled for that afternoon had been called off. All the players were told the reason and while there was an honourable clamour to visit their ailing colleague, it was deemed right and proper that just Norman F. Billington, Sammy's wife and club captain Dave Carter would drive down to Cheshire in the afternoon to see the patient and try to establish more clarity.

The journey was mainly undertaken in an uneasy silence. Conversation was sporadic and difficult, guilt, remorse and embarrassment abounding. Angela, still feeling mighty rough, had apologised to Norman F. Billington in private before they had set off. She was sorry she had sounded off at him down the telephone, explaining that she would never have reacted that way if she had been aware of the full circumstances. Norman F. Billington was tact and diplomacy personified. He reassured the poor lady that her husband was in good hands and would soon be well again, benders behind the timbers before they could say Brian Johnston.

Angela smiled weakly. She really didn't have a clue what he was talking about.

Cheveland Royal Hospital was low, modern and white and set in its own grounds of tidy lawns intersected by neat lines of small box shrubs which fittingly been clinically trimmed.

Two magpies squabbled on the roof.

The female receptionist at the front desk directed the gang of four along a narrow corridor running next to the laboratories and told them to follow the signs to the tropical disease unit at the end. She said she would telephone ahead so they could be met.

A black doctor almost wholly covered in a gleaming white and green gown was standing in front of the door marked 'private.' He smiled, removed his surgical gloves and shook hands with all the visitors before introducing himself as Leading Consultant Moses Catanaya. His colleagues, he informed them with a small smile, simply called him Dr Cat.

Before he was prepared to discuss the patient's condition there was the important issue of identification.

'Is the next of kin here with us today?' he asked.

Angela stepped forward: 'I'm his wife,' she said.

'Excellent,' replied the doctor, pushing his hands together as though in prayer. 'Normally just the closest relative is the only person we ask to identify an unknown patient, but under the circumstances, I think we will all go in together. You will all need to wear masks, gowns and gloves. We try to keep the isolation ward as germ-free as we can.'

Norman F. Billington considered the doctor's words

carefully as he pushed his arms into the surgical gown being held in front of his chest by a stern-looking nurse.

'Under the circumstances' and 'isolation ward' were most unsettling expressions he mused, but nothing the doctor could have said would have prepared Norman F. Billington for the vision he was about to encounter.

Dr Cat opened the door and ushered the visitors inside. The first startling sight that greeted them was the size of the bed supporting the patient. It was truly enormous. Norman F. Billington took a step closer before realising it was actually two single beds pushed together. Across them was sprawled a motionless Sammy, a huge, bloated, motionless Sammy, his body at least twice its normal size, his face swollen and puffy and a peculiar shade of dappled light purple. His head had rolled to one side, releasing a lifeless tongue and the only discernible movement was a slight, but unsteady raising of his chest.

Above him had been erected a surreal-looking contraption which bore an alarming resemblance to a giant squid poised to attack. A host of interconnected metal rods formed its body while its legs were the tubes descending on to its hapless prey below before entering the body at what seemed to be every conceivable angle. Fluids flowed along some of the tubes. Behind the bed lurked a bank of blinking, flickering monitors. The visitors also blinked, disbelief and astonishment in equal measure etched on all their faces. Angela put her head in her hands and started to weep quietly. No-one spoke.

The silence was broken by Dr Cat.

'Firstly, may I apologise for the strange bed arrangement. I'm afraid one of our single hospital beds just wasn't, err, large enough to accommodate the patient, so we had to come up with this, err, compromise. Angela, I assume that this is your husband and without wishing to sound impertinent in any way, I also assume he's not usually this size.'

Angela screwed her damp handkerchief into the palm of her hand and sobbed: 'Yes it is Sammy and no, he's not normally so big. He usually weighs about fourteen stones. He must be twice that now. What on earth has happened to him?' she wailed.

Dr Cat placed a reassuring arm around Angela's shoulders.

'The reason he's increased in size so much is because of the vast amount of fluid his body has produced, presumably as some kind of defence mechanism against what ever it is that's making him so ill.'

'Exactly how ill is he?' interjected Norman F. Billington. 'He would appear to be in a coma. Is he in a coma?'

Dr Cat replied: 'The patient is deeply unconscious. In this instance, a coma is difficult to define because although there is plenty of brain activity, there are few life signs elsewhere. You can squeeze his hand as hard as you like, even stick a pin in the back of it and there is no visible reaction. To be honest we don't really know what's wrong with him yet or what may have caused him to be this way. We're running numerous tests, but these take time. Hopefully this is where you may be able to help us. Can any of you help shed some light on what might have happened to your colleague? Has he done or taken anything that could have caused him to be this way?'

Norman F. Billington looked at Wobbler who tried not to look completely blank and totally useless before speaking: 'Sammy's been seriously down in the dumps for these last couple of days, quite depressed really I suppose, but not really ill. On the food and drink front, he's been through much the same as all of us, has been to all the same places and no-one else has even caught a cold, let alone....'

Wobbler's voice trailed off before he added, 'I'm sorry, but I suspect I can't really be a great deal of help.'

Dr Cat replied: 'I appreciate this is most upsetting, so I think we'll leave it at that for the moment.

'We shall continue to run the tests and monitor the patient, but there's not a lot more we can do for him at the moment. His condition shall have to remain a mystery, for the time being at least. But do let me know immediately if you think of anything that might help us.'

Angela started to cry again as the consultant led them to the door.

FORTY-FOUR

It was a pleasantly warm early evening, but Gazelle had still lit a fire at home. On his first day back he was grateful for the comfort rather than the heat it afforded, especially now that the full extent of Sammy's illness had been graphically outlined to him by Norman F. Billington on the telephone earlier.

But it required more than the reassuring glow of burning coals to banish the groundsman's many nagging worries. Gazelle was shouldering an onus of responsibility for Sammy's condition and it weighed heavily. He was the last one to have been with him before he had been so mysteriously struck down and felt personally responsible despite the many assurances from Norman F. Billington that he wasn't to blame. If only he had been more assertive, if only he had stood up like a man and insisted that Sammy get back into the mini-bus at the services and complete the journey home then surely none of this would have happened.

Or would it?

Gazelle had his own theory as to the cause of Sammy's

mystery illness and there was one person he wanted to share it with.

His drug-taking lodger from Australia.

FORTY-FIVE

Stuey stepped off the train from Bristol, flicked his heels and decided there and then that this new life in England suited him just fine.

His night with Laura had been passionate and fulfilling, the day after spent hand in hand exploring the cafés and bars of the bustling city, the couple embracing with mutual tenderness and affection before Stuey had caught a late afternoon train home. As they would have said back in Australia, everything was fair dinkum. He was the hero of Renwick, Laura loved him – possibly – Norman F. Billington loved him – certainly – while he was even looking forward to returning to Gazelle's quaint little house despite the owner's outlandish domestic habits.

Stuey climbed out of the taxi outside Gazelle's home and enquired as to the fare. 'How much!' he exclaimed and, while he was sorely tempted to ask the driver if by any chance he was related to Ned Kelly, decided against it.

His mood was even better than he thought.

He opened the front door and greeted Gazelle with a cheery

hello. Gazelle shifted slightly in his chair and issued a low grunt as Stuey abandoned his luggage at the bottom of the stairs, shimmied across the carpet, leapfrogged over the side of the comfy chair before settling down alongside his landlord in front of the fire.

'Great tour Gazelle,' he chirruped. 'Absolutely marvellous, a spiffing time had by one and all old boy, that's what I reckon you English guys would say.'

'You've not heard then,' replied Gazelle sullenly without looking up.

'Heard what?' replied Stuey.

'Heard about poor Sammy?'

'No, why, what's happened?'

Gazelle described Sammy's fate in intricate detail, his bizarre behaviour on the motorway, the police involvement and his subsequent hospitalisation given a full airing. He concluded by telling his rapt audience of one that the best doctors in the land had yet to establish what was wrong with him, the dramatic effect at the end perhaps a touch overcooked. If Gazelle had intended to shock Stuey, he had succeeded. He then delivered a stunning blow.

'Norman informed me that the consultant has asked if we can shed any light on what's wrong with Sammy. Perhaps you may be able to help them out on that one.'

'Me?' gasped Stuey incredulously. 'I wasn't even with you guys on that last night.

'How on earth have you worked out that I might be able to help?'

Gazelle drew a deep breath and said: 'Well, you were the one who gave him those illegal drugs that night in the toilets in the Swan. God only knows what they did to him. It's not as though he was used to them or anything.'

Stuey looked at Gazelle in amazement as a cold tidal wave of reality crashed up on to a beach which only minutes earlier had been bathed in warm, dappled sunshine.

He thought briefly before slowly replying.

'So, let's have this right. You reckon that the grass Sammy smoked at least three days before he was taken ill has left him flat out across two beds in a tropical disease unit looking like Moby Dick on shore leave. That has to be the most ridiculous theory I've ever heard in my life. I smoked exactly the same grass that night and look at me, I'm fine, so work that one out Doctor Kildare.'

'Yes, but you're always smoking the stuff and Sammy's not,' protested Gazelle vehemently. 'According to the specialist at the hospital, something's poisoned him and the only different thing he took during that week on tour were your drugs. Now he's in a tropical disease unit and that cannabis stuff is tropical isn't it? It all makes sense to me.'

'The cannabis stuff as you call it came from some place called Chorlton-cum-Hardy, if that's what you mean by tropical,' scoffed Stuey defiantly, again staring intently at Gazelle and wondering exactly how narrow-minded and naive his landlord could be.

But if Stuey was honest with himself, he was inwardly troubled by the accusations being levelled at him, even if they did come from a chap who had barely dipped a toe in the sea of life, hence the discernible concern in his voice as he made his next point.

'I hope you've not aired these views with anyone else Gazelle. I thought we had an agreement,' he added quietly.

Gazelle replied: 'No, I've not talked to anyone else about it. No-one else knows. Your secret is still safe with me, but I can't tell you how uncomfortably all this lot sits with me. It nags at me all the time.'

'Well, don't let it nag. Sammy will be fine,' replied Stuey. 'Can we talk about something else now?'

Gazelle grunted, stared dolefully into the mid-space between him and the coal fire and said nothing.

FORTY-SIX

Matt Fairacre had been in bed for more than an hour and sleep was still a distant dream.

Earlier that evening, Norman F. Billington had returned from the Cheshire hospital with a medical report on Sammy that had deeply upset him. The chairman hadn't laboured the point, but he had mentioned the doctor's appeal for help into tracing the cause of the mystery illness. Even as he lay on the pillow Matt Fairacre winced, bit his lip and cursed himself for being such a wimp and a serial ditherer. He knew why he had kept his secret of course, the vast quantities of embarrassment that would descend on all concerned – not least himself – should he blow the whistle on the shabby drug scene that he had witnessed take place in the Swan. His own shady role was reason enough to keep quiet, but Stuey, Sammy and even Gazelle would all have to be named and shamed if he made his discovery public. He shuddered at the very thought, but the more he thought about it the more he realised that he had to come clean. If Sammy was to die and one Matt Fairacre hadn't mustered the strength of character to tell the medical authorities what he had learned on that fateful night in the washroom then his own life would barely be worth living.

His mind was made up. The bucketfuls of disgrace, shame and embarrassment would have to be ignored. The drugs story would have to be told. Matt Fairacre punched his pillow yet again, closed his eyes tightly and resolved that he would inform Norman F. Billington of the whole truth in the morning.

His sleep was fitful, littered with horrible dreams and ghastly images, and while the waking reality was alarmingly forbidding, it still came as a merciful release. It was only 6.30am, but Matt Fairacre was more than happy to clamber out of the torture chamber that had been his own bed. He felt far from refreshed and even less enthused by the daunting task that lay ahead, but the will-power was still strong. The alternative, which was to do doing nothing, could no longer be considered. After several cups of strong tea and even more deep thought he telephoned Norman F. Billington at home around 8.30am and initially asked about Sammy's health. The chairman reported that there had been no contact from the hospital which he assumed meant nothing had changed.

'I urgently have to see you this morning Norman,' said Matt Fairacre, draining his body of its last drop of courage. 'It's about Sammy and something that happened on tour which I think you ought to be aware of.'

'You'd better come to my house right away,' replied Norman F. Billington, somewhat taken aback. 'I'll see you in about half an hour.'

FORTY-SEVEN

From the vantage point of Norman F. Billington's back sitting room, Matt Fairacre could espy about half his beloved cricket club over the garden wall. He suspected the place would never be quite the same again after he had told the chairman what he needed to.

Norman F. Billington placed two cups of tea on coasters on top of a pristine pine coffee table, pinched, then pulled up his trousers above the knee, settled on to the sofa and cast his guest an anxious look.

'Right then, what do you want to talk about Matthew?'

'This isn't going to be easy Norman and I hope you will forgive me for not telling you earlier, but hopefully you will understand the reasons when I've told you the whole story.'

He gulped and swallowed hard.

'Some of the guys didn't just stick to alcohol and cigarettes on tour.'

'No, so what else were they up to then?' asked Norman F. Billington with a puzzled look on his face.

'Err…some of them were smoking dope, you know, that cannabis drug. In light of what's happened to Sammy I thought you'd better be in the picture because I know for a fact that he smoked it too. Now he's flat out on a hospital bed with tubes sticking out of him and I can't shake off the feeling that taking these illegal drugs may have something to do with his illness. The doctors want to know if we can help so that's why I had to tell you what I know and let me add that it hasn't been easy.'

Norman F. Billington stared at the nervous young man opposite him in a state of utter disbelief.

The euphoria of winning a simple cricket game against his old foe and friend in Bristol just a few days earlier suddenly seemed like a lifetime ago. Now he could see only huge problems, complications and dilemmas descending on him from a dizzy height. Inwardly he groaned and heaved, but outwardly he tried to remain calm and circumspect.

'So, Sammy was just smoking this stuff on his own in front of everyone in the hotel bar then was he'? he asked.

'Err no, not quite,' replied Matt Fairacre.

'He was smoking it in the toilets with err, Stuey, and err, well, Gazelle was with them too.'

'Stuey!…Gazelle!' exclaimed Norman F. Billington. 'And you were in there with them as well I assume?' he demanded.

Matt Fairacre's stomach tightened as he prepared to lay bare the stark embarrassment contained in the small detail. 'Well, yes and no,' came a stammering reply. 'I was locked in one of the toilet cubicles. I just overheard them talking about doing it then I suppose smelled them actually doing it. I don't think Gazelle actually smoked any, but he seemed to know exactly what was going on. He certainly didn't sound surprised.'

'So let me go over all this again,' gasped Norman F. Billington.

'You'd gone to the gents just to use the toilet, locked the door, then these three came in and started smoking cannabis while you sat there and said nothing.'

'That's about the long and short of it,' nodded Matt Fairacre, staring bleakly at the carpet and wanting the world to end. 'But like I said before, I don't think Gazelle actually smoked any.'

'And I suppose it was that rascal Sammy who had the stuff in the first place,' retorted Norman F. Billington.

'I don't think so actually,' replied Matt Fairacre, who was now squirming in his chair.

'As far as I could work out, and you have to remember that I couldn't actually see what was going on, it was Stuey who seemed to have the stuff. I certainly heard him offer it to Sammy and he accepted.'

At this point Matt Fairacre felt like crying. Norman F. Billington wasn't far behind him.

'Oh my God, not Stuey,' he blurted out. 'How on earth could such a fine young sportsman like him be so stupid as to take drugs? What are we going to do now?'

'I think we should tell the hospital,' replied Matt Fairacre. 'Whatever the rights and wrongs of what these guys have been up to, surely Sammy's health comes first. If what he smoked is linked to his illness then the doctors ought to know.'

Norman F. Billington found himself nodding in agreement. At least Matt Fairacre had come up with a positive, practical step forward. What would happen after he'd told the doctors really didn't bear thinking about.

'I'll ring the hospital straight away,' he said.

Norman F. Billington walked purposefully into his hallway, dialled the number of Cheveland hospital and asked for Dr

Moses Catanaya. After what seemed an eternity, the doctor's voice broke the silence on the other end of the line.

Norman F. Billington cleared his throat and drew a deep breath.

'Ah, doctor, good morning. Norman F. Billington from Crawford cricket club speaking. How's the patient?'

'Much the same. He's stable, but there's nothing too encouraging to report I'm afraid.'

Norman F. Billington cleared his throat once again: 'After you asked us for our help in trying to trace the source of Sammy's condition, I've met with some of the colleagues with whom Sammy shared the, err, recent holiday and we feel there's something you ought to know.

'Fire away,' said Dr Cat.

'We know for a fact that Sammy was taking illegal drugs a few days before he was taken ill and we think it's most important, indeed imperative, that we pass on this information to you,' said Norman F. Billington.

'What kind of drugs would those be then?' asked the doctor.

'He was smoking cannabis,' Norman F. Billington's hushed voice dropping a further couple of decibels as he delivered the devastating news.

Dr Cat – not averse to the sporadic puff of marijuana himself – did not gasp in amazement to the slight surprise and even disappointment of the former solicitor on the other end of the line.

'So you think this could have contributed to the patient's poor state of health?' replied Dr Cat.

'I certainly do,' added Norman F. Billington. 'This is an illegal, mind-altering substance we're talking about here. God only knows what it can do to a person.'

'Well, it's certainly an interesting theory,' responded Dr Cat, privately re-calling a particularly powerful batch of home-grown grass he'd smoked back home in his native Jamaica during his early student days.

'I must say that I've never come across cannabis rendering anyone unconscious before, but that doesn't mean to say it's not relevant. We're running blood tests at the moment and we shall certainly test for all narcotics, legal or illegal, including cannabis. We'll let you know. Is there anything else I can do for you?'

Norman F. Billington, slightly non-plussed by what he regarded as the medic's rather dismissive attitude, found himself struggling for words: 'Err, no, that's fine for the moment, but you will inform me of the results of the tests as soon as possible won't you?'

'I certainly will. Good morning then,' replied Dr Cat.

Norman F. Billington placed the receiver back on its cradle and walked back into the lounge where Matt Fairacre looked up anxiously in anticipation.

'Are we on to something then?' he asked.

'Not too sure actually,' replied Norman F. Billington.

'The doctor didn't exactly hot-foot it over to the laboratories or anything, but they are going to investigate. And that's what we should do as well. I need to know precisely what's been going on here. So I'd like you to ask Bernard and Stuey to come to the club at 7.30 prompt this evening for a special meeting with me. We'll keep everybody else out of this for the time being at least, but perhaps you ought to attend as well Matthew.'

Matt Fairacre looked at the chairman completely crestfallen.

'Me? Do I really have to come?' he pleaded.

'Under the circumstances I think it's for the best', responded Norman F. Billington sternly. 'We have to get to the bottom of this. The most important factor is that Sammy's seriously ill in hospital which means that everybody involved should be, well, involved, and it was you who brought this drugs issue to light after all.'

'Don't I just know it,' mumbled Matt Fairacre, sullenly shaking his head slowly from side to side as he rose to his feet.

'Right Norman, I'll see you at the club this evening then. I'll push a note through Gazelle's front door on my way to work. Good bye.'

And with that, Matt Fairacre trudged disconsolately out of the lounge leaving his untouched cup of tea stone cold on his host's immaculate coffee table.

FORTY-EIGHT

Gazelle pushed his way through his front door in the late afternoon and stepped on an envelope lying mid-ships on the door mat. He didn't recognise the rather neat hand-writing on the front, but he certainly recognised the enormity of the message contained within.

Half an hour later, he slid the note past the sugar bowl to Stuey who read it while eating on the opposite side of the kitchen table.

'What's this meeting all about then?' asked the Australian as he liberally applied dollops of relish sauce to his prawn crackers from the take-away. 'And who else is going?'

'I don't rightly know,' admitted Gazelle. 'But you can bet your last beer voucher that it's something to do with Sammy and the reason he's flat out in a tropical disease unit.'

'You're not going to let me forget that are you?' snapped Stuey. 'Something tells me you still think I'm responsible for what's happened to that lad,' he added, pausing as he lifted a large spoonful of fried rice out of its metal tray. 'Do you know something that I don't Gazelle?' he added, narrowing his eyes and fixing his landlord with an icy stare.

'If this meeting is about Sammy, then I'm the last witness that ought to be called. I've told you before, I wasn't even out with you lot on that last night in Bristol. That's me completely not guilty your honour, unless you've been sharing your stupid killer cannabis theory with anybody who cares to listen that is.'

'And I've told you before, I've not breathed a word to anyone, I swear,' protested Gazelle. 'The only other person who knows about your sordid little secret is Sammy and he's hardly in a position to tell the world about it is he?'

Stuey again eyed his landlord suspiciously, but carried on crunching his way through his prawn crackers.

FORTY-NINE

The atmosphere at Crawford cricket club had plunged to an all-time low.

Early week evenings were rarely bustling, but on this particular Monday night, the place was more funereal than fun-packed. Sammy's empty stool by the bar was a constant reminder of the reason misery and despondency had descended, the place just wasn't the same without the lecherous one and his mischievous grin operating somewhere beneath the thicket hedge aboard his top lip. The gloom barely lifted as Gazelle and Stuey entered a deserted lounge.

'There's nobody in the place,' remarked Stuey as he wandered over to the bar. 'There's not even anybody to serve us a drink.'

'I'll get you what you want,' announced a disembodied voice as Matt Fairacre pushed open the cellar hatch and emerged unexpectedly into the half-light cast by the lager pump. 'Norman's in the back room ready and waiting. I'll get you a couple of beers and we'll all go through.'

Stuey looked around the room as though willing company to appear out of the woodwork. 'Is there nobody else here? Where's Wobbler, Meat Loaf and Pete Skidmore?' he asked.

'I'm afraid we're the only ones invited. Come on, let's go in and get it over with,' replied Matt Fairacre.

Stuey looked at Gazelle in puzzlement and trepidation. Gazelle, equally bemused, shrugged his shoulders, picked up his glass and made his way into the games room.

Norman F. Billington had established himself in the middle of the long top table used for committee meetings and looked every inch like a high court judge ready to hand down life sentences. He invited all three defendants to sit down and without offering a single pleasantry, started to talk: 'I'll get straight to the point. I've asked just you three here tonight because you all share something in common. I'm led to believe that you all know exactly what Sammy got up to on tour and quite possibly the reason why he's so seriously ill in hospital.'

Stuey and Gazelle looked at each other in bewilderment and then back to Norman F. Billington, both in need of further explanation.

It came speeding down Devastation Highway at an alarming rate of knots.

Norman F. Billington drew a deep breath and continued: 'I had better tell you straight away that I know both Stuey and Sammy were smoking cannabis on tour while I have reason to believe that you, Bernard, had something to do with it. I also believe it is the reason that poor Sammy is flat out on a hospital bed, his life possibly in danger.'

Norman F. Billington's startling revelations shook both Stuey and Gazelle to the core. Stuey turned and glowered at an ashen Gazelle, the young Australian now completely convinced that his turn-coat, quisling landlord had blabbed, while Gazelle was once again seconds away from turning into a complete emotional wreck as had so often been the case ever since Stuey had come storming into his life.

From his lofty seat, Norman F. Billington sensed the smouldering animosity and cleared his throat to intervene. But before he could do so, Matt Fairacre looked up from his shoes for the first time, turned in his chair and addressed both Stuey and Gazelle.

He spoke in hushed, faltering tones: 'I am the reason Norman knows all about the cannabis,' he mumbled, his voice trembling.

'You!' exclaimed a stunned Stuey. 'How on God's own earth can that be?'

Matt Fairacre drew a deep breath: 'When Sammy and you were smoking the stuff in the Swan hotel toilets on tour I was locked in one of the cubicles and heard exactly what went on. I wasn't spying on you guys, honestly, what you did just kind of took place before I realised what was happening. I swear that in normal circumstances, I wouldn't have breathed a word to anyone, but in light of what's happened to Sammy, I felt that I needed to tell someone. So I told Norman. I'm so sorry guys. So truly, truly sorry. But if it helps Sammy, then surely I did the right thing, didn't I?'

Matt Fairacre's startling admission was met with an aghast, two man silence as both Stuey and Gazelle tried to come to terms with the enormity of the confession laid bare before them.

Norman F. Billington attempted to recover composure and control. He said: 'Matthew has done us a favour with his straight-talking and honesty. Now I expect the same of you two. This conversation will not go beyond the walls, I promise you, but I must have the complete and utter truth with an assurance that nothing will be concealed or kept from me. A young man's life could be at risk here. Do I make myself abundantly clear?'

Both Stuey and Gazelle nodded gravely, Stuey pulling his hair roughly through his fingers before placing his head in his hands.

Norman F. Billington continued: 'I believe that Sammy and Stuey both took this drug on the first night of the tour, three days before you all went to Bristol. Is that right?'

The pair nodded.

'And it was Stuey who supplied the drug. Is that right too?'

'Jeez, Norm, supply's a bit strong,' protested Stuey immediately.

'It was just two mates who had drunk too much lager sharing a joint in the sit-downs. It wasn't some kind of heavy duty drugs scene.'

'Be that as it may,' continued Norman F. Billington, aware that he was beginning to sound like some pompous prosecution brief, 'but it was you Stuart who had the drugs in the first place and it was you who took them into the washroom and shared them with Sammy wasn't it?'

'Yeh, right, whatever', replied Stuey, shaking his head in disbelief.

Norman F. Billington, looking to strike a more positive note, continued: 'But on the night out in Bristol, the night before Sammy fell ill in fact, Stuey wasn't with you, so I assume Sammy had no cannabis to smoke?'

Stuey paused before giving a reply he really didn't want to. 'Well, that may not be true actually,' he confessed. 'I gave Sammy a couple of joints before he went out on the town with the guys. I was only trying to help. He just seemed so miserable.

I thought they might help cheer him up.'

It was Norman F. Billington's turn to place his head in his hands. The former solicitor realised that he didn't know too much about cannabis. He had rarely encountered it during his career as a solicitor, conveyancing and messy divorces had been his professional food and drink.

Now he needed to time to think and he could hardly do so in the present company. Rising to his feet, he decided to bring the meeting to an end. 'Is there anything else that any of you three would like to add?' he asked.

Three sullen shakes of the head answered his question.

'Right then, we'll call it a night. Enough has been said, for the time being at least. As I said before, it would be prudent for all concerned if this conversation isn't repeated beyond these four walls. The doctors at the hospital already know that Sammy had been smoking drugs and are working on it. I need to think what to do next. But for the moment it might be best if we all went home and tried to catch a few hours sleep.'

Matt Fairacre grabbed his coat and the opportunity to flee. The last thing he wanted was a grilling – particularly from Stuey – after his fly-on-the-toilet-wall confession and he gratefully scampered out into the warm evening air and his waiting car.

As Stuey and Gazelle slowly made their way out in his wake, Norman F. Billington spoke again. 'Err, Bernard, may I have a quick word…in private,' casting Stuey a nervous glance.

Stuey, now totally disillusioned and wholly brassed off with the events of the night, was past caring what anybody said or thought anymore. 'I'll wait for you in the car park then Gazelle,' he said. 'I assume the villain of the piece is at least entitled to a lift home.'

'Err, yes, right, I won't be a minute,' replied Gazelle before Stuey thrust his hands in his pockets and stamped out of the room.

Norman F. Billington stepped down off the high table and addressed Gazelle face to face. He remained mystified, indeed intrigued, by his groundsman's role in this distasteful affair and decided that a direct approach might shed more light on it.

'Well, Bernard this is a right old to-do isn't it?' was his opening gambit. 'But I gather, from what I've been told, that you've known about Stuey's – how shall we say? – secret habit for some time, but have never actually taken any of the drugs yourself. Strictly between you and me, is this the case?'

'Err, that's about right Norman,' stuttered Gazelle. 'Stuey told me about his err, bit of a habit, shortly after he'd arrived from Australia, but I've never tried any myself.'

'So I assume he's been smoking the stuff in your house with your permission then?' added Norman F. Billington.

'Well, yes, I suppose so,' added Gazelle feeling distinctly uncomfortable and ill at ease. 'Why, does it matter?'

'Well, yes, I'm afraid it does rather,' replied Norman F. Billington, his mind wandering back to his legal training all those years ago. 'It's against the law for someone to allow a third party to take an illicit drug in his or her place of residence. It makes you as guilty as the person smoking the stuff.'

Gazelle thought he was going to faint.

Norman F. Billington added: 'Did it never occur to you that what you were both doing was wrong? Didn't you try to explain this to him or stop him?'

Gazelle suddenly felt the need to get several weighty issues off his chest and surprised himself by the forthright tone he produced as he gushed forth. 'Look Norman, I never knew that

I was doing anything illegal. I knew what Stuey was up to was wrong, but he was adamant he was going to do it anyway. He kept what he did very much to himself and said it would be our secret which it surely would have stayed had it not been for what happened to Sammy down in Somerset. And to be honest, nobody seemed to be suffering and nobody was getting hurt. So I just kept my trap shut and let him get on with it. He told me about it when he first arrived and if I'm being honest, he offered to pack his bags and leave if I objected.'

'And why on earth didn't you take him up on his offer?' demanded Norman F. Billington.

'I certainly thought about it long and hard believe you me,' replied Gazelle. 'But in the end I decided that I had too much to lose. The offer that you made me, Norman, was one of the best things that's ever happened to me in my entire life. In return for providing Stuey with somewhere to stay, I got regular rent money, a full time job and a place on the tour. Those things meant a lot to me and I knew how much having Stuey over here playing for the team meant to you as well. So, having weighed up that lot, I decided to overlook his secret habit as you call it and carry on as though everything was normal which it was until the tour and Sammy and everything else that's gone so horribly wrong since.'

Gazelle's voice started to falter and break as a wave of guilt and pity washed over Norman F. Billington. His groundsman's frank confession had made the club chairman realise that some of the blame for what had happened could even be laid at his own door. Norman F. Billington placed his arms around Gazelle's shoulders, coughed gently and spoke slowly. 'I didn't realise you had been forced to take that decision Bernard and in light of what you have just told me I fully understand why you did so. I suppose Stuey just keeping his habit behind closed doors so that nobody else knew must have been reassuring for you in a way. Did he smoke a lot of this stuff? Thank God he didn't bring it into the club.'

'Well, if we're all being totally honest about things as you asked us to be, then I have to tell you that he did in a way,' replied Gazelle.

'After most home matches he would sneak around the back of the club house and have a quick smoke when nobody was looking. But then he would nip back and just blend in and be the same old affable Stuey, the life and soul of the party as usual. Taking this drug didn't seem to affect his cricket or his social life and nobody seemed to notice'.

Norman F. Billington swallowed hard as the ramifications of Gazelle's most recent revelations hit home. He spoke slowly and deliberately and was only just audible: 'So, you mean to say that when Stuey was talking to me in the bar after games he did so, well, as they say, stoned, as in under the influence of illegal drugs.'

'Err, that's right. Most of the times you spoke to him after weekend games he'd just been smoking his hay as he called it,' replied Gazelle. 'I always suspected this was the case, but then he told me as much himself after he'd been smoking one night at home. That was the thing with Stuey, taking this cannabis stuff didn't really seem to change him all that much and the fact that you never noticed surely backs me up. In fact when we stopped in at night on our own together, he would often be more chatty and forthcoming after he'd rolled up. We had a right good laugh at times.'

Norman F. Billington looked at Gazelle in utter amazement. He couldn't work out which was the more astounding fact just laid bare before him: A middle-aged groundsman admitting that he preferred talking to his lodger who was stoned or a blissfully ignorant retired solicitor discovering that he had regularly been a willing party to the analysis of bowling averages with a young blade off his head on illegal narcotics.

Norman F. Billington was in danger of information overload and desperately needed to retreat to the sanity of his own home and mull things over. Again.

'Right then Bernard. Many thanks for your time this evening, it's been – how shall we say – more than illuminating. But I think that's more than enough state secrets for one night. Let's draw down a curtain on this for the time being.'

'What are you going to do next?' asked Gazelle half-heartedly.

'Nothing for the time being,' replied Norman F. Billington. 'Sammy's health remains priority. You'd better go and take young Stuey home. He'll be wondering where you are.'

Norman F. Billington made his way around the cricket square as soon as Gazelle's Triumph Herald had disappeared from view leaving a haze of blue, oily smoke in its wake.

The light was still half-decent so the club chairman opted to embark on a couple of laps of the field to further engage in his most recent full-time occupation, thinking deeply about the events of the last couple of days and trying to work out exactly what to do next. He felt baffled, bemused, disappointed and amazed in just about equal quantities, yet it was disappointment which constantly bubbled to the surface.

In almost every regard, Stuey had turned out to be everything he was hoping for and even a little bit more. On both sporting and social fronts, the young Australian had matched every expectation asked of him, bettered most of them in fact. High-flying Renwick had been beaten, leaving his former comrade-in-arms Ronald Richardson chewing on a rather large slice of humble pie, mainly thanks to Stuey's heroic efforts on the oval and as the end of a most successful league campaign loomed, promotion was a real and distinct possibility. Stuey had secured the admiration and respect of all his peers by dint of his charisma and athletic prowess, and now an unseemly drug scandal threatened to wreck everything.

Norman F. Billington shook his head and reflected ruefully on the gross unfairness of it all as he lifted the latch on his back gate and pushed his way through into the garden.

He also fervently hoped that Mrs Billington hadn't embarked on an early gin frenzy.

FIFTY-ONE

Sergeant Jon Swindells pushed his legs under his desk at the start of his night shift and scowled at the usual mound of paperwork as he had done so often in the past.

Crimes and misdemeanours of the last few days littered the bottom of his in-tray, the policeman lifting them out with a vexed flick of the wrist before sifting through them with an eye for the important and scant regard for the not so. Several of the reports needed following up and the file on the guy found slumped unconscious over the table at the motorway service station fell into this category. The sergeant scanned the report before dialling the number of Matt Fairacre, the young man answering the call and subsequently suffering his now customary rush of palpitations every time he encountered a brush with the law. He explained to the policeman that Sammy was still unconscious in hospital and that the doctors were still trying to establish what had happened and indeed the cause.

The sergeant's next words quickened his pulse and banged up his blood pressure even further: 'In the light of what you've told me, we shall have to investigate further,' explained the sergeant. 'If this gentleman's life is in danger, which it seems it may well be, then we need to try and establish what went on during the hours before he was taken ill. Who was the last person to see him before he was found at the service station?'

Matt Fairacre was rather relieved that the sergeant's line of questioning had ventured down this particular track. He replied: 'Sammy made the journey from Bristol in a mini-bus with another gentleman called Bernard Gazelle who was driving the vehicle. He, err, kind of dropped his passenger off before completing the journey on his own, so he was the last person to see him.'

'Why on earth did he leave his friend at a motorway service station in the first place?' asked the sergeant.

'Well, it's all a bit confused,' replied Matt Fairacre. 'It seems that Sammy was in a foul mood, possibly depressed about something and decided that he just wanted to be alone. So that's what Mr Gazelle did. He just left him there. I don't think he had a lot of choice in the matter to be honest.'

'We need to speak to this chap rather urgently,' added Sergeant Swindells. 'What did you say his name was again? Mr Gazelle? That's an unusual name.'

'Yes it is rather,' agreed Matt Fairacre. 'I'll get you his number.'

FIFTY-TWO

The bright red plastic telephone in the hall rang noisily in the early evening and Gazelle cursed softly under his breath.

The latest new fangled piece of modern technology was a real pain as far as Gazelle was concerned. It was Norman F. Billington who had insisted it be installed and it was only the club chairman who ever rang him, usually to tell the groundsman that the heavy roller would be needed at the weekend or to pass on some other piece of work-related trivia. Gazelle wondered what the pestering one wanted now, especially as he had just settled down in the kitchen with the evening newspaper shortly after his tea.

The voice on the other end of the telephone was a strange one.

'Is that a Mr Bernard Gazelle,' enquired a distinct Birmingham accent.

'It is. Who's that?' asked Gazelle.

'This is sergeant Jon Swindells from Birmingham Central police station speaking. May I beg a few minutes of your precious time please sir?'

Gazelle gulped, felt his heartbeat increase rapidly and his saliva turn to dust as he waited for news of the drugs bust to arrive.

But the sergeant had other matters on his mind. He asked Gazelle to confirm that he was the last member of the cricket team to see the character called Sammy before he was taken ill and having established this to be the case, asked if he could shed some more light on to his passenger's mysterious malaise. Gazelle explained to the officer that he had already given his bizarre, unscheduled motorway stop much thought, but had failed to come with any facts that might help his investigations.

Sergeant Swindells added: 'Your colleague Matt Fairacre informs us that Mr Samson was upset about something, depressed even. Do you have any idea what might have been the cause of that?'

Gazelle had one big idea all of his own, but there was no way he was about to share his illicit drug theory with an officer of the law no matter how deep his suspicions ran. 'Well, Sammy was indeed in a foul mood when I last saw him,' confessed Gazelle. 'But he'd been like that the night before and none of us could really work out why. We tended to leave him on his own and let him get on with it if the truth be known,' he added.

'Was he drunk the night before?' the officer asked.

'He'd had quite a lot to drink, it was our last time together on tour after all, but nothing too outlandish, not by Sammy's standards anyway,' Gazelle replied.

He considered adding that Sammy had managed to shin up a 40 feet high builder's ladder, climb through a third storey bedroom window and shimmy across a Dutchman's bed to gain access to his own hotel, but hastily decided that the waters were muddy enough already.

'Right, so not much further on then,' added Sergeant Swindells.

'However sir, I'd still like you to go over this old ground again if you don't mind. Just think about those last few hours you spent with Sammy and see if you can remember anything at all that might help us. Talking to the doctors at the hospital it would seem they're working on the theory that your friend has possibly been poisoned, so if you can assist us in any way it might prove useful. Sometimes even the smallest detail can lead to something quite unexpected.'

Gazelle promised the officer he would do just that.

'OK, I'm here until after midnight for the next few nights so don't hesitate to ring,' added Sergeant Swindells.

Gazelle issued his farewells and walked into the lounge where Stuey was leaning forward in his chair rolling a joint in front of the fire.

'I can't believed you're still smoking that stuff in light of all that's happening and especially as that was the police on the telephone.'

'I wasn't to know it was the police,' replied Stuey, feigning a certain amount of indifference.

'What did they want anyway?'

'They're still trying to work out what happened to Sammy and as I was the last of us guys to speak to him they want me to help them.'

'I hope you didn't share your ridiculous cannabis theory with them,' snarled Stuey, lighting the joint as he did so.

'No I didn't. But they want me to trace over the last few hours and see if I can come up with anything that might help them.'

'I don't see how that's going to help much,' added Stuey,

flicking ash into the glowing embers. 'I suppose it was just you two travelling along in silence most of the time up a boring motorway.'

'It wasn't even that,' replied Gazelle. 'Sammy didn't even travel in the front seats with me. He was in the back on his own with all the kit bags.'

'Strewth, you're joking!' exclaimed Stuey, blowing smoke towards the chimney. 'What on earth possessed him to do that?'

'Dunno really,' replied Gazelle. 'He was in a stinking mood and insisted he was staying on his own in the back.'

'How weird,' replied Stuey, inhaling a large lungful of smoke. 'What did he do, just get his head down?'

'Well, I thought so at first,' replied Gazelle. 'But after a while there was all this banging and crashing. It sounded as though he was moving the luggage about or something.'

'Even stranger,' added Stuey 'Why on earth would he do that?'

Both men stared into the flames as they licked the back of the chimney, Stuey mellowing as the cannabis kicked in, Gazelle frowning and concentrating diligently on events leading up to Sammy's swift exit at the motorway services as the police officer had requested. Gazelle closed his eyes and tried to picture the exact scene when Sammy and he had parted company on the M6. He gripped his forehead with his right hand, massaged it gently and remembered that Sammy wasn't wearing the jacket he had worn in Bristol the night before although possibly the same set of clothes beneath. Clothes. Now there was a thought. Gazelle dug deeper into his memory banks and recalled the exact moment he had opened the rear doors of the van to let Sammy out.

He remembered that he was dishevelled and dragging his suitcase behind him. A further furrowing of the brow brought up the mental picture of his last sight of Sammy. He was sitting on the grass verge near the motorway services unzipping the suitcase.

Why had he done that?

'Hey up,' he called across to Stuey who appeared to be in a world of his own, that world focused on the centre of the fire as the hot coals sparked and glowed. 'I think I might have come up with something.'

'What might that be then?' asked Stuey, reluctantly drawing himself away from the myriad of private thoughts coursing through his own mind.

Gazelle chose his words carefully.

'When Sammy got out of the minibus he was carrying his suitcase. Then, as I left him at the motorway services, he was sitting on the grass unzipping it as though he was about to take something out. What do you reckon that might have been then?'

'Dunno,' replied Stuey.

Gazelle resumed his deep thinking audibly: 'Every time Sammy sat down on grass he was usually boozing. Let's face it, when he wasn't playing cricket, he was usually boozing.'

Stuey took a last draw of the joint before flicking the end into the fire where it burst immediately into flames. At almost the same time there was a spark in his brain.

'That's it,' he almost shouted. 'You've got it. Booze. Do you remember the lunch time before we set off to play cricket in Bristol? We all met up in the bar at the Swan and Sammy was late because he'd been shopping. You lot were all intrigued because you'd never known Sammy go shopping before and you demanded to know what he'd bought. He told us that he'd bought cider. Real farmhouse cider he said. And he was keeping it all for himself.'

'That's right,' replied Gazelle, slowly nodding his head in agreement. 'And he'd been to pick it up in the kit bag minibus. He must have hidden it in the back of the van which meant it was still there when we drove up from Bristol on the way home.'

Gazelle suddenly shot forward in his chair. 'If he did take the cider with him to the motorway services, it would explain all the banging about in the back of the minibus as we drove towards Birmingham. He was probably chucking all the kit out of the way trying to get his hands on it.'

The light bulb burning brightly in Gazelle's brain suddenly turned into Blackpool illuminations. He was so excited he clambered to his feet.

'Got it,' Gazelle cried out. 'It would also explain why we found some of Sammy's clothes in the back of the van when we got back home. That's it. Sammy took out the clothes so he could fit the cider into the suitcase and then carry it. Didn't he say he'd bought two flagons of the stuff? It's all starting to make sense.'

'It's still not all making sense to me,' interjected Stuey. 'What's all this about clothes in the back of the van?'

'Oh, you weren't there, were you?' replied Gazelle. 'When we arrived back to the club and all the guys had taken out their kit and luggage, some of Sammy's clothes, a rugby shirt, socks and the jacket he'd worn on our night out in Bristol were found strewn all over the back of the minibus. I brought them home with me after I'd taken the mini-bus back to the depot. It was Meat Loaf who found them. Do you remember that Brisbane Broncos rugby league shirt that Sammy was always wearing in the cricket club bar at night? He'd even left that behind.'

'Yeh, good call, it was a great idea to get rid of that. He'd have been far better with a Sydney City Roosters jersey in the first place,' replied Stuey. 'They're a far superior team.'

Gazelle looked with some dismay at his lodger, not quite believing he could be so flippant when they were discussing such important detective work. He put it down to Stuey's recent drug intake and quickly moved on.

'The point here is that there's every chance that Sammy took that cider out of the suitcase and drank it there and then on that grass verge before he collapsed. Did you ever consider the distinct possibility that it was the cider that made him so ill?'

The enormity of Gazelle's last sentence suddenly hit home.

Between them, straight landlord and stoned lodger had worked out what may well be a reasonable, logical explanation as to the cause of Sammy's illness and suddenly Stuey felt energised, not least because Gazelle's return of memory took some of the heat off the prime suspect...the cannabis as provided by one Stuart Latham.

Stuey tried to concentrate and add some joined-up dots to the hazy picture that Gazelle was painting.

He continued: 'Sammy also told us that he bought the cider from some farm that didn't usually sell the stuff And if he did drink it all himself as you're suggesting, then it may even explain why no-one else, err, collapsed. It's starting to all makes sense to me. The question is, what do we do now? Tell Uncle Norman perhaps?'

'I think we should tell the police straight away,' replied Gazelle, amazed at his own forthrightness and newly-discovered decision-making. 'And looking at the state of you, I think I'd better do it. One word from you and the battering rams will be coming through the front door.'

Stuey looked at his landlord forlornly and shrugged his shoulders in despair.

On the drugs front at least, progress was still painfully slow.

FIFTY-THREE

It was 10.30pm, still a bit early for the inevitable hauling in of late night miscreants when Sergeant Swindells' telephone trilled loudly.

On the other end of the line, Gazelle closed his eyes, concentrating on being as precise and concise as possible as he outlined to the policeman the newly-remembered events on the motorway which hopefully would cascade much light on the cause of Sammy's illness.

When he explained his theory about the cider, the Sergeant listened intently and made several encouraging clucking noises. 'Great stuff, well done Bernard,' he said. 'Do you know what's happened to Mr Samson's suitcase?

'I haven't got a clue,' replied Gazelle. 'I haven't seen it since I got back. I don't think anybody has.'

'Right, leave this with me,' replied the sergeant. 'I'll ask the duty officers who were called to the service station and then take it from there. I might even get back to you later this evening. Will that be OK?'

'That will be fine,' replied Gazelle, resolving to make sure that he answered the telephone himself due to the chemically-induced torpor afflicting his zapped-out tenant only a few feet away. 'I won't be going to bed early.'

Sergeant Swindells put down the 'phone and picked it straight up again.

He managed to speak to one of his patrol officers who had tried to revive Sammy and establish that they hadn't come across a suitcase. But they did have the name of the duty manager who had called them and when Sergeant Swindells rang the service station and asked for him by name, a fellow Brummie accent was soon being more than co-operative on the other end of the line.

The manager, a Mr Ken Dodd – who was quick to explain that all the jokes had already been cracked – went away to check with lost property and returned with positive news. 'There is a suitcase here,' he said. 'Bit of a turn-up that. Folk leave lots of bizarre things out of their bags, but rarely the bag itself, although I think this one has stuff in it as well. Do you want me to open it and see what's in there?'

'If you don't mind,' said Sergeant Swindells.

The sound of unzipping then noisy rummaging could be heard via the telephone laid on the manager's desk before Mr Dodd returned it to his ear. 'Hello again officer,' he said. 'There are plenty of personal belongings in here, mainly clothes and some dirty cricket flannels, so it looks very much like it's the right suitcase. And rather unusually, two large stone flagons of what appears to be farmhouse cider, although I suspect they're both empty.'

Sergeant Swindells smiled briefly as an early smidgeon of success brightened his evening, but he was soon back on the case, both literally and metaphorically.

'Right, Mr Dodd, this next bit is important. You say that both flagons are empty, but are you absolutely sure about that? Might there be some dregs left in the bottom of either of them? Have a look, but if there is, whatever you do, don't drink them.'

'One of them still has a cork pushed in the neck,' replied Mr Dodd, 'so I'll investigate further,' the service station manager rather warming to the spot of amateur detective work being pushed his way. He shook the flagon and was pleased to hear a faint splashing noise with its origins in the bottom of the container. He removed the cork and gingerly poured a drop or two into the palm of his hand before sniffing it. The colour reminded him of a urine sample his teenage daughter had once taken from her horse to send to the vet and the smell wasn't too dissimilar either.

The horse had been in perfect condition.

Mr Dodd picked up the telephone again and related what he hoped could only be good news to the policeman.

'There is some left and it certainly smells like cider,' he added, declining to reveal what he really thought it smelled like.

'Good man,' replied Sergeant Swindells. 'Now I want you to replace the cork and put the flagon somewhere safe. I'll send one of my men round later to pick it up. I know there's not much left, but it might just be enough.'

'Enough for what?' asked Mr Dodd.

'Enough to establish if this is the stuff that flattened our friend from up north.'

FIFTY-FOUR

The red telephone in Gazelle's hallway rang for second time that night which in itself was a first.

Gazelle sprang out of his chair to answer it before Stuey could, the fact that his almost horizontal tenant hadn't moved a muscle in his comfy chair for the best part of an hour completely lost on Gazelle. He recognised the sergeant's voice immediately and listened intently to the news of the success the officer had achieved.

'I'll ring the club chairman and tell him right away about these developments,' he jabbered at the police officer excitedly.

'You'd better inform the hospital as well,' replied Sergeant Swindells. 'Tell them that we'll arrange to have a sample of this cider sent to them for laboratory tests as soon as we can. I reckon we could be on to something here.'

'Is the cider the prime suspect then?' asked Gazelle.

'I would say so,' replied the officer. 'Why, is there some other suspect that we don't know about?'

'No, no, not at all,' gushed Gazelle, perhaps a tad too hurriedly. 'Good work Sergeant. Now we all just want to see Sammy back on his feet again.'

FIFTY-FIVE

Dr Cat was reminded of playing pass the parcel when he was a young boy.

Layer upon layer of brown paper had been carefully swaddled around a container which had arrived by special delivery overnight. Beneath the paper were wads of cotton wool held in place by swathes of sticky tape and bubble wrap and lurking at the centre of it all this padding was a glass vessel on which was inscribed the legend: 'Property of Birmingham Police.'

The doctor smiled at the utilitarian use of the urine sample bottle which had been pressed into service to send him five fluid ounces of farmhouse cider.

But he was secretly impressed as well.

He had received the bottle intact having survived the Post Office's overnight courier service, although there was every chance it would have survived if it had been dropped from the top of the Empire State Building. So this was what they called police protection.

Dr.Cat surveyed then sniffed the murky fluid as he swilled

it around the glass vessel in the sharp morning light pouring through the French windows in his office. It smelled of cider, but also reminded him of lighter fluid. The boys in the laboratory would soon suss it out.

He passed the patient's room on the way to the analyists' department and looked at Sammy through the small glass window in the door. Sammy lay motionless, bloated and as helpless as ever across the two beds. Tubes dripped, monitors blinked and lights flickered.

Dr Cat frowned and continued his journey.

FIFTY-SIX

Sydney Cricket ground was bathed in brilliant sunshine as the thermometer mercury touched 90 degrees, the early afternoon sun starting to slowly casserole a capacity crowd alive with expectation.

Up on the hill, the highly-charged home fans were banging on their drums, waving their flags and blowing the froth off a few tinnies on the first day of the first Test between Australia and New Zealand.

In the Australian dressing room, deep under the main stand, opening batsman Alan 'Sammy' Samson stretched his hamstrings, flexed his biceps and tweaked his 'tache before padding up to prepare for his debut international appearance. His partner, another Test debutant called Stuart 'Stuey' Latham, embarked on a series of similar stretching exercises before checking his hair in the mirror.

Nervous tension filled the air. A crushing burden of responsibility bore down heavily on both men.

Captain Allan Border, having won the toss and electing to

bat, was also padded up ready to take to the field at number three. He addressed his side with a solemnity and gravitas fitting the occasion of an opening Test match between these two great rival nations.

'I surely don't need to tell you boys the depth of pride and commitment that must be shown by every one of you out there in the colours of your country today. Many of you are no strangers to Test cricket and will be aware of the monumental onus of responsibility resting on our collective shoulders. But there are two guys in our midst on deboo today, our openers, Sammy Samson and Stuart Latham and they are charged with the task of laying the bedrock of a fine innings, one which can lead us to a great win here in Sydney and ultimately a series triumph over these Kiwis who frankly deserve nothing less than a fair dinkum thrashing. Let's get out there and do all of Australia proud.'

Sammy felt an exhilarating surge of pride begin to course through his body, rising from the very home soil on which he stood, sending his stomach all aflutter before the adrenaline flow engulfed his entire body. He closed his eyes briefly to amass his thoughts and harness the power within.

When Sammy opened them again he trained them on Stuart Latham, his partner in the front line ready to face what they both knew would be a merciless assault, both mental and physical from a fully loaded New Zealand strike force.

Sammy briefly admired the taut and muscular body of his fellow antipodean, the dashing blonde rinse, the fine cut of his sporting attire before quickly dismissing such thoughts as unwanted distractions.

The door of the dressing room was pushed open by a stadium official who barked that the game would commence in less than fifteen minutes.

Sammy and Stuart headed out of the tunnel into the dazzling sunlight and a stadium arena brimming with emotion. Thousands of white hats were flung in the air, flags fluttered, bare chests glistened with sun tan oil. Tanned young girls wore bikinis, drank beer with the boys and flaunted their bodies. Seagulls yapped.

Sammy took his mark from the umpire and prepared to face his first ball. He sensed hostility and got just that, the opening delivery, short of a length and dripping with venom, demanding last-second evasive action from the batsman to avoid a broken nose. Sammy raised his head, turned to the bowler and issued several threats in language that turned the air blue.

His Kiwi tormentor laughed and strode manfully away.

The next ball was short of a length too, but Sammy had the measure of it this time, stood his ground and pulled it out of the air towards the boundary.

A sprinting fielder stopped it short of the rope and hurled it back to the wicket, but not before Sammy had galloped three runs, leaving his young partner to face his first ball.

Stuey called for middle and leg before settling in at the crease. Gardening was at a minimum on the rock-hard, sun-baked surface. The first three balls he allowed to fly harmlessly through to the 'keeper, his nonchalant arrogance raising the bowler's blood pressure who let fly with his last delivery of the over.

With anger came inaccuracy and Stuey whacked the ball to the boundary without even bothering to run before strolling down the wicket and patting down an imaginary flaw in the russet brown track.

Sammy met him half-way to talk tactics.

'Stay calm and keep a focus is the way to deal with these jesters,' remarked Stuey. 'Play safe with the balls you have to, leave the rest and smash the soft oranges into Queensland,' he added glibly.

Sammy nodded sagely in agreement before returning to his crease.

His admiration for his partner had deepened after just one over while he was more than willing to take on board tactics that made eminent sense, the bowlers soon starting to wilt in the draining heat, their frustration and ire increasing as both batsmen selected their shots with a tiresome yet effective attention to detail. The two debutants' fledgling opening partnership grew, blossomed and matured. Sammy, striving to emulate his partner's controlled élan, took his time by his own swashbuckling standards, but still reached half a century first, the proud antipodean's raised bat acknowledging the raucous cheers of an appreciative audience.

Stuey soon struck 50 too which meant more willow pointing towards the heavens and as the afternoon heat slowly dissipated, the crowd sensed they were about to witness one of the finest opening partnerships in the annals of Australian Test cricket.

They were not to be disappointed.

Sammy, even more measured and guarded as a rather special page of sporting history was turning, allowed his partner to take the lead role, Stuey reaching a splendid century with a straight six back over the bowler's head as the fans fell over each other in inebriated glee.

The celebrations didn't last too long though. Stuey was caught on the boundary three deliveries later, those fans still capable of doing so affording their hero a standing ovation all the way back to the dressing sheds.

Sammy, now on 98 not out, was joined at the wicket by Allan Border and beckoning the new bat down the track for a short council of war, offered his somewhat bemused captain a slice of sage counsel.

'Play safe with the balls you have to, leave the rest and smash the soft oranges into Queensland,' he advised before returning to his crease and smoothing down his moustache with some aplomb.

By way of demonstrating the tactic – and of course in tribute to Stuey, the great cricketing philosopher himself – Sammy allowed the next four deliveries to pass by his stumps with scant regard before dispatching the final ball of the over into a pitch side lager advert with a resounding thump.

Most of the crowd once again scrambled to its feet in collective adulation, Sammy raising his right hand to all four corners of the ground before nodding in deep appreciation to the applauding Allan Border, the greatest recognition of his feat he could ever have wished for.

Ebullient and relaxed with his century safe on the scoreboard, Sammy decided to demonstrate his vast array of dynamic shots to his adoring fans, a rash tactic that was to prove his undoing. Sammy was also caught out on the boundary in the next over, a fate which seemed surprisingly fitting and failed to upset him even a tad.

He followed slowly in Stuey's footsteps all the way back to the pavilion – Sammy drinking deeply of every clap, every cheer, every shout of appreciation – the rapturous reception continuing in the Australian dressing room where the back-slapping and glad-handing was led by the legendary Rodney Marsh.

This was truly the stuff dreams are made of.

Sammy threw down his bat, ripped off his gloves and pads, accepted an ice-cool tinnie and surveyed a dressing room that was surely a part of heaven itself.

'Strewth, I'm as hot as a pair of Ghandi's sandals,' he quipped to no-one in particular before stripping down naked.

'And I could really use a shower. Where's Stuey by the way?'

'He's already gone through to the wet room,' replied a grinning Rodney Marsh. 'He's waiting in there for you.'

Sammy padded barefoot into the showers, but even though hot water cascaded from every wall fitting, there was no-one to be seen. He peered through the rising steam before tentatively calling: 'Stuey, Stuey, are you there?'

There was no reply, but through the gathering condensation, Sammy could make out a strange door on the far side of the room. It was covered in pink crushed velvet, had a gold handle in the shape of a leaping porpoise and was slightly ajar. Sammy felt a pressing need to open this intriguing portal to the great unknown, to explore what it contained, body and mind beckoned and lured towards it with an urgency he just knew was irresistible. He pushed it open expectantly, surprised by a heavy scent of sweet perfume which pervaded the slightly misty air and took in a sight which stopped him in his tracks.

In the middle of the room, Stuey was sprawled across a huge, king-size bed, naked apart from a small towel covering his private parts. He smiled sweetly at Sammy and waved him towards his writhing body laid provocatively on silky, rustling sheets which were also pink. Sammy stood transfixed before a surreal sensation took over him. He felt himself lifting off the ground, rising slowly upwards before he came to a halt, hovering high in the slightly sickly air above Stuey who continued to wave and preen and flaunt his attractive, sun-kissed body.

Sammy felt himself being overwhelmed by a desire to descend on the vision of loveliness below him and as his desire grew, so he started to slowly fall, inching towards Stuey who continued to wave, lure and preen.

But as Sammy slipped through the air, he heard other voices coming from the door.

It opened slowly and through it flew three other figures, Sammy's wife Angela and their two sons Rod and Ben, all three of them drifting in to hover above Sammy in some kind of family holding pattern.

Angela looked down at her husband and as he looked up, tears cascaded from her eyes and fell to form rivulets on Sammy's cheeks and chest.

'Don't go down there, Sammy,' she pleaded, reaching out her arms in tortured anguish. 'Come back to me. Come back to the family. Come back and make us whole again. We all love you. Please, please stay.'

'Please come back Dad, please,' cried his sons in unison. 'Don't leave us. We need you. Who's going to teach us to play cricket if you're not here for us?'

Sammy lay on his back suspended in mid-air. Below him Stuey purred seductively, above him his sons were now also crying and clinging on to their mother.

He looked around him in a state of total bewilderment.

On the wall he saw shimmering visions of straw trilbies, a rusting Morris Marina, a Somerset cricket pitch deep under water and flagons of farmhouse cider.

What was this room? What was happening to him? What was he expected to do next?

He looked up at his weeping wife and was overwhelmed by a tidal wave of compassion, guilt, remorse and love. He reached out his arms to her and as he did so, he rose while Angela and the boys started to sink towards him.

They met in mid-air and started to embrace. First Sammy hugged Angela and the boys and as he too started to weep, suddenly they all started to plummet downwards, plunging towards the bed in free-fall. The fall should have taken seconds, but it lasted much longer, long enough for Sammy to look down at the half-naked body lying on the bed below, Stuey's face now contorted by a leer of anger and frustration.

'We're all going to land on him and crush him,' thought Sammy.

But he didn't care. Stuey was part of this conspiracy, this stupid test or whatever it was, and if he had to pay a price, then so be it.

But as Sammy, Angela and the boys hurtled towards him, Stuey suddenly disappeared in a cloud of hazy perfume and all four of them landed softly on the bed as if dropped by parachute.

Sammy turned to Angela, kissed her softly on the lips, drew the two boys close in and clung on to them all. He clung on to them as though he was never going to let them go.

The monitors above Sammy's motionless body in the hospital bed jumped and flickered into life.

The patient's left hand closed in a tight grip and then opened again.

FIFTY-SEVEN

The telephone rang in Norman F. Billington's lounge.

He clucked in exasperation because he had already tucked it away behind the curtains. It was only 7.00pm, but he wasn't expecting any calls.

He picked it up and crisply dictated his number.

'Hello Norman. Dr Cat speaking. I hope you don't mind me calling you Norman, but my informal nature might be a hint of the good news I have to impart. It's Sammy. He's awake and conscious. We have to run some more tests and these are early days of course, but we think he's going to be OK.'

Relief coursed through Norman F. Billington's body.

'Thank the dear Lord for that,' he said. 'It was that horrible cannabis stuff wasn't it?'

'Err, well, still not too sure about the exact cause at the moment,' replied Dr Cat. 'Like I just said, these are still early days and we're still running tests. I've already spoken to his wife and she wants to come and see him straight away. It's a bit unorthodox and Sammy is still very weak, but under the circumstances I think we can allow it. Perhaps you might like to come too and perhaps you can bring her in your car.'

'I'll ring Angela straight away and we'll be there in less than an hour,' replied Norman F. Billington.

'Thank you so much doctor for all you have done. I can't tell you how much this means to so many people'

'Don't thank me,' replied Dr Cat. 'The patient hasn't received any real treatment apart from monitoring and the saline drips because we really haven't tracked down the exact cause of his illness. Sammy seems to have come through this ordeal all on his own and we're still not sure why he came round when he did. But all the life signs are good and hopefully we're going to see a steady improvement. I'll see you in an hour.'

Norman F. Billington and Angela drove south in the fading light and barely spoke a word. They didn't need to. A mutual happiness meant the long silences were quite comfortable and they arrived at the hospital in expectant high spirits.

Dr Cat met them in the reception and let them through to a dressing room near where Sammy lay. As they pulled on white gowns and gloves, the doctor explained what to expect: 'Sammy is conscious, but he's very weak and tired. He's asleep at the moment and we haven't really tried to engage him in conversation. I thought we would leave that to you. So in we go then. Just a few minutes perhaps.'

Dr Cat pushed open the door and led them into the room. Nothing much had changed apart from the extra activity in the monitors above the bed and the fact that Sammy was snoring loudly.

'That's more like it,' smiled Angela. 'Can I try to wake him?'

'Yes, but gently and no shocks.'

Angela lifted her husband's hand just as she had done so often during the many long and anxious vigils by his bedside, but on this occasion she did so with hope and optimism.

'Sammy, Sammy, it's me Angie. Are you awake love? Can you hear me?'

Sammy stirred and snorted in his sleep, turned his head awkwardly and uncomfortably, opened his eyes, looked around in bewilderment and croaked: 'I never touched him ref.'

Angela giggled nervously, Norman F. Billington smirked and Dr Cat coughed politely into his pristine white sleeve.

Sammy looked at Angela, smiled and tried to reach out to his wife with both his hands. He failed miserably so Angela placed her hands around his huge waist and hugged him gently.

'Oh Sammy it's so good to have you back.'

'Where have I been?' croaked Sammy wearily. 'Oh, I remember, Sydney, no Somerset. Where am I now? What is this place?'

'You're in hospital because you've been seriously ill,' said Dr Cat who took Sammy's hand off Angela and felt his patient's wrist for the pulse count.

'Tell me Sammy, what's the year?'

'Err, let me think...1981.'

'Yes, good, and what's the last thing you remember?'

Sammy closed his eyes to concentrate on distinguishing between reality and fantasy. The memory of himself cascading towards Stuey's semi-naked body on a pink bed was vivid, but even though confusing, he realised this was a dream, yet a dream that was important and one he already knew he would never forget.

He furrowed his brow to concentrate further.

'Take your time Sammy,' said Dr Cat. 'It's not that important if you can't remember. Do you re-call going on this cricket tour?'

Sammy spoke slowly and deliberately.

'I do and I can remember going to Bristol then coming home in the back of the minibus.'

He paused and frowned. 'I got out at a motorway services in a rotten mood and left Gazelle on his own. I shouldn't have done that should I?'

'It doesn't matter any more,' said Dr Cat. 'What matters is that you make a full recovery. Now I think you ought to rest.'

Dr Cat turned to Angela and Norman F. Billington both of whom were close to tears. 'He's going to be alright, I'm sure of it. Let's leave him now. You can come back tomorrow.'

As all three left turned to leave the room, Sammy made a great grimacing effort to turn his head to one side and said: 'Angie, I really do love you. Will you tell the boys that I love them too.'

Angela smiled, nodded, pulled a screwed-up handkerchief out of her palm and patted her tear-stained cheeks.

FIFTY-EIGHT

The splendid news of Sammy's amazing recovery coursed through Crawford cricket club.

Gazelle celebrated by treating the wicket to a double dose of the heavy roller and despite the imminence of an important championship game later that day – it was a Saturday – there was a universal agreement that Sammy should be visited by the entire team that morning. Meat Loaf's suggestion that they take along a large Botham shandy for the patient by way of a special pick-me-up was summarily dismissed. Norman F. Billington pointed out that restrictions limited the number of bedside visitors at one time, but his half-hearted protests were brushed aside by one and all which meant a convoy of cars heading down the motorway as soon as Gazelle had laid out the boundary rope.

Tour trilbies, somewhat battered and ale-stained, were dug out, dusted down and donned by one and all.

Dr Cat was somewhat taken aback by the arrival of what appeared to be a posse of titfer-clad racketeers invading his ward, but he didn't have the heart to muster much of a complaint. 'The patient is clearly a very popular person and has many friends,' he opined. 'He's had a restful night and is much improved, so under the circumstances I'm going to allow you all in to see him. His wife and sons have been to visit already today, but before you do go in, I have a bit of interesting news for all concerned. We've finally discovered what made Sammy so ill.'

Matt Fairacre's heart missed yet another beat while Norman F. Billington raised a most worried eyebrow. Revelations about Sammy's illicit drug-taking were about to receive a most public and unwanted airing, but before the chairman could do anything to halt proceedings, Dr Cat started to address his audience again. 'It is, I believe, thanks to much help and information provided by Bernard Gazelle and Stuart Latham, plus some astute detective work by Birmingham police officers that we have been able to establish the cause of Sammy's, err, ailment.'

Norman F. Billington closed his eyes, hid them behind his hands and wanted the world to end. Matt Fairacre edged towards the door and seriously considered running out of the building before booking a one-way passage on a slow boat to the Dutch West Indies.

Dr Cat continued: 'Thanks to the efforts of all these good parties I came into possession of this.'

The doctor dipped into his pocket and lifted a small glass laboratory test tube into the air. In the bottom lurked a murky, apple-green liquid. 'This, gentlemen, is a small measure of what used to be two flagons of rough farmhouse cider which Sammy consumed shortly before collapsing at the motorway service station. Lab reports have now confirmed that it is toxic and possibly even fatal if taken in high enough doses. It certainly laid your colleague low. However, despite all he's been through, I think we can safely say he's going to make a slow but full recovery. He's a very fortunate young man.'

There was a collective gasp from the gathering.

'I was right all along', triumphed Pete Skidmore. 'I told him they put dead rats in it.'

Norman F. Billington opened his eyes and blinked as a heady mix of bafflement and bewilderment overwhelmed him. He glanced across at Matt Fairacre who was either talking silently to himself or finishing off a prayer.

This latest development – while certainly not unwelcome – had somewhat bamboozled the club chairman. When Gazelle had earlier informed him of the poisonous cider theory he had been rather dismissive. It was surely far more likely that an illicit drug was the cause of the Sammy's illness he had reasoned, but now his logic had seemingly been challenged and from a respected member of the medical fraternity no less. He decided to take Dr Cat to task there and then.

'Excuse me doctor, but if it is the cider, have you come up with an antidote that has brought about Sammy's recovery?'

'We haven't found an antidote as yet,' replied Dr Cat. 'Sammy seems to have pulled through on his own, but the lab boys have established that the cider was toxic and are working on an antidote. They've also contacted the local police in Somerset to tell them what they've discovered and I daresay they'll want a word with Sammy when he's well enough. We certainly don't want anyone else poisoned from the same source. Does anybody know exactly where he got it from?

'No, not really,' said Pete Skidmore. 'Sammy went off on his own in the van and said that the farmer who supplied the cider didn't normally sell it. I reckon the old boy just sups it himself and is immune to it by now. He probably eats wurzels too. I'm surprised he's still alive.'

Norman F. Billington intervened to keep the morning on track. 'Well boys, it's great news that Sammy's going to be OK. Shall we go in and see the patient now?'

The cricketers filed silently into the room, removing their hats as they did so.

'It's only a pity the fine system's not still up and running,' mumbled Wobbler. 'I could really have filled my boots.'

Sammy was slumbering contentedly as the door was pushed open, his enormous bloated frame still straddling two beds. He stirred and raised his head with some difficulty as his fellow cricketers shuffled nervously around his considerable perimeter, most of them taken aback by the sheer size of their unfortunate colleague, Meat Loaf allowing himself a smug little smile as he was no longer the biggest bloke in the room.

Dr Cat spoke first: 'Right gentleman, your good friend is on the road to recovery and will eventually lose most of the unwanted weight he's gained as his recuperation continues. He will be staying with us here in hospital for a while yet and I suspect he won't be playing cricket again this summer, but otherwise the prognosis is a sunny one.'

The medic's attempt at gentle humour was lost on everyone as all eyes focused on the blubbery, bleary-eyed, bed-ridden wicketkeeper.

'Hey up Sammy, this is a rum old do isn't it?' piped up Meat Loaf. 'Have you weighed yourself since you woke up? I'm laying odds on about 27 stones.'

'Pack it in Meat Loaf,' snapped Wobbler. 'Show some respect and ask the poor lad how he is. What odds are you offering by the way?'

Meat Loaf coughed and mumbled into his sleeve. 'How you doing me old mate?'

'Not too bad under the circumstances,' croaked Sammy. 'It's good to see so many of you boys by my bedside. I never realised I was so popular.'

'Does Sammy know what's made him ill yet doctor?' interjected Wobbler.

'Err no, not yet,' replied Dr Cat.

'Right them I'll tell him', cried Wobbler, far too gleefully. 'Sammy, listen to me. Do you remember that farmhouse cider that you bought, the stuff you refused to share with anyone else and drank all on your own on the way home because you're so tight?'

Sammy closed his eyes to aid memory recovery before replying. 'You mean the stuff I picked up in the van and supped at the motorway service station? Yes, I do remember that. In fact, it's possibly the last thing I remember. Why?'

'It was the cider that made you ill,' triumphed Wobbler. 'It was highly toxic.'

'As poisonous as an adder's armpit,' added Pete Skidmore. 'I did warn you.'

'Oh my God,' groaned Sammy and attempted to shift his bloated frame but with little success. 'What have I done?'

'Do you remember the farm you bought it from?' asked Dr Cat. 'I only mention it because the police are bound to ask me or you the same question, eventually anyway.'

'I'm not sure I could find it again easily,' whined Sammy. 'I drove around for ages and I don't remember seeing any advert or anything. All this thinking is making my head hurt.'

Norman F. Billington decided to draw stumps as it were. 'Right boys, perhaps we'd better all set off for home now,' he said, casting a querulous glance across at Dr Cat who nodded in agreement. 'Sammy needs to rest some more now and let's not forget that there's a cricket game to be won this afternoon.'

After the cricketers had issued their fond farewells to their stricken colleague and strolled outside into the car park, Stuey espied his chance. He took Norman F. Billington gently by the arm and led him to one side.

'Can I have a word in private Norman?'

'You may indeed Stuart.'

Stuey took a deep breath and spoke: 'Good news about Sammy then Norman?' a statement of fact which was in fact little more than a gentle introduction to what he really wanted to say.

'That's right,' replied Norman F. Billington. 'It's given us all a real lift.'

'And what about that cider being poisonous? Jeez, a real bonza turn-up for the book that one don't you reckon?'

'Mmm,' agreed Norman F. Billington. 'Quite an eye-opener.'

'Err, so that's me and you sweet,' ventured Stuey, tentatively and a little nervously. 'As good as gold again.'

'I'm not quite sure what you're trying to say Stuart. Please try and be a little more precise.'

Stuey shot the chairman an exasperated glance before trying again: 'I mean, that's me off the hook then. The doctor just explained that it was the cider that flattened Sammy and not the, err cannabis, so, like I said before, that's me off the hook then.'

'The illicit drug that you supplied may well have contributed to Sammy's illness,' replied Norman F. Billington haughtily.

'That's not what the bloody doctor said,' protested Stuey, raising his voice. 'You heard him. He said it was all down to the cider. Weren't you listening Norman?' Stuey added angrily, his eyes flashing.

Norman F. Billington felt aggrieved too and spoke his mind. 'It doesn't alter the fact that you still took then supplied an illicit substance to a third party and in the eyes of the law that is wrong. In my eyes it's wrong too and I just can't brush it to one side and pretend it never happened which is clearly what you want me to do.'

Stuey felt his stomach churn and his frustration rise, but he couldn't contain his emotions. 'So exactly what are you going to do then?' he demanded. The abrupt reply startled and momentarily ruffled Norman F. Billington, but the young Australian's bellicose manner rankled with the former solicitor who quickly regained his composure and again stood his ground.

'I don't rightly know at the moment, but I don't think you should play for the team this afternoon until I've decided what to do.'

Stuey stared at him aghast before speaking. 'But this is our first game for two weeks and what about the big push for the championship that you're always banging on about?' he replied.

'Sometimes there's more to life than even cricket,' said Norman F. Billington.

'And how am I supposed to explain my absence to the boys?' added Stuey.

'Tell them you're injured, or ill, or whatever, I really don't care,' replied Norman F. Billington. 'Now if you don't mind I'm going back to my car to drive home. I daresay we shall speak again'.

And with that Norman F. Billington walked stiffly away, climbed into his vehicle and drove off with Wobbler pushing his contorted face against the glass and grinning inanely out of the back window. Stuey clambered disconsolately into the front passenger seat of Gazelle's car, shook his head and turned to Matt Fairacre who was sitting in the rear of the Triumph Herald.

'Norman's not letting me play cricket this afternoon,' he muttered sullenly.

'Why on earth has he done that?' asked Gazelle.

'Well, as there's only you two in the car I suppose I can tell you the real reason. He's still got a major issue with the fact that Sammy smoked my cannabis. He still thinks it's got something to do with Sammy's illness even though the doctor guy himself stood there and told us all that it was the fault of that poisonous cider. I just can't believe that he won't let go of this. And if the rest of the guys get to know what's been going on then I'm never going to hear the last of it. What a stinking mess.'

Matt Fairacre nodded vigorously in total agreement, not least because the last thing he wanted was his own sorry role in the sordid affair to come out in the wash. He frowned and thought hard as Gazelle drove slowly up back up the motorway then said: 'Right then, here's an idea. I'll tell the rest of the team that Stuey's not too well because Gazelle's breakfast didn't agree with you. Gazelle, you've really got to stop feeding him those terrible tinned pilchards.

'Then, after the game, I'll try to have a word with Norman on my own to see if I can't make him see sense. Let's face it, none of us want this lot out in the open. Norman will come round eventually. He has to. Drop me off at the club Gazelle and then if you don't mind, take Stuey back to your place before you come to the club to watch the game.'

Stuey reluctantly mumbled his agreement before Gazelle grunted, nodded and pushed his grumbling Triumph Herald up to its top speed of 58 mph.

Gazelle, too, had fervently hoped that the doctor's diagnosis would draw a line under recent events, and not for the first time in recent days, found himself wishing that he'd never gone on tour in the first place.

FIFTY-NINE

Stuey's absence from the team that afternoon made a hole in morale, dented confidence and considerably reduced the ability quotient.

Despite the heartening news of Sammy's progress, the weakened Crawford side could only manage a lacklustre draw against Upper Dalton, applying a handbrake to the team's rise up the league table. Gazelle had watched the game from the long grass near the scoreboard and after he had roped off the wicket and trodden down a couple of divots in the outfield, decided against a drink in the pavilion bar, opting to drive straight back home instead.

He kept wondering who had been actually harmed by his lodger's illicit habits and now that it had been proved that Sammy was recovering from a dodgy cider-related poisoning, he had to reach the conclusion that no-one had really suffered, apart from himself and poor Matt Fairacre of course, relatively innocent on-lookers if ever there were two.

Gazelle pushed open the front door of his house shortly after 7.00pm and wondered if Stuey had been indulging early.

Gazelle would be the first to admit that sometimes it was difficult to tell – as Norman F. Billington would surely testify – but on this occasion the pungent smell that pervaded the air in his front parlour was proof positive that Stuey had been heavy on the herb early in the evening.

Despite the relative warmth of the late summer evening, the fire was roaring in the hearth. For a chap who had poured so much scorn on a real fire when he had first arrived, Gazelle noted with a quaintly satisfying inner smile that Stuey was most keen on focusing a blood-shot eye into the depths of a glowing ember these days.

He had even filled the coal scuttle last weekend.

'Hey up,' chirruped Gazelle, 'a bit early on the old weed tonight aren't we?'

'I'm smoking to forget,' replied Stuey, without turning his head. 'Can't say it's really working though. I can't stop thinking about Norman and his atrocious attitude. What's wrong with the guy? Why can't he just let it drop?'

'I think he's just a bit old-fashioned like me,' replied Gazelle. 'A couple of pints of flat rib and fish and chips on the way home was about as exciting as it got when I was the same age as you,' Gazelle added as he lowered himself into the other comfy chair. 'Gosh, it's warm in here.'

'Mmm, that's right,' added Stuey, absent-mindedly. 'What on earth is flat rib?'

'Mild, a kind of dark, weak, draught beer. Pretty gruesome stuff if the truth be known. It's almost impossible to get drunk off it.'

'If Sammy had stuck to flat rib then we wouldn't all be in this bloody mess,' Stuey replied ruefully before reaching for his cigarette papers on the floor.

SIXTY

Back at the clubhouse, Stuey was being missed both on and off the field.

Matt Fairacre had done a reasonably convincing job of blaming tinned fish for the Australian's absence, but there was still surprise among the players when Stuey didn't turn up for the evening's socialising, even if he was feeling rough. The atmosphere in the clubhouse had never been quite the same since Sammy's enforced absence and now Stuey wasn't part of the mix as well, the wit and laughter levels had dipped noticeably.

Norman F. Billington was sitting alone at the end of the bar perusing the day's scorebook and didn't look particularly happy. Matt Fairacre grabbed his chance and pulled up a stool alongside the chairman.

'That was a game we should have won Norman,' he ventured. 'We needed the points if we're going to secure promotion.'

'I can't disagree with you there Matthew,' replied Norman

F. Billington. 'The boys weren't really on top of their game today were they? I mean, look at Dave Carter's bowling figures. They're quite disgraceful really.'

'Well, he didn't have Stuey backing him up at the other end did he?' replied Matt Fairacre. 'Wobbler picks up most of his wickets after Stuey's half-terrified the batsmen to death. They're so glad to see the back of him they drop their guard when they see Wobbler's layers of lard trundling towards them and he uses this deception to his advantage. I'm sure he would be the first to admit that. I think the lesson to be learned here is that we need Stuey back in the team straight away,' added Matt Fairacre, cautiously laying one of his larger trump cards on the table.

Norman F. Billington eyed the young accountant suspiciously and paused before replying: 'So you also think his misdemeanour should be overlooked and we all carry on as normal as though nothing had happened. May I remind you, Matthew, that it was you who brought this sorry cannabis smoking affair to my attention in the first place and now it is you who appears to be asking me to forget all about it. Would I be right?'

'Well, you know the reason why I felt compelled to tell you in the first place Norman, and now that it's been proved that Stuey didn't do anything wrong, perhaps we should all move on,' replied Matt Fairacre, although his tremulous voice was hesitant and unsure. He had rather hoped the club chairman might be easier to break down than this.

'Didn't do anything wrong!' exclaimed Norman F. Billington. 'This rascal, a young man whose wages and accommodation are paid by us, has taken an illegal drug under my nose here at the club, at Bernard's house and on tour. That's quite a lot wrong in my book,' he scoffed.

'He wasn't responsible for Sammy's illness though and a lot of people think Stuey's the best thing to have happened to this club for a long time,' retorted Matt Fairacre quietly. 'Sammy and Laura think the world of him, Gazelle's managing to share a house with someone for the first time in his adult life and I suspect that even you Norman must have a sneaking admiration for the lad, even if it is only because he's the best cricketer at the club.'

'I don't deny that I respect and admire him as a cricketer, but we mustn't let sporting prowess cloud the issue here,' snapped Norman F. Billington. 'I really don't understand why he feels the need to take illegal substances, but he certainly felt the need to keep it a secret or at least try and keep it a secret anyway. But now it's out and even though Stuey would appear to have been a victim of unfortunate circumstances, what he has been doing behind my back will not go away. It haunts me like a ghost. It gnaws at me, I think about it all the time and the more I think about it, the more let down I feel. I appreciate that Stuey and his illicit substances weren't responsible for Sammy's illness, but I can't just leave it at that. Some of my best friends are still practising solicitors and lawyers. I had a justice of the peace over for drinks last Wednesday night. What if Stuey were to be prosecuted by the police and it leaks out that I knew about his drug-taking all the time? Well, your honour, it's like this you see. Stuey is a fine cricketer, a splendid chap and the absolute darling of our social circle, so I decided to overlook his illegal drug-taking and let him get on with it. How does that sound? I would be the laughing stock of the legal profession.'

Matt Fairacre listened to the chairman's diatribe with his toes curled tightly half way up his trainers and his finger tips white as they clenched his half pint of mediocre cooking lager.

'But it doesn't need to get out does it?' he replied, trying to sound relaxed, composed and not completely desperate. 'Apart from Dr Cat, only me, you, Sammy and Gazelle know about it and Gazelle's kept quiet about it for months.'

'Yes, quite a disappointment that too', replied Norman F. Billington. 'I might have expected more from such a sober-minded pillar of society.'

Matt Fairacre suddenly felt a wave of helplessness wash over him.

Trying to reason with Norman F. Billington would appear to be getting him nowhere. In cricketing terms, his entrenched opponent was shoving everything back down the wicket with a dead bat and digging in with a dogged determination.

Matt Fairacre shifted uncomfortably on his stool and looked Norman F. Billington in the eye and said: 'So, if you won't change your mind, what are you going to do then? If Stuey misses another game next weekend then the questions will really start to fly thick and fast.'

'I appreciate that some kind of decision will have to be made soon,' replied Norman F. Billington with a deep sigh, snapping the scorebook closed with an exasperated flick of his hand. Rising to his feet he added: 'I've got a few more days to think further about this whole sorry affair, during which time I shall also consult a few learned colleagues. I'm going home now Matthew. I don't feel like socialising much this evening. The short walk will hopefully help clear my mind. Thank you for your time and good evening.'

Norman F. Billington walked briskly out of the club and then around the cricket field in the near darkness, but the short stroll to his house did nothing to improve inner clarity. He opened the front door of his house and walked through to the back parlour where he found his wife asleep in the chair, an empty half bottle of gin on the floor. He tutted and was about to wake her, but stopped abruptly as his hand reached for her shoulder.

It was only 10.00pm and an idea had suddenly struck. His old RAF pal Ronald Richardson would be back home from a day's cricket in Bristol and surely still up and about. When Norman F. Billington had earlier told Matt Fairacre that he was to seek sage counsel from learned friends, he felt forced to admit to himself that he wasn't really sure who exactly these friends might be. He was still acquainted with many peers in the legal profession, but on this issue at least, felt a more softly, softly approach was required. Ronald was a man of the world and a trusted comrade. He would know what to do and Norman F. Billington felt sure this was the right time to ask him.

He checked that his wife was still asleep – reflecting ruefully to himself that she seemed to have managed to fall into a coma not dissimilar to the one that had flattened Sammy – walked back to the hall where he picked up the telephone, pressed 'R' in the plastic pop-up personal directory and rang the number. After a few shrill trills, Ronald Richardson's patrician tones wished the caller a good evening.

'Ronald? It's me, Norman.'

'Billers old boy, grand to hear from you, absolutely top class!' Ronald Richardson guffawed. 'But if you've come on to indulge in another free gloat after that win on tour then I'll be replacing the receiver straight away,' he added with a muffled chortle. 'You would never have won that game without that Johnny Foreigner in your ranks. Mind you, those Australian chappies were shoulder to shoulder with us when the balloon went up in the war, so I've no complaints there. How is young

Stuey by the way? My God, Norman, you've landed yourself a fine catch there. What a truly remarkable cricketer. Tell me he's still playing as well.'

'Actually, it's about Stuart I'm ringing,' replied Norman F. Billington.

'I get it', interrupted Ronald Richardson, 'he wants a proper English club to play for, so he's asked for a free transfer to us. Send him down Billers, we'll look after him for you,' came a second chuckle down the line.

Norman F. Billington sensed an imminent low warning light on his small tankful of patience and felt the urgency to get to the point without hacking his way through too much unnecessary detail.

'Actually Ronald, I've encountered a couple of problems with Stuart and I was rather hoping you would lend me an ear and offer me some advice.'

'Fire away Billers, always ready to help an old chum, you know that.'

'Well,' said Norman F. Billington, 'the sad fact is that it's been brought to my attention that Stuart has been taking illegal drugs.

'Mmm, what's the rascal been up to then?' replied Ronald Richardson softly.

Norman F. Billington steeled himself: 'He's been smoking cannabis, not just at home, but behind the club house after games as well and I'm so very disappointed to say the very least. Frankly, I don't really know how to handle the situation or what to do and as a fellow club chairman, I wondered if you had any thoughts on the matter.'

Norman F. Billington awaited his old pal's response. He was at the very least expecting a volley of disapproving tuts,

243

several sharp intake of breath or even some choice expletives to accompany his colleague's shock and disdain, but no such reactions were forthcoming.

'So, I suppose it's been affecting his game and he's been missing nets has he?' came Ronald Richardson's less-than-explosive response.

'Err, err, well, no, not really,' stammered a somewhat taken-aback Norman F. Billington. 'If I'm being honest, it doesn't seem to have detracted from his game and he still attends nets regularly.'

'So everybody knows about it and the police are on his case then,' replied Ronald Richardson. 'Could be a tricky one that Norman.'

'Actually Ronald, only a handful of people know about it and the police aren't on his case. I've found out about what he's been up to by accident, shall we say from a third party, and I'm wondering what to do next. I must say that you seem very relaxed about this Ronald. I expected you to be surprised to say the least.'

'Well, to be honest, a couple of years ago I might have been surprised, appalled even, but something happened last season which opened my eyes a bit,' replied his old RAF chum wistfully. 'We had this West Indian lad join us here at Renwick and he was a Rastafarian. Donovan was his name – yep that's right, Donovan – and he had this plaited hair which went on for ever, but the most remarkable thing about him was his cricket. He was a superb all-rounder, possibly up there in Stuey's league. Well, he didn't even try to make a secret of his fondness for his hashish as he called it. He even claimed it was part of his religion. I didn't believe him at first, but I did some research and it's true. My God, he would smoke the stuff in the clubhouse in front of the members. Some of the ladies were aghast. One of the old dears got a lungful one night and fainted. Anyway, I needed to have a word with Donovan and basically we came up with a kind of compromise arrangement. He agreed just to smoke it in private and I agreed to keep it a secret I suppose, not that he was particularly bothered who knew about it as I mentioned before. But it worked a treat and I have to say that taking this drug never seemed to have a detrimental effect on his cricket. He even used to tell me it made him play better. I was never too sure about that, but he was still one of the finest left-handed spin bowlers we'd ever had.'

'I don't remember him playing against us,' replied Norman F. Billington curtly.

'Well, you wouldn't, because this all happened last season and he's left us now,' replied Ronald Richardson. 'Poached, would you believe, by those absolute bounders at Dennington in north Somerset. Bloody cheek. They must have made him an offer he couldn't refuse. Probably the use of a secret marijuana plantation hidden deep in the Mendips.'

'So they know he takes drugs as well?' remarked Norman F. Billington, singularly unimpressed by his old friend's attempted humour.

'I wouldn't have a clue,' replied Ronald Richardson. 'But he's still at the club and he took five wickets last weekend. So that's about it. Hope that's been of some help Norman.'

Norman F. Billington was tempted to tell him that it had been of no help whatsoever, but quickly resisted. 'Well, it was an interesting perspective Ronald and one I must admit I wasn't expecting.'

'Have you sat down and spoken to Stuey about it? That might help,' interjected Ronald Richardson.

'Well, I have, kind of talked it over,' replied Norman F. Billington uncertainly. 'He just wants me to forget all about it and just carry on as before, but I'm not sure I can do that.'

'It strikes me that in many ways, Donovan and Stuey are hewn from the same piece of cloth,' offered Ronald Richardson. 'So perhaps, like me, you would do well to leave things just as they are because you can't afford to lose a talent like that.'

'What I can or can't afford to lose Stuart is a matter that I shall decide on,' replied Norman F. Billington rather stiffly.

'Have it your own way,' replied Ronald Richardson. 'But if you are going to boot him out then let me know straight away will you because we'll have him down here at Renwick like a shot.'

'So the fact that Stuart takes illegal drugs doesn't bother you at all?' retorted Norman F. Billington.

'Like I said before, it might have done a few years ago, but young Donovan opened my eyes to all this and I suppose I'm more of a live and let live kind of guy these days. The fact that he's a damn fine cricketer might also have swayed my judgment.'

Norman F. Billington felt strangely deflated. The strong urge to talk over this polemic issue with his old RAF chum, one which only a few minutes earlier had felt so irresistible, was suddenly jaded and unwanted. Or perhaps he just hadn't got the answer he'd been looking for.

Following an awkward few seconds' radio silence between the two former RAF buddies, Ronald Richardson decided to change tack completely. 'By the way Billers, how's that delightful wife of yours. Not seen or heard much from her of late. Is everything alright?'

'Yes, fine. She's fast asleep actually,' said Norman F. Billington, only too aware that his reply, although not a lie, masqueraded more home truths than he would ever be prepared to put his name to.

'In fact, I really ought to go and see how she is, so I'll thank you for your time and say goodnight Ronald.'

'Delighted to be of assistance. I'd stick with Stuey if I were you old boy. I've put down smoking hashish as a youthful indiscretion and we've both shared a couple of those in the past haven't we old chum?'

'Perhaps,' replied Norman F. Billington morosely. 'Goodnight Ronald.'

And he put down the telephone.

SIXTY-ONE

Back at Gazelle's house it was nearly midnight and Stuey wasn't so much slumped in his comfy chair, more sprawled horizontally across it.

He knew that he had smoked far too much marijuana and Gazelle – still by his side in front of a roaring fire – had tempted him with more narcotics in the shape of a litre bottle of red wine, lashings of imported Australian lager and a side portion of two fresh scuttles of coal. To be fully prepared and to demonstrate full understanding of his lodger's every need, Gazelle had also placed two fresh cheese and onion pasties on a metal tray to warm next to his slippers on the hearth.

The evening's arrangements, if the truth be known, suited both man and boy.

Even after all the strife drug-taking had brought them both, Gazelle still found Stuey far easier to talk to after he had been smoking weed and the two of them had spent nearly four hours in front of the fire engaged in deep conversation. Television treats such as Match of the Day and Test Match Special had passed by unnoticed.

For his part, Stuey found Gazelle a good listener and a chap without prejudice. His landlord made no comment as to how stoned his young friend might be, did not criticise him, nor did he try to pass judgment, unlike a certain Norman F. Billington.

However, the club chairman had been the prime focal point of their attention for most of the evening. Stuey told Gazelle of the conversation he had held with Norman F. Billington outside the hospital then whined long and hard about how completely unreasonable Norman was being. After all, he argued, sparking up his third joint of the night, had it not been for Matt Fairacre being locked in a pub lavatory at a most inconvenient moment – both Stuey and Gazelle had laughed out loud at that one – then history would have taken a different course completely.

But gravitas soon returned, Gazelle reminding Stuey that the issue had still not been resolved and that Norman would have to decide soon what action, if any, he was going to take. As Matt Fairacre had pointed out only that afternoon, Stuey had effectively been dropped from the side. The rest of the players had so far accepted the food-poisoning explanation, but another weekend with no Stuey in the team and some serious questions would be asked.

Stuey nodded his head gravely in agreement and looked across at Gazelle.

'I still don't know what else I can do though,' he added. 'Norman doesn't seem willing to budge. He's completely blinkered to common sense as far as I'm concerned.'

'He's old-fashioned like me, that's his problem,' replied Gazelle.

'Yeh, but you don't have a problem with me smoking my hay do you?' replied Stuey. 'Do you?'

'Well, I don't now', answered Gazelle honestly. 'I did at first though, but I had other reasons to overlook your habit.'

'What exactly do you mean by that?' asked Stuey, his bloodshot eyes narrowing and just about focusing on his landlord.

Gazelle, wriggling somewhat uncomfortably in his chair, realised immediately that he had strayed into previously uncharted territory, but decided it was perhaps the right time to come clean anyway.

'Well, it's like this Stuey. Norman offered me certain incentives so that I would take you on as my lodger.

'Such as?'

'The club pays me your rent which you know about already obviously, but they also sweetened the pill in other ways.

'Sweetened the pill?' asked Stuey, stubbing out the last quarter inch of his third joint in his multi-coloured ash-tray on the floor. 'What on earth does that mean?

'Perhaps it's an English expression, but they made it worth my while is a simpler way of putting it', replied Gazelle.

'What else did you get then?' probed Stuey.

'Well, they made my job at the club full time, so more wages, and let me go on tour to play cricket. That's a first for a groundsman I believe.'

Stuey surveyed his straight-talking landlord across an undulating terrain of half-burned coal, warming pasties and toasting slippers and said: 'So let me get this straight. You only let me stay here because Uncle Norman was filling your tinnies from the free tap. That's an Australian expression by the way.'

'No, no, not at all,' stammered Gazelle. 'I value your company. Always have done.'

Gazelle realised that his rushed, unrehearsed reply was far from what he had actually wanted to say, but silence had descended on Stuey who once again was staring deep into the burning fire.

His mind was racing.

Gazelle, he mused, had a couple of secrets squirrelled away after all. Stuey had often wondered if this simple soul had anything covert in the closet and now it was out in the open. Stuey decided it was time to come clean as well. He realised that the surfeit of cannabis in his bloodstream was partly responsible for his sudden candour, but chose to overlook it. He drew a deep breath and spoke: 'Well, Gazelle, I've got a bit of a confession to make myself.'

Gazelle poured himself another glass of wine and listened intently as Stuey continued: 'When I first moved in with you, I didn't like it here one bit and wanted to move out. I told Norman as much, but he wouldn't listen, so I tried to get you to chuck me out instead by confessing that I smoked cannabis. To be honest, that is exactly what I thought you would do and I suppose even hoped you would do. But you didn't and I'm still here. I've been meaning to tell you for a while, but never thought the time was right. Now I know that there were other factors which may have influenced your decision. So the question is this: If you didn't have so much to lose, would you have kicked me out back at the start of the summer?'

Gazelle averted his eyes from Stuey and also stared into the bank of flickering flames before replying. 'I suppose I would. Your drug-taking habit was a shock to me and I suppose I would have reacted just how Norman is doing now. The difference is that I've grown accustomed to you rolling up and used to how this drug affects you. And if I'm being honest here at confession time, I think I actually prefer talking to you when you're stoned which is something I never thought I'd hear myself say. But it's true. You're better company, more interesting, more amusing and possibly even more truthful. Look at us here now, gassing away like two wash ladies over the back garden wall and it's well past midnight.'

Stuey pulled himself up from horizontal mode and sipped his warming wine.

'Perhaps you ought to take up smoking weed Gazelle. Think of the long evenings we would have then. Non-stop banter followed by chapter upon chapter of guilty secrets. Saturday nights would never be the same again.'

Gazelle smiled wanly at Stuey before an awkward silence descended. Stuey suspected his landlord felt ill at ease and changed the subject.

'So you've no plans to kick me out just yet then?'

'Nope, you're welcome to stay as long as you like,' replied Gazelle.

'Or as long as Norman lets me stay,' added Stuey softly.

'Norman will come round. You mark my words,' replied Gazelle. 'Now young man, do you want one of these pasties or would I be correct in assuming that you want both pasties followed by a couple of packets of crisps, a jumbo bag of salted nuts and an entire family bar of fruit and nut chocolate?'

'Bring it on Gazelle, I could eat a cane-backed chair,' Stuey chuckled.

Gazelle smiled to himself as he shuffled into the kitchen to ferry through the rest of his lodger's late night munchies.

If only Norman could see him now.

SIXTY-TWO

If Norman F. Billington could had seen him, the two-man party in Gazelle's parlour would have left the club chairman feeling more like an outcast than he already did.

Support for his anti-drugs stance was hard to come by and he was somewhat at a loss where to turn next. Gazelle, Matt Fairacre and now even Ronald Richardson had shown much sympathy for Stuey and he wasn't convinced that Sammy would be opening the batting for the Norman F. Billington XI once the full background details of his illness were laid bare. The easiest option, he reasoned, would be just to throw his hands in the air, ignore Stuey's misdemeanour – if indeed he could ever convince himself that illegal drug-taking was no more than that – and let life carry on as it had done before.

But deep down this hurt.

It rankled that he had been deceived. The trust, money, admiration and even affection that had been channelled the young Australian's way by so many people – himself included – had, in his book, been betrayed. Stuey was surely everything he needed to be without the need to take illicit narcotics, yet he had done so in profusion and had shown little in the way of remorse when he had been found out.

He had merely asked for a pardon enabling him to carry on as before, and if Norman F. Billington were to grant this pardon as it were, then he would not only be soft in his own eyes, but also soft in the eyes of the law and those contemporaries who were fully aware of the nefarious deeds Stuey got up to in his leisure time.

He knew that he would always struggle to rest easy with this knowledge. His university grounding in the laws of the land had not preached leniency because of a handful of sympathetic banner-wavers. Even if the secret did not seep out to a wider audience, close associates such as Gazelle and Matt Fairacre would always regard Norman F. Billington as a chairman who would recruit and tolerate illegal drug-users as long as the person smoking the spliff was a decent sportsman and a stout fellow. Sitting alone in a darkened lounge at home, he shook his head in despair and asked himself if he could ever afford to take such a risk. He decided that he would call a special meeting at the club later in the week.

Norman F. Billington sighed and sank the dregs of a small whisky before wearily climbing the stairs to bed, stubbing his toe on yet another empty half-bottle of gin as he crossed the half-landing.

SIXTY-THREE

The list of those instructed to attend the special meeting at the club two days later was short on content, but long on deliberation.

After much soul-searching, Norman F. Billington had decided to keep the number as small as possible, inviting Stuey, Gazelle and Matt Fairacre – those already in the know – and, after much hand-wringing, Dave Carter. As club captain, Wobbler ought to be kept informed of events and Norman F. Billington's lengthy telephone call to the skipper the previous night had painted a full picture of prior events and the terrible dilemma facing the chairman.

Wobbler's cup of sympathy for Norman F. Billington's plight hadn't actually overflowed either, but the chairman was growing accustomed to waging war with embattled opposition. The rest of the committee would be told of developments after the weekend. Whether or not they would be told the whole truth remained to be seen.

The mood at the meeting, not unexpectedly, was a sombre one.

Norman F. Billington summoned the gang of four into the back games room, noting that the strongest drink on the trestle table was an orange cordial. This was serious.

'Gentlemen,' said Norman F. Billington. 'Let me say straight away that it gives me no pleasure whatsoever to have to summon you all here this evening, but the gravity of the situation has left me with little choice. You all share something in common. You are all connected in some way to a certain activity which went on while you were on tour. Prior to last night David Carter was not aware of what happened, but now he is fully informed because I've told him.'

Wobbler blushed and looked fierce as Norman F. Billington continued.

'Because you are all in the picture as it were, there's no need to trawl our way through all the gruesome detail. All that concerns me is that certain members of this cricket club have been under the influence of illegal drugs both on and off the club premises and on the recent tour. I have good evidence that both Stuart and Sammy have smoked cannabis, and while I am reasonably satisfied that this illicit drug did not cause Sammy's illness, the very fact that trusted members of my cricket team chose to indulge in this activity while representing the club is something I find totally unacceptable. I do not intend to pass this matter on into the hands of the law, but I do intend to deal with it in-house as it were and will deal with Sammy when he is well enough to leave hospital. As chairman of Crawford cricket club, I organised and offered a contract of employment to Stuart Latham, but after this unfortunate sequence of events, I feel I have no alternative but to withdraw and terminate that contract forthwith. Stuart Latham is no longer employed by the club, is no longer a member of the team and will not play for us again. That is my decision and my decision is final.'

A deathly silence descended on the room. Norman F. Billington scanned the small, stunned gathering for some kind of reaction, but there was none forthcoming.

Wobbler stared at the floor while Matt Fairacre opted for the ceiling. Gazelle's eyes were hidden behind two ranks of tightly closed fingers. The silence was broken by a wooden chair being pushed noisily backwards across uneven wooden floorboards. Stuey was on his feet and spoke with some authority.

'Right then guys, if I'm not wanted then I'm off. I'll try and book a flight home as soon as possible, this weekend hopefully, so that way I'll not be an embarrassment or a nuisance for much longer. It's been good knowing you all.'

And with that, Stuey propelled the chair another two feet backwards, ran his fingers briskly through his hair and stamped out of the room.

A second, even more intense silence descended.

Wobbler and Matt Fairacre switched their focus to the chairman who, rather startled, cleared his throat to speak, but Gazelle beat him to it. 'I'll go after Stuey', he said. 'He might speak to me about his…decision,' he said.

'I hope you won't be trying to change his mind,' said Norman F. Billington croakily.

'I wouldn't dream of trying Norman,' replied Gazelle, 'I somehow imagine that's not going to happen now.'

And with an authoritative step never before seen, Gazelle marched briskly out of the room in the wake of his lodger. He caught up with him half-way across the cricket square, slowing to a walk as he jogged up behind his lodger's back.

'It's a long way to walk home Stuey. Don't you want a lift?'

'I'd rather walk if you don't mind,' replied Stuey without turning.

'Do you mind if I walk with you?' asked Gazelle.

'Not at all. We'll take the scenic route around the back of the gas works.'

Gazelle drew up alongside Stuey and rested his arm on his shoulder, stopping him in his stride.

He spoke quietly and softly: 'Stuey, I just want you to know that Norman didn't speak for us all back there. Certainly not for me anyway. If it was up to me you could stop. But I think you know that already.'

Gazelle's little speech tailed off uncertainly, his voice faltering with emotion.

Stuey came to his rescue.

'I know that Gazelle,' he said with a reassuring smile and placed a hand on his landlord's arm. 'But it looks like Uncle Norm's got it in for me good style and perhaps it's for the best.'

The two walked into the fading light in silence, Gazelle's mind racing.

He had a myriad of questions he wanted to ask, but one in particular burned into him. He steeled himself inwardly, coughed and spoke.

'Do you mind if I ask you a personal question Stuey? One you might not like me asking?' said Gazelle.

'Fire away. I'll be the judge of whether I like it or not.'

'It's Laura. You two seem pretty close and now you'll have to explain to her why you're going back early to Australia. Didn't you once tell me that she didn't know that you smoked your, err, stuff. Is that still the case and if so, what are you going to do?'

Stuey stopped and turned. 'Pretty good questions those Gazelle. You're right. She doesn't know. She didn't even twig all those times when I met up with her after home cricket games, although I do remember that she was amazed late one night back at her parents' place when I almost emptied the kitchen cupboards. I even ate the cornflakes and it wasn't even midnight. I had to tell her fat boy Wobbler had scoffed my cricket tea at the club.'

Stuey allowed himself a flickering smile as the memory returned before continuing to talk. 'But you're right Gazelle. I'll have to tell her the truth and she'll probably want no more to do with me after that anyway. She may well do an Uncle Norman on me.'

'I doubt that somehow,' replied Gazelle. 'She may be so sorry to lose you. Won't you feel the same? You two have been together for quite some time now.'

'I suppose I will', replied Stuey, 'but I was always going home at the end of the season anyway. I was going to worry about it then, but it looks as though I'm going to have to worry about it now instead.'

The two continued to walk along side by side, Gazelle still anxious to fully understand the true depth of Stuey's feelings.

'So that's it then? You seemed to make a snap decision back there in the meeting. Are you sure it's the right one and what do you mean it's for the best?'

Stuey drew a deep breath before replying: 'It might have seemed that way, but actually, it wasn't a spur of the moment decision. I've been thinking about it a lot recently and decided that if Norman doesn't want me then I'm not going to kick up a big fuss about it. I'm not staying where I'm not wanted and if I'm being totally honest, I really can't be bothered with all the attention and bother heading my way when my drug-taking secret is on the open market which it surely be will now that people like bucket-mouth Wobbler know all about it.'

'So get out the place quickly with not too many questions and no regrets, is that it?' added Gazelle.

Stuey sighed before replying: 'Lots of regrets really I suppose, but there's not a lot I can do about any of them now, so the sooner I leave the better.'

Gazelle coughed, nodding his head rapidly in understanding before the two traipsed off into the darkening night, Stuey's arm resting gently on Gazelle's shoulder, the two of them looking for all the world like father and son.

SIXTY-FOUR

Norman F. Billington sipped at his cup of early morning tea in his back parlour, furrowed his brow and looked forlornly over his garden wall at the cricket pavilion in the near distance.

He had done exactly this many times before, but the pleasure and satisfaction that the view had so often provided had been replaced with inner turmoil and consternation. He hadn't slept at all well after delivering the news of Stuey's dismissal, his mind filled with doubts, daggers and dark thoughts, not least the nagging suspicion that, within the confines of Crawford cricket club at least, he had managed to turn himself into public enemy number one, two and three.

His gaze was averted by the trundling into view of a rusting Morris Marina which Norman F. Billington immediately recognised as the personal transport of club captain Dave Carter.

Wobbler halted his car on the top car park, clambered out rather unceremoniously, tucked in a wayward shirt flap, scowled and proceeded to blunder his way around the field edge to the rear of Norman F. Billington's house where he roughly pushed open the back gate and walked in.

Norman F. Billington met him half-way up the garden path, greeting him with a half-hearted smile.

'Hello David, shouldn't you be on your way to work?'

'Yes, I should, but I've arranged to go in a bit later so I can have a talk with you. Can I come in?'

'Please do,' replied Norman F. Billington, stepping aside on to his lawn. 'I suspect I already know what you want to discuss.'

Furnished with a mug of tea, a serviette and a Fred Trueman commemorative coaster in the bright and airy back parlour, Wobbler seemed edgy and nervous.

'I suppose it's that bounder Stuart Latham you want to talk about?' said Norman F. Billington, settling down on the opposite sofa and sensing his guest's unease.

'Yes, it is Norman and in a way I feel personally responsible for what's happened.'

'Why should that be?' replied Norman F. Billington. 'This bother is all of this young man's own making so I don't know why you should be beating yourself up about it.'

Wobbler frowned, fixed his eyes on the coffee table and started to make a paper plane out of his serviette as he spoke again. 'Well, all this trouble came to light on tour and I feel responsible because I know that you were relying on me to keep good order which clearly I didn't and I'm still feeling guilty about it.'

'Well don't,' replied Norman F. Billington firmly. 'As I said before, Stuey took those drugs on tour so no-one else is to blame.'

'Well, that's another thing,' added Wobbler, smoothing out the shape of the right wing between forefinger and thumb. 'I don't claim to know much about drugs, but I was amazed when you told me that Stuey used them. I mean, I would never have realised. I must have spent hours with him when he was err, under the influence, on tour and on Saturday nights back at the club as well and I never would have known. I always thought drug addicts lived in squats, slept in gutters and talked drivel. That was never Stuey by any stretch of the imagination.'

'So, what exactly are you trying to say David?' asked Norman F. Billington, trying to disguise his increasingly exasperated tone.

'Well, I realise the lad has clearly been a great disappointment to you, but don't you think sacking him is a bit, well, hasty? Couldn't you discipline him or something? Suspend him for a couple of weeks perhaps or stick him in the glasshouse like you brave boys in the RAF used to do?'

Norman F. Billington sighed before replying: 'Suspension would be useless because then everybody will want to know why he's been suspended and will have to be told.'

'Everybody will want to know why he's going home early as well,' retorted Wobbler.

'That is undoubtedly true,' said Norman F. Billington, 'but Stuart Latham will be back in Australia by the time the gossip mill starts to churn and that will suit everybody just fine.'

Wobbler picked up his paper plane off the table. It looked more like a Wellington boot than a Wellington bomber. He threw it gently towards the bin, but it crash-landed belly-up into the fireside companion set three feet away.

'I'm not convinced it will suit Sammy fine when he finds out,' remarked Wobbler before rising to his feet. 'I may be mistaken, but I reckon that lad's got a bit of a soft spot for young Stuey.'

'It will have to be pure unadulterated love if it's to reach all the way to another hemisphere,' replied Norman F. Billington, before immediately regretting his flippancy. 'Look David,' he sighed, 'I don't like this whole sorry state of affairs any more than you do, but the decision has been made and I'm sticking with it. I know that I'm not exactly mister popular around these parts at the moment, but I believe that what I'm doing is for the best and I'm not changing my mind.'

Wobbler rose to his feet with a slow resignation before walking over to the patio doors to let himself out.

'Right then, I'm off. Just one last thing, a bit of good news. I've heard Sammy's going to be at our home game this Saturday. Apparently Dr Cat and some of the hospital staff are bringing him up for a special day out or something like that. Angela was supposed to be keeping it a secret, but she blabbed on the telephone late last night. It was meant to be a surprise, but under the circumstances I thought I'd better let you know.'

'You didn't tell her about Stuey leaving then?' asked Norman F. Billington.

'No. I thought I'd leave that to you,' replied Wobbler sheepishly. 'But there is one more thing. Stuey's booked on a flight home to Australia on Sunday. Gazelle also rang last night and told me. He seemed quite upset about it actually, but he asked me to tell you and says they'll both be at the home game on Saturday for a last day together. So I told him about Sammy's surprise appearance with the medical guys from the hospital.'

'Why didn't anybody ring and tell me about such major developments?' demanded Norman F. Billington.

'Don't rightly know,' replied Wobbler. 'But, like you say, you're not exactly mister popular at the moment.'

Wobbler paused, finished his tea and stood up to bring an end to an awkward silence. 'Err, that's it. I'll, err, say goodbye then. Bye.'

Wobbler seemed quite oblivious to the devastating effect of the two bombshells he'd just dropped on his club chairman's doorstep as he pulled open the door and made his way back up the garden path.

A speechless and stunned Norman F. Billington managed a half-spirited wave, but his head was bowed and shaking sadly as he turned back towards the house.

SIXTY-FIVE

Dr Cat closed the file of papers on his desk and allowed himself a small smile. The report on Alan Samson was just about complete and it made for mostly satisfying reading. The cause of the illness – poisoned by the rough farmhouse cider – had been identified and although an exact medical diagnosis had yet to be defined, the patient was making meritorious progress on the way to what would appear to be a full recovery. He had lost much of the bulky weight gained during the depths of the illness, and was back in one bed again, reducing embarrassment levels on many fronts.

Dr Cat had rather taken to this particular patient since he had re-gained consciousness and started to speak. Although slightly abrasive at times and drifting in and out of a barely credible Australian accent, Sammy seemed genuinely glad to be back in the land of the living. He had spoken with much affection about his early up-bringing in Adelaide, his love for his wife and two sons, and how much he had missed his family both on tour and during his illness. Dr Cat had also been impressed with the splendid show of support from his patient's fellow cricketers and their collective concern for the loveable old rogue in ward nine and nearly ward ten.

Hippocrates probably wouldn't have approved, but the doctor thought that a small treat wouldn't go amiss. Having consulted with and gained the approval of the patient's wife, he and two nurses had organised one of the smaller ambulances to transport them and Sammy north that weekend to watch Crawford entertain Jarvis Hall in a crucial promotion game.

Sammy would still be confined to one of the larger wheelchairs, but Dr Cat felt the fresh air and the re-union would be of much benefit to all concerned.

Norman F. Billington could not have agreed less. Although his conscience told him that he was behaving in a most underhand manner, he would have been much happier if Stuey had just slipped off home without the blowing of too many trumpets.

Now it seemed there would be a full fanfare, not only that, but the chairman would have to explain Stuey's absence – and his early departure the day after – to virtually all of his star player's admiring peers and various hangers-on in one job lot.

And then there was Sammy. He too would have to be fully informed, news that hardly qualified as a tonic for the ailing invalid. And what exactly had Dave Carter meant by Sammy having a 'soft spot' for Stuey?

Saturday loomed large and as Norman F. Billington shook his head sadly, he was already quite convinced it had all the makings of the worst day of his life.

SIXTY-SIX

Gazelle took up his usual position in his comfy chair by the fire at 7.30pm on Friday night and opened up the evening paper with a vigorous rustle.

He and Stuey had purchased large portions of fish, chips and mushy peas each from the local chip shop by way of a farewell supper. Gazelle felt like he'd eaten a beach ball and slackened off his belt accordingly to accommodate the swell.

Stuey was concentrating studiously as he rolled his first joint of the night, Gazelle neatly folding the evening newspaper to a quarter of its original size and pushing it under the cushion on his chair before starting to speak.

'So, our last weekend together then young man. It seems like a long time ago since you first moved in and a lot has happened since then.'

Stuey replied without looking up. 'That's right. Do you remember those terrible tinned pilchards? Jeez, you're lucky I'm still here.'

Gazelle smiled and reflected on the chain of circumstances

that had thrust them together and now the fickle hand of fate that was tearing them apart. A sudden sadness engulfed him. He was struck by a realisation that a chapter of his life was about to come to an end, a chapter that had been so eventful, so colourful, a chapter that could never happen again.

'Have you told Laura that you're leaving yet?' he said, trying to distance himself from the unwanted invasion of such forlorn thoughts.

'No, not yet', admitted Stuey blushing slightly. 'She's still in Bristol and I rang last night with the intention of telling her all about what had happened, but then my nerve went. I suppose I knew deep down that I shouldn't be telling her such news on the telephone anyway, and if I'm being honest, I was afraid what her reaction might be. But then I was saved because she told me that she's coming home this weekend anyway, so I'll be seeing her at the match tomorrow.'

'It's a bit late to be telling the poor girl that you'll be flying back to Australia the day after', remarked Gazelle.

'I realise that and it's really not what I wanted,' replied Stuey sadly. 'Then again, none of this is what I wanted. But as you know already I don't think I'm to blame because I still think I've done nothing wrong. If there was any justice in the world, Uncle bloody Norman would be explaining it all to her, not me.'

Gazelle nodded ruefully in agreement and said: 'He'll have enough explaining to do to Sammy and the rest of the crew when they find out you're not playing and then he'll have to explain why you're going home, assuming of course that all this information is going to be on general release.'

'What? Sammy's going to be at the game as well?' asked a surprised Stuey.

'Err, well, yes, he is,' stammered Gazelle, taking his turn to blush. 'Wobbler told me on the telephone the other night. It was supposed to be a secret, but well, it isn't any longer.'

Stuey furrowed his brow before replying:'It's certainly going to be quite a day for all concerned. Sammy, Angela, I presume, Laura, Norman, me and you and all the guys. Quite a gathering.'

'Dr Cat's coming too,' blurted out Gazelle.

'Dr Cat !' cried Stuey, looking up for the first time. 'What on earth's he doing here?'

'He's bringing Sammy up from the hospital. You're really going to be the centre of attention tomorrow, quite a celebrity really. Doesn't it bother you, especially when your big secret comes out?'

'I suppose it should, but I still don't think I've done anything wrong, and if Norman's going to stick to his small-minded principles, then so am I,' replied Stuey defiantly.

'I've done nothing to feel ashamed of.'

And with that he pushed his bare feet nearer to the blazing fire, wriggled his toes to aid the warming process and lit the joint.

SIXTY SEVEN

Stuey's last full day in England dawned bright and sunny.

As ever, Gazelle was first at the club shortly before lunch, laying out the boundary rope then rolling the wicket with his customary high level of care and attention. Matt Fairacre was the next to arrive and while routine dictated that he should go straight to the bar to roll up the shutters and clean the pumps ready for the staff, instead, he parked his car and walked briskly across the mid-field wicket to Gazelle. He pulled a sheet of paper out of his back pocket as he approached the groundsman.

He jabbed an angry finger at it held it up in front of Gazelle and said dolefully: 'Stuey's not in the team that Norman read out to me over the telephone this morning.'

'Well, did you expect him to be?' replied Gazelle. 'You heard what Norman said.'

'I suppose not, it's just that, well I suppose I thought, hoped, prayed that he might have had a change of heart and that this whole horrible business would just go away,' said Matt Fairacre, his face creased and etched with worry. This was a young man on the verge of tears.

Gazelle felt a deep sympathy for the young accountant.

On his shoulders rested an onus of responsibility far greater than anyone else's for this whole sorry episode, yet his role was no more than a most unfortunate victim of quite surreal circumstances. Gazelle could have wept with him.

'The thing is that as soon as the rest of the players see the team sheet on the notice board, they will want to know why Stuey's not playing and the questions will start to fly,' wailed Matt Fairacre. 'What do I say? What do I do? Do I tell them the whole truth about my role in all this? And if I don't, is Norman going to tell them all anyway? What a mess. Do you know I've hardly slept at all since Norman dipped in his big fat oar. Isn't it about time he took a bit of control over all of this? It was his decision to sack Stuey after all. I'm going to have to tell him what I think when I see him.'

'It looks as though you're going to get the chance quite soon,' replied Gazelle glancing over his shoulder. 'He's on his way over right now.'

Norman F. Billington closed his garden gate behind him and made his way across the cricket field. He was dressed immaculately in a grey three piece suit, he was freshly shaven and his small moustache had been neatly clipped that very morning. His greying hair was smoothed down along both flanks with the aid of a gentleman's dressing tonic.

Yet as he crossed the outfield, Gazelle thought he looked older.

'Good morning gentlemen,' Norman F. Billington announced as he approached them, Gazelle half-heartedly returning the greeting. Matt Fairacre declined all pleasantries, reached for his back pocket instead and thrust the team sheet directly into the chairman's line of sight. 'As soon as I stick this on the noticeboard with no Stuey in the team Norman, all hell will break loose. So what are you going to do about it?'

Norman F. Billington was rather taken aback by his first lieutenant's brusque attitude, but he was well prepared for more than one bruising encounter that day. 'You can hand the team sheet to me and I will deal with it', he replied assertively. 'As soon as all the senior players are here I will call a meeting in the dressing room to clarify the circumstances of Stuart's absence today and the reason he will not be playing for us again.'

'And you're going to tell them the whole truth, all the gruesome detail including my role I suppose?' demanded Matt Fairacre, his voice quavering and faltering.

'They will be told as much as they need to know and no more,' added Norman F. Billington. 'But let me say that the innocent parties in all this, that is to say you Matthew, and you Bernard, will not be implicated in any way. Sammy might eventually have one or two questions to answer when the time is right, but as far as I'm concerned the only guilty party at the moment in all this sorry affair is one Stuart Latham.'

And with that Norman F. Billington folded and inserted the team sheet neatly in the top pocket of his jacket and briskly headed off towards the pavilion.

'That's quite a relief I can tell you,' sighed Matt Fairacre as the chairman disappeared into the distance.

'Personally I don't care less if everybody knows everything about my role in all this,' snapped Gazelle irritably before aiming a flailing foot at an imaginary divot three yards from the popping crease.

Matt Fairacre looked at him with some surprise.

It was the first time he'd ever heard Gazelle utter a rebellious word.

SIXTY-EIGHT

About an hour before the commencement of play at 2.00pm, Norman F. Billington marched into the Crawford dressing room and called for the all the players' attention.

He did so by rattling a cricket stump along the radiator.

But the noise was quickly overwhelmed by a far more raucous din from outside as an emergency vehicle siren started to yap and wail. Meat Loaf pulled down an old sash window, stuck out his head and started to jabber excitedly. 'There's an ambulance making its way around the field with all its lights flashing and its siren blowing. And there's this bloke hanging out of the window waving some kind of flag in the air. Bloody hell! It's Sammy!'

As the ambulance approached the pavilion, the team members rushed past Norman F. Billington like a tsunami wave, the players crashing into the open air to greet their long lost chum, leaving Norman F. Billington still clutching his wicket, message undelivered and reflecting that the timing of Sammy's entry could not have been, well, more untimely.

As the crowd gathered at the end of the car park, Norman F. Billington stepped outside where he spotted Stuey and Laura strolling along the edge of the field towards the club house hand in hand.

The squad, as it were, was complete.

Dr Cat was the first to clamber out of the ambulance, the Jamaican quite taken aback by the large reception committee awaiting them. He stood in front of the gathering, called for order, secured a semblance of one and spoke: 'Gentlemen, I have here a very special guest for you today and there are no prizes for guessing who it is. Your very own Sammy is back among his dear friends for at least one day. Another week or so and he will be back with you for good. But before you bestow your best wishes upon him, may I first invite Angela and the boys over to greet their much-loved and much-missed husband and father.'

Angela, Rod and Ben, waiting in the doorway of the pavilion, walked across to the ambulance, the players parting to let them through. Sammy though still weak and overweight, clambered out of the vehicle unaided and started to rub his eyes to hide his emotions. He took Angela in his arms and hugged her like he had never hugged her before. He kissed her like he had never kissed her before. He hugged his boys like he had never hugged them before. He kissed them like he had never kissed them before.

At the back of the throng Meat Loaf poked Pete Skidmore in the ribs and whispered: 'Bloody hell, Sammy's changed. I've never seen him kiss and hug his missus like that.'

Finally, Sammy stepped away from his family and turned to face his cricketing peers, salty tears now cascading down his bloated, half-shaven cheeks.

'It's truly great to be back boys,' he blubbed. 'I'll be buying you all a Botham shandy, but I'm afraid it won't be this week.'

Pete Skidmore turned back to Meat Loaf and grunted: 'He's not changed that much then.'

Norman F. Billington, who had pursued a solo path to the back of the gathering, interrupted proceedings. 'Would you all mind making your way over to the home dressing room for a few minutes. I would still like a word with you all.'

'Does that include the ladies as well Norman?' blurted out Angela.

'Err, yes, well of course,' stammered Norman F. Billington, who suddenly felt tremendously nervous. 'You and Laura are more than welcome. In fact you ought to be there.'

And with that, Norman F. Billington, cricket stump still in hand, led the throng back to the pavilion, Meat Loaf pushing Sammy in his wheelchair and jabbering excitedly in his ear while Dr Cat and the two nurses excused themselves before sitting down on a nearby grassy bank to take on board some early afternoon sunshine.

The party entered the dressing room, Sammy pushed to the front, most of the cricketers standing on the long wooden perimeter seat and securing themselves by hanging on to their kit pegs.

Norman F. Billington stood on top of a small, up-turned wooden box at the far side of the room, cleared his throat and started to speak: 'Ladies and gentlemen. Thank you all for allowing me a few moments of your precious time and may I start by welcoming our old friend Sammy back to his family and into our cricketing fraternity. This past few weeks have been a traumatic time for us all, particularly Sammy's wife and children, but we can all take great pleasure from the fact that our esteemed wicket-keeper is well down the road to recovery and for today at least, back among his nearest and dearest here at Crawford cricket club. Perhaps we can toast his good health later, but for the moment, perhaps a round of applause would be in order.'

Loud clapping and raucous cheering filled the Crawford dressing room, Meat Loaf tumbling head first into a kit bag on the floor after releasing his grip on the wall peg much to the amusement of all.

Norman F. Billington waited for the kerfuffle to settle, coughed nervously, called for order and continued to address the gathering: 'I'm afraid, ladies and gentlemen that I have some bad news to impart as well.'

A hush fell over the room.

'As a few of you are already aware, our overseas professional Stuart Latham is not included on the team sheet for today's game. He hasn't been selected to play and in fact will never be asked to play for Crawford cricket club again.'

A low murmur rose towards the ceiling.

Norman F. Billington braced himself and continued: 'This is because of his completely unacceptable behaviour on our recent tour of Somerset and by mutual consent he will shortly be returning home to Australia. In fact he will be flying home tomorrow.'

A deathly hush descended on the room. Stuey stared at the wall, Laura stared at the side of Stuey's head, Matt Fairacre studied a poster on the wall, Meat Loaf started to sweat profusely while Gazelle glared angrily at Norman F. Billington.

The stunned silence was broken by Pete Skidmore who blurted out: 'What's Stuey done wrong? What on earth happened on tour that's got him the sack?

'We were all as good as gold and we wouldn't have beaten that team in Bristol if it hadn't been for Stuey.'

Norman F. Billington sighed before drawing the deepest of breaths.

'You might as well all know now because you're sure to find out sooner or later anyway. It has come to my attention that Stuart took illegal drugs on tour and in my book that is totally unacceptable. He smoked cannabis if you want to know the exact detail and I will not tolerate such behaviour from any member of this club, whoever he is, so his contract has been terminated.

'I appreciate that some of you may feel this punishment is harsh, but that's the way it is and the sooner Stuart Latham is on his flight home, the better it will be for everyone so this whole sad episode can be put behind us. I'm only sorry that the news had to be broken to you this way and I feel particularly sorry for Sammy who has learned of this development after a long and worrying illness and on a day when we should be celebrating our colleague's return. I also feel extra sympathy for Sammy because I know that he and Stuart were so close.'

All eyes fell on Sammy who struggled to shift his still considerable bulk to one side in his wheelchair to prepare himself to speak.

On the back row Pete Skidmore again whispered to Meat Loaf: 'Sammy's going to blow his stack. He'll completely do his nut. Norman's not going to know what's hit him.'

Sammy stared intently at Norman F. Billington, waited for a few seconds, then with some considerable effort started to speak quite slowly: 'Close?' he said. 'Who said Stuey and I were close? I know Stuey had some illegal drugs and if Norman's decided to punish him by sending him home then that's fine by me.

'I don't have a problem with that.'

Astonishment bounced off all four walls, disbelief was etched on many faces while Stuey grimaced in pain as sharp fingernails dug into the flesh on his upper arm. Laura gripped her boyfriend tightly as a cauldron of emotions erupted within, incredulity, betrayal, sadness and anger all fighting for immediate attention.

She hissed in his ear: 'How long has all this been going on? Why didn't you tell me?'

Stuey put his arm around Laura's shoulder, but she pulled away.

'Perhaps we'd better go outside on our own,' he said.

'Yes, perhaps we'd better,' she replied coldly. Stuey and Laura pushed their way out of the dressing room in front of a dozen pairs of staring eyes, leaving behind a rising tempo of frenzied gossiping and a salvo of unanswered questions straining to be unleashed.

SIXTY-NINE

The warm sunshine outside the cricket pavilion contrasted sharply with the dank and dreary dressing room, but neither Laura nor Stuey appreciated it.

Stuey stared sullenly at the ground, unable to look Laura in the face, suddenly realising how stupid he'd been not to tell his girlfriend the truth right from the start and how understandably shocked and let down she was so entitled to be.

Laura grabbed Stuey by the chin, turned his head and made him look at her.

'Are you really going back to Australia tomorrow?' she demanded, although her voice was wavering and strained.

'Afraid so,' replied Stuey. 'I'm so sorry. I never wanted it to end like this.'

Laura started to cry. Stuey placed his arm around her shoulders again and this time she did not resist.

'Let's go and sit over there on the field behind the boundary rope. I'll tell you everything,' he said.

And tell her everything Stuey did. From the start of his drug habit back home in Australia, how he had struck a deal with Gazelle to stay and smoke in his house, the blame he had got for Sammy's illness after the tour, how he and Gazelle had worked out that the toxic cider was the real culprit, even Matt Fairacre's unwanted role as Norman's secret grass after his unintentional espionage in a shabby hotel toilet.

Laura listened intently, and as the story unfolded felt a little compassion and sympathy dent her anger and disbelief.

'But why didn't you tell me all this was happening?' she demanded to know again.

Stuey shook his head: 'I realise now that I should have done. But I was worried how you'd react if I told you, afraid I suppose, scared that you wouldn't want to see me anymore because some people won't tolerate any kind of drug use as you now know, Uncle Norman being the classic example.'

Laura smiled sadly and took Stuey's hand.

'For an illegal drug user you're still an OK kind of guy.'

Then she started to cry again.

SEVENTY

Crawford cricket team performed woefully that afternoon.

Stuey's absence had taken a heavy toll, but it was Norman F. Billington's bombshell speech that had knocked the spirit out of the side. Jarvis Hall romped to an easy victory with four wickets and an hour to spare, ending Crawford's slim hopes of promotion and Norman F. Billington's dreams of life in a more elite sporting lane. Sammy had stayed until the end of the game before Dr Cat and the nurses shoe-horned him into the ambulance and drove him back to the hospital.

There were other notable absentees.

Stuey had abandoned his spectator's perch to shake hands with all the players at the end of the game and then had left early with Laura to avoid embarrassing questions. Matt Fairacre had made his excuses and left for much the same reason and when Gazelle appeared in the bar after his tidying-up duties outside and in the dressing rooms, he found the atmosphere awkward and cold.

Norman F. Billington was sitting at the bar flicking

mindlessly through the season's scorecards conspicuously short of company while the players were sitting in huddles of small groups in the far reaches of the room talking in hushed tones about the drama of the day.

Gazelle bought himself a pint of bitter at the bar, ignored Norman F. Billington completely – hoping to make some kind of point – before scanning the room for the least intimidating company. He settled for Wobbler who had formed a small scrum in a corner with Pete Skidmore and Meat Loaf. He asked to join them and had barely pulled up a stool before Meat Loaf was on his case.

'Did you know about all this drugs outrage Gazelle?' he wheezed excitedly, the sweat dripping off his forehead in even more profusion than usual.

'Did you let Stuey smoke cannabis in your house? Did you have any? When did he smoke it on tour? Where did he get it from? How did Uncle Norman find out?'

Gazelle smiled weakly and realised he was in the wrong place at the wrong time, quite unable to cope with this onslaught of questions and the three expectant faces bearing down on him.

'I'll tell you when you're a bit older Meat Loaf,' he said, pushed his untouched beer into the middle of the table, stood up and walked out.

SEVENTY-ONE

It was about 10.30pm and Gazelle had been home for about two hours when he heard the key turn in the door and Stuey shuffle his way into the house.

'I wasn't sure I would see you at all tonight,' Gazelle said as his lodger flopped into the chair alongside him. 'How's Laura?'

'She's not too upset. We went back to her parents' house and we had a long talk in private about, well, about you know what. We're still friends, just about. I think she's more brassed off that I never told her what was going on in the first place if the truth be known.'

Gazelle nodded knowingly.

'I've handled it all wrong. I realise that now,' continued Stuey. 'But it's too late to do anything about it. Anyway, we're going to stay in touch and we'll have to see what the future holds.'

Stuey slumped down in his chair, thrust back his head, expelled a deep breath and stared at the ceiling.

Gazelle sensed the mental turmoil within and felt only

sympathy. He stood up, chucked some coal on to the struggling fire and said: 'Not smoking tonight then?'

'No, not tonight,' replied Stuey, sitting back up straight in his chair and rubbing his eyes vigorously. 'It's got me in enough bother already and I'm not in the mood anyway. I need to get up early tomorrow and it's going to be a long day.'

'What time's your flight?' asked Gazelle.

'Late afternoon, about four o'clock I think,' replied Stuey.

'Do you want a lift to the airport?' asked Gazelle.

'No thanks mate. Norman has insisted that he's taking me. I could do without it really, but he was adamant and I really couldn't be bothered arguing. It will be his last chance to deliver a big sermon on the dangers of vicious, evil drugs and the disastrous consequences of taking them.'

Stuey glanced across the room and caught Gazelle looking straight at him. There was an embarrassing moment before they both turned their attention back to the flickering flames.

'Norman should have spent an evening here with you when you've been smoking your vicious, evil drugs. He might have changed his mind then,' remarked Gazelle.

'Do you really mean that Gazelle? I didn't know you thought that way,' replied a surprised Stuey.

'Well, I must admit that I was scared witless when I first agreed to let you smoke your stuff here in my home, but now, all these furlongs down the track, I really can't work out what all the fuss is about and I never thought I'd say that about any kind of drug. But had some right good laughs at times and we never did get to watch Test Match Special did we?'

Stuey smiled and chuckled: 'Perhaps I'd better skin up after all then.'

Gazelle smiled too before rising to his feet.

'I'm having a cup of tea. Do you want one?'

'No thanks', replied Stuey yawning, 'I'm going to bed in a minute. I'm walking over to say my last goodbyes to Laura early in the morning and Norman's picking me up here at lunchtime. You'll be on groundsman's duty for the game at the club by then, so it will be just me and Uncle Norman for the last lap of this rather surreal adventure.'

Gazelle paused before he sighed deeply and said: 'So this really is it. Our last night under the same roof.'

Gazelle stood up, walked the few feet to his lodger's comfy chair, stood in front of him and offered his hand.

'I'm going to miss you Stuey,' he added, mumbling awkwardly and shuffling his feet on the rug as his eyes welled with tears.

'And I'm going to miss you too Gazelle,' replied Stuey, rising to his feet before shaking his landlord by the hand and biting his bottom lip until it hurt.

'And your little house and your little coal fire.'

SEVENTY-TWO

Norman F. Billington's grey/green Rover pulled up punctually outside Gazelle's house at noon the day after as arranged.

The club chairman felt tense and ill at ease. He had forgotten that Gazelle wouldn't be there and his absence somehow made life that little more difficult.

When he had volunteered his services only the day before, taking Stuey to the airport had seemed like a good idea, the right thing to do in the circumstances as it were, the chance to explain himself more fully perhaps, but now he wasn't too sure.

Stuey was barging his way through the front door with his luggage before Norman F. Billington had even found the time to turn off the ignition. He dragged two suitcases and an enormous kit bag around the back of the car and waited until Norman F. Billington arrived with the key to open the boot.

'Good morning Stuart,' chirruped Norman F. Billington, turning the lock.

'Err, yeh, right, err, g'day' replied Stuey unenthusiastically, pushing both suitcases into the boot and avoiding any eye contact. I'll have to put the kit bag on the back seat if you don't mind. It's not going to fit into the boot.'

'I doubt it will fit into the hold of the plane,' replied Norman F. Billington, chuckling nervously.

The chairman's attempt at gentle humour elicited no response from Stuey who merely walked along the side of the car and climbed into the front passenger seat. Norman F. Billington felt relieved Stuey hadn't opted for the back seat next to his kit bag.

The chairman started the car and set off down the road in silence. At the first set of red traffic lights he coughed and started to speak.

'In the light of recent events Stuart, I would just like to say that the decision I took to, err, end your contract was nothing to do with you personally. It was an issue of ethics and standards and not because of who you are and the kind of character that you are. If the truth be known, I still respect you and certainly admire your cricketing skills.'

'But not my social ones,' replied Stuey sullenly.

'Well, no, I suppose not,' said Norman F. Billington, fiddling unnecessarily with the indicator stalk. 'But we're not going to let such issues come between us are we Stuart?'

'It looks like they've come between us already,' replied Stuey. 'That's why I'm sitting next to you in your car on the way to the airport before the season's ended.'

'Yes, well, that's true' replied Norman F. Billington reddening slightly. 'But you must be aware that I can't tolerate the use of drugs in any circumstances.'

Stuey had never wanted to debate the drugs issue with Norman F. Billington.

Ever since the club chairman had declared he was to kick

him out, Stuey had decided to quit quickly with the minimum of fuss. If he and his habit weren't wanted, then he wasn't going to be there. This was his philosophy and he was sticking to it. Yet there was one issue that nagged and clawed at him. Above all others, there was one point he felt he ought to make, and before he could stop himself, he found himself gushing forth.

'Yes, but you do tolerate drug-taking quite a lot of the time, don't you Norman?'

'I certainly do not,' rasped Norman F. Billington in reply, his raised voice bristling with indignation.

'Oh yes you do, both at the club and at home,' replied Stuey in a low, slightly intimidating tone.

'I think you'd better explain yourself straight away young man or you may find yourself walking the rest of the way to the airport,' barked Norman F. Billington angrily.

Stuey let fly: 'You tolerate drinking in the club bar, excessive drinking at times and you even encourage it. You knew there would be loads of alcohol abuse on tour, while I believe your good lady takes to the gin bottle at home on more occasions than is good for her.'

Norman F. Billington shot Stuey a dismayed glance before replying:'That's alcohol and it's legal and I would appreciate it if you left my wife out of this.'

'It may be legal, but alcohol is still a drug and it's a dangerous drug as well,' replied Stuey. 'Look at what it did to poor Sammy. A spot of weed wouldn't lay anyone flat out across a hospital bed in a million years. It's just a pity you didn't appreciate that at the time Norman. That's the trouble with law-makers and guys like you who lecture guys like me. It wouldn't be too bad if you knew what you were lecturing everybody about in the first place, but you can lay your bottom dollar that the vast majority of politicians and judges who decide which drug is wrong or right, harmful or harmless, have never smoked a spliff in their lives. Where's the sense in that?'

Norman F. Billington listened intently to the longest speech he had ever heard Stuey make.

He was appalled that the young Australian was aware of his wife's chronic drink problem, even more appalled because he knew it must have been the other cricketers who had told him. He had long suspected that they gossiped about his dark secret behind his back. Now he was certain.

Norman F. Billington steadied himself inwardly before replying: 'In the eyes of the judiciary the drug you took is illegal and therefore you broke the law of the land. You should think yourself lucky that you didn't find yourself in deeper trouble young man.'

'Yeh, right', replied Stuey, before resting his head against the window and staring intently at the passing rows of terraced houses. He had always known it was pointless trying to reason with Uncle Norman, but at least he had tried.

The rest of the journey was spent in a painful, uncomfortable silence, but Norman F. Billington's mind was racing.

Stuey's short but stout self-defence had jangled a few raw nerves.

His wife's gin habit had grown from a fondness in social circles to a terrible home alone addiction in only a few, short years and Norman F. Billington knew that he constantly denied the gravity of the problem to himself and others. His wife didn't even make it over to the club house these days.

And in a way Stuey had been right. Norman F. Billington

didn't have a clue about the effect of cannabis or any other illicit drug for that matter. He just knew they were all illegal and that was it. That had always been enough.

The car pulled up in front of the airport departure lounge. Stuey bounded out with undue haste, legged it round to the boot and started to pull out his suitcases.

With some effort, Norman F. Billington dragged the huge kit bag out of the back seat and met Stuey at the back of the car. The two men looked at each other apprehensively before Norman F. Billington pushed out his right hand and spoke: 'Despite what's happened Stuart, I want to thank you for all your cricketing efforts representing the Crawford club, especially your contribution in Bristol and wish you all the best for the future. Can we shake hands on that at least?'

Norman F. Billington pushed out his hand even further.

Stuey looked at the outstretched hand and then looked up at Norman F. Billington.

A decent up-bringing had taught the young Australian respect and manners, yet there was a fire of rebellion burning fiercely in his belly. He had to fight a tangle of surprisingly fraught nerves and a sparring partner of better judgment, but when it was delivered, his response was exactly as he wanted it to be. He looked Norman F. Billington straight in the eye and said: 'Sorry Norm, no can do. Goodbye.'

And with that he hurled his kit bag over his shoulder, ran his fingers through his hair, grabbed his luggage and strode over to the two sliding doors leading to the check-ins.

Norman F. Billington withdrew his unshaken hand and watched in dismay as Stuey passed through the doors. He thought his young cricketer would turn and wave an acknowledgement before entering the building. But he didn't.

Stuey just marched steadfastly forward before blending with and then disappearing into the throngs of fellow travellers.

Norman F. Billington waited for several seconds before walking slowly back to his Rover with a heavy heart.

He clambered in wearily, placed his hands on the steering wheel, bowed his head and wept.

SEVENTY-THREE

Gazelle inserted the key, turned the front door lock and entered his terraced house at 7.30pm that same night.

It was a rather pleasant Sunday evening in mid-August, but it may as well have been a wet Wednesday afternoon in deepest February.

The day's cricket had again been a complete disaster, Crawford collapsing to 67 all out, team spirit non-existent, no Sammy, no Stuey, the rest barely interested. Not even Norman F. Billington had turned up.

Gazelle had ploughed through his after-match duties quickly and hurried straight home, but now he had arrived, he really didn't know what the urgency had been.

He entered the lounge in a disconsolate mood and looked moodily around the room with a critical eye. Stuey had been right about the place. It was shabby and dull and as Gazelle's gaze rested on the pile of dead grey ashes in the grate, he reflected on how much they looked for all the world like a funeral pyre of life's missed chances. His own missed chances.

Gazelle glanced at the dreary clock on the mantelpiece and the discoloured pair of socks secured beneath it, dangling over the front edge in drying position.

Stuey had been right about his laundry habits too.

Gazelle moved the socks and the ashes, re-filled the coal scuttle and gathered up three stained tea-cups. He glanced over at Stuey's empty chair. The smoking burns on the arms which had once so upset him now only filled him with a wistful nostalgia.

Gazelle needed to cheer himself up.

He lit the fire even though it was a mild evening, drew the curtains across the windows, sat down again and unfurled the previous day's evening newspaper. He read the bits he hadn't already read before making himself a cup of tea and switching on the television. He flicked through the handful of channels, decided it was all rubbish, turned it off and once again gazed forlornly around the room.

Gazelle had never experienced emotions such as these before. He felt uneasy, restless, totally brassed off, but more than anything, so, so alone.

He had, of course, been alone for most of his life, but it had never got to him before like it was getting to him now. His loneliness burrowed into him, nagged and hectored. Even the flickering fire did nothing to relieve his simmering discontent that seemed to envelop his dispirited body.

Gazelle stood up and wondered what to do next.

Without any real purpose or reason, he climbed the stairs and wandered aimlessly into the empty spare room. Stuey's room. Yet Stuey's room no more. He didn't expect to find much had changed, so wasn't disappointed when it hadn't. Stuey had made the bed and tidied up, quite neatly Gazelle noted, leaving no sign that a knavish young antipodean had ever laid his head there.

The curtains still didn't fit the window properly and the creaky old wooden wardrobe remained off kilter, still covering the damp patch on the wall. The left hand door of the wardrobe was closed, the other half open.

Gazelle walked over to close it, but before he did, peered inside the dark closet. At the far end of the wardrobe, some clothes were hanging on the rail. Gazelle frowned curiously, opened the left hand door and carried out a closer inspection. Hanging up there was a Brisbane Broncos rugby league shirt, various t-shirts, a couple of jumpers and a jacket. Gazelle yanked the jacket off the rail, held it up to the light and looked it up and down. He felt sure it wasn't Stuey's and then suddenly he recognised it.

It belonged to Sammy. It was in fact the jacket Sammy had been wearing on that fateful last night out together in Bristol and as Gazelle put the pieces together, the picture came into focus. The clothes were the ones Sammy had taken out of his suitcase to make room for his toxic cider, and along with the jacket, left in the kit minibus after he had been rendered unconscious at the motorway services. It was in fact Gazelle himself who had brought the clothes home all those weeks ago and now he remembered what he had done: He had stored them on the top shelf of the spare wardrobe in Stuey's room before forgetting all about them. Clearly Stuey had found them when he was packing to leave and hung them up for Gazelle to find. Sammy could have them back now.

Gazelle threw the jacket on to the bed, but as it landed, a small white flash caught his eye. Puzzled, he pulled the jacket towards him from the bottom and as he did so there was a second flash and what looked like a small white torpedo slipped out of the top pocket.

Then another.

Gazelle leaned over to inspect the strange objects further and as he did so, his heart missed a beat. There, lying on the beige cloth of Sammy's second best jacket were two cannabis joints. Gazelle blinked rapidly and looked again. Joints rolled by Stuey, thin at the bottom, wide at the top with the excess paper tweaked into a small bow shape. He had seen them dozens of times, so was sure they were Stuey's work. So why did Sammy have two of Stuey's joints in the top pocket of his jacket? He knew they had both smoked together on that fateful night in the Swan, but what were these drugs doing here?

He frowned, thought hard and long and then he remembered. During that meeting at the club, when Norman dropped the bombshell that he knew about the drugs, Stuey had also confessed that he had given Sammy two joints for the cricketers' last night out in Bristol, the night that Stuey didn't attend. Clearly Sammy had never smoked them, but it really didn't seem to matter now.

Gazelle suddenly felt quite weak, his stomach heaved, his knees trembled and his armpits started to perspire. But it was the reason for this overwhelming wave of nausea that was so worrying. He tried to rid himself of this new, all-pervading thought, cast it from his mind, banish it to a dustbin of forgetfulness.

But he knew it wasn't going to go away.

Gazelle found himself pacing up and down the bedroom and behaving quite irrationally. He closed the curtains even though it was still light and then picked up the joints and walked up and down the room carrying them in his trembling open hand like unexploded hand grenades. Maddened by his own gormless dithering, he hid them in the top drawer of the bedside cabinet.

Then he began to talk to himself.

Why had he done that? he asked. In case somebody called round, he reassured himself.

When was the last time anyone had ever called on lonely old Gazelle on a Sunday evening? Never, as far back as he could remember, was the wholly correct answer.

But there was still the off-chance of a visitor. He scurried down the stairs, double-locked the front door with the bolt on the inside, checked the back door was secure and took the telephone off the hook. No-one had ever rung him on a Sunday night either, but what the hell.

It wasn't yet dark outside, but did it matter? Gazelle didn't know, so he closed the curtains in the lounge and sat down in his chair, his armpits sweating like Meat Loaf locked in a steam room, his mouth dry, his blood pressure rampant.

Gazelle closed his eyes and ordered himself to calm down. He took several deep breaths before he walked into the kitchen and poured himself a glass of water from the tap, sipping it noisily. He walked back into the lounge, sat down again and tried to think about anything other than those two small white tubes of intrigue hidden in the spare bedroom.

He couldn't.

His mind was wholly embraced by their presence. Relaxation was impossible. Escape was impossible. Gazelle placed his hands over his eyes before opening them slightly and looked at the slowly ticking clock for the third time in five minutes. It was 8.30 pm. Stuey had always maintained that 9.00pm was the best time.

Gazelle couldn't wait that long. His nerves couldn't possibly hold out that long.

He climbed slowly up the stairs, his legs still weak, his mind still racing. He lifted one of the joints out of the bedside cabinet and carried it slowly towards the stairs on the palm of his hand as gingerly as if it were a rescued baby bird unable to fly. This is quite ridiculous Gazelle mused to himself as he stepped off the landing, but caution still haunted his every wary step as he made his way down the stairs. He entered the lounge, placed the joint on the side arm of his chair and sat down alongside it. He looked at the empty chair where Stuey should have been. Deep sadness and a sense of total injustice combined to overwhelm him and stir within an inner strength, a strength he had never encountered before.

Gazelle dragged Stuey's multi-coloured ash-tray from underneath the other chair. Taking one of his fire-lighting tapers off the mantelpiece, he lit it on the blazing coals and sat down. He took one last look around the room. As far as he was aware, everything was in place for the most audacious act of his life.

And with that, Gazelle placed the joint between his lips, lit it with the flaring taper, inhaled deeply, closed his eyes and waited for the world to change.